Kitty Hawk and the Tragedy of the R.M.S.Titanic

Book Four of the Kitty Hawk Flying Detective Agency Series

Iain Reading

This page is dedicated to everyone who thinks that
Charlie and Kitty Hawk belong together

To Zoe!

Thank you so
Much. I hope You

LOVE this Book!

29 April 2015

Other books by this author:

Kitty Hawk and the Curse of the Yukon Gold
Kitty Hawk and the Hunt for Hemingway's Ghost
Kitty Hawk and the Icelandic Intrigue
Kitty Hawk and the Tragedy of the RMS Titanic
The Guild of the Wizards of Waterfire
The Hemingway Complex (non-fiction)

www.kittyhawkworld.com
www.wizardsofwaterfire.com
www.iainreading.com
www.secretworldonline.com

TABLE OF CONTENTS

Prologue
A Lost Soul Set Adrift

I found myself surrounded by an all-consuming blackness so thick that it felt as though I could touch it. It was such a deep inky blackness that it made me realize that even when we *think* we're in complete and utter darkness, there is almost always light emanating from somewhere: light in the hallway sneaking under the doorway, perhaps, or the light of the stars on a moonless night in the wilderness. But this inky blackness wasn't like that at all. It was so dark, as the saying goes, that I couldn't see my hand in front of my face. It was so intense and absolute that the longer I stood there, the more I felt it seeping into my pores.

To make matters worse, it was also cold—bitterly cold. And while I stood there waiting, I was forced to pull my jacket more tightly around me in a vain attempt to protect myself from the freezing air. Just a few days earlier, I'd been in the tropics, wearing shorts and sandals and suffering in the oppressive, sweltering heat of equatorial Africa. But now I'd returned to the colder climate of Ireland by backtracking north on commercial airliners along the path I'd already taken across Europe and Africa.

Six months earlier, I'd filled out an entry form on a whim, and that's how I found myself standing there on that cold December morning, but I wasn't alone. Surrounding me on all sides were others waiting with me for the sunrise. I could feel their presence somehow, and I could hear them breathing the icy air. They were even close enough for me to feel their warmth, but in the invisible blackness, they might as well have been a million miles away. I felt isolated and alone as though I were a lost soul floating aimlessly through the universe.

I looked up at the ceiling. I couldn't see a thing in the darkness, but I knew it was up there—the writing that we'd discovered so many months ago—the final clue that had unlocked the secret to everything.

I had to remind myself that I was supposed to be looking down, not up, so I peered down toward my feet where at any moment the light of the rising sun would begin to carve its way across the floor of the chamber.

Just imagine being in this place so many thousands of years ago when it was first built, I thought to myself in wonder as I stared blindly into the black. *Far underground, cold and frightened, and probably wondering if the sun would ever rise again, but they knew it would. That's why they built this place. And with the rising sun their world would be reborn.*

My breath caught suddenly in my throat as I thought I caught a glimpse of light in motion in the endless dark. Was it the first rays of the sun breaking over the distant horizon? Or was it just a trick of my imagination?

The seconds passed, and my eyes detected a flicker of light in the gloom as the curtain of darkness slowly lifted from my eyes. Seconds turned into minutes, and I stared in utter amazement as a thin rapier of pure liquid light knifed its way across the stone floor and poured a golden heavenly luminescence into the crowded chamber, filling it with light and warmth.

My mouth was hanging open in complete astonishment at the sheer and absolute beauty of it. I glanced around me and saw that the others were every bit as breathless as I was. It was the most beautiful thing I had ever seen.

It was numinous.

It was sublime.

But in truth there were absolutely no words to describe it, and yet my mind raced to find some linguist hook upon which I could anchor the experience and never forget it, not that I ever would. I would remember it for the rest of my days.

As the heavenly fire continued to fill every nook and cranny of the underground chamber, I couldn't resist lifting my head again to look at the ceiling. Somehow, I just had to be sure that the writing was still there, and of course it –was; it had been there for many, many years before I ever laid eyes on it, and it would remain there for many years more, perhaps for all eternity. But I just had to know for sure, so for a quick moment I tore my eyes away from the radiant beam of light splitting the floor and glanced upward.

It took a moment to orient myself and find it again, but there it was, waiting to be found again.

So many months and a thousand memories had passed since I'd last been inside this underground temple of light, and yet it felt like yesterday.

With a lump growing in my throat and tears of emotion in my eyes, I lowered my gaze and watched the dagger of light slowly recede across the floor. Before I knew it, and as mysteriously as it had arrived, the beam soon retreated up the tunnel and out into the reborn world outside, plunging our underground world into the same thick and utter blackness from which we'd just emerged.

And then there was silence. A silence so complete that not a single one of us dared to breathe. For a moment, I was a lost soul again, set adrift in the universe and floating on the memory of the adventures that had led me to this place so many months before.

Chapter Zero
A Flying Blob of Sumo-Wrestling Wasabi

From: Kitty Hawk <kittyhawk@kittyhawkworld.com>
To: Charlie Lewis <chlewis@alaska.net>
Subject: A Flying Blob of Sumo-Wrestling Wasabi

Dear Charlie,

You should see my plane! It looks completely ridiculous! Every time I passed low over a cargo ship or fishing boat on the flight from Iceland to Ireland I couldn't help but wonder what in the heck they thought of me, flying overhead in my bright red plane with its new bright green Wasabi Willy painted on the side. I think even the whales and dolphins were laughing at me.

Just kidding Charlie. Well, sort of kidding, anyway. I am sure all of those people are still laughing but I don't care. If that's what it takes to continue my flight around the world, then it's perfectly fine with me.

I can never thank you enough for everything you've done for me and all the trouble you went through to make sure I could keep on flying. I will never forget it. Thank you.

I am thinking of you, always. Talk to you soon.

k.

Chapter One

Welcome To Wasabi Willy's

"Ladies and gentlemen!" the sharply dressed man at the podium said excitedly. "Welcome to Dublin and the grand opening of the Grafton Street location of Wasabi Willy's Family Sushi Restaurant!"

The crowd cheered and clapped enthusiastically. And this was understandable since they would soon be sampling some free sushi as part of the opening ceremony activities. I have to admit that I was a bit less enthusiastic as I watched the man address the crowd. The man's name was Kevin O'Donnell, and he was the head manager of the Wasabi Willy's restaurant chain in Ireland.

"We have a lot of exciting things lined up today for you guys," Kevin continued, "including some free sushi giveaways for anyone who wants to try a few of the delicious items from our menu. But first I would like to welcome a very special guest to today's grand opening. This young lady has come to visit us all the way from Canada, and she's stopping here in Dublin to have some sushi before she continues on her amazing solo flight around the world. Ladies and gentlemen, will you please welcome the incredible and remarkable young female pilot, Ms. Kitty Hawk!"

The crowd burst into another round of energetic applause and cheers— fueled, I suppose, by the promise of free sushi and not so much by the prospect of meeting me. With a big smile I stepped into view and struggled to wave to the crowd as I waddled across the stage toward Kevin in the gigantic inflatable sumo wrestler suit that I was wearing to help celebrate the grand opening.

"Thank you very much," I said after I reached the center of the podium and Kevin handed me the microphone. "Thank you for such a warm welcome to your beautiful country. I am thrilled to be here to support this grand opening of a restaurant that I know and love so much."

I was reciting some pre-written text that Kevin and I had agreed upon earlier, but I really *did* know the Wasabi Willy's restaurant fairly well. I had eaten there twelve months earlier, before my adventures took me up the Chilkoot Trail and into the Yukon where I was doing humpback whale research in Juneau, Alaska. The restaurant atmosphere was great and the food even better, but I did have my doubts about their colorful mascot, a giant blob of maniacally smiling wasabi in a sumo-wrestler loincloth.

Of course, I didn't say anything to Kevin about my feelings toward their mascot. The company was, after all, financing my flight around the world in exchange for my promoting the company and participating in events such as this grand opening. Oh yes, and let's not forget that they had painted their giant smiling wasabi logo on the side of my De Havilland Beaver seaplane.

My friend Charlie in Alaska had made all the arrangements for me with the Wasabi Willy's advertising department, and for that I was eternally grateful, but as I wobbled and teetered precariously onto that stage in my enormous sumo suit, I did have to wonder how in the world I'd gotten myself into this situation.

I looked out across the small sea of smiling faces and did my best to smile as I handed the microphone to Kevin so that he could continue with the grand opening festivities. As I scanned the crowd, I noticed a handsome young man standing by himself off to one side. He was wearing a dark suit with a pale gray tie, and his forehead was wrinkled in a slightly worried expression. I watched him for a few moments, wondering why he was looking so serious while everyone else in the crowd was smiling. After a few seconds, he noticed me looking at him and immediately broke into a wide smile as he nodded in my direction.

Busted! I thought to myself and quickly tried to look elsewhere, pretending that I hadn't been staring at him so intently. In my embarrassment, I blushed bright red and averted my eyes, but I was smiling to myself as I did so. Whoever he was, he was very good looking, and who can help but be happy when someone like that smiles at them?

"Thank you, Kitty," Kevin said as he continued with the opening ceremony. "We're happy to have you here with us in Ireland, and I hope that you'll join us for some free sushi in just a few minutes."

"I certainly will," I replied, keeping my eyes forward, resisting the urge to look out of the corner of my eye where I could see the young man in the dark suit standing there.

"But first," Kevin continued, his voice deep and booming loudly through the microphone like an announcer in a boxing match, "it's time to introduce your opponent for today's sumo wrestling challenge. Ladies and gentlemen, in the opposite corner, weighing in at a staggering three hundred and forty seven kilograms, please allow me to introduce the reigning heavyweight champion—Wasabi-i-i-i-i Willy-y-y-y-y-y!!!"

I resisted the urge to roll my eyes as dramatic music began to play and Kevin gestured flamboyantly toward the opposite side of the stage.

"Y'all ready for this?" Kevin bellowed to the crowd. "Let's get ready to rumblllle!!!"

As the pulsing electronic beat of a dance mix filled the air, I turned to look to the side of the stage where a gigantic Wasabi Willy was pounding up the steps and out onto the podium. I couldn't help but laugh as I watched the enormous costume make its way to center stage. I knew that underneath the huge inflatable costume there was a tiny young woman named Ciara, whom I'd met before the show. I was amazed that despite her very small size she was able to move around in the Wasabi Willy costume as if it didn't weigh a thing.

As Wasabi Willy broke into a comical dance, the crowd below us clapped and danced along to the deafening beat of the music. Above our heads, confetti cannons exploded a deluge of tissue paper wasabi blobs into the air, and as they showered onto the crowd, a cheerleading squad in short wasabi green skirts erupted from both sides of the stage and joined Willy in his ridiculous dance.

There was a time in my life when I probably would have nearly died of embarrassment from being involved in such an outlandish spectacle, but it was so completely insane and over-the-top that I simply couldn't help but laugh at the craziness of it all.

"Be aggressive! B - E aggressive!" the cheerleaders cheered as they kicked and flipped their way around the stage. "Whoop, there it is! Whoop, there it is!"

The cheerleaders continued their frenetic dance, and then just as quickly as they'd appeared, they circled around and disappeared backstage. At the front of the stage, Wasabi Willy led the audience in one final cheer as the music faded, and then he (or really she) lumbered to the side of the wrestling ring where he crouched in a traditional sumo wrestler's stance.

"You're up," Kevin said, grinning as he slapped me on the back of my inflatable sumo suit. "Good luck."

Still laughing and smiling, I waddled over to my side of the circle and tried to lean over in a proper wrestling stance. The whole thing was crazy, but if this was what Wasabi Willy's restaurant wanted me to do in exchange for funding my flight around the world, then who was I to complain? I was going to enjoy every second of it even if they expected me to sumo wrestle a ridiculous big-head costume version of their mascot. And that, of course, was exactly what I was about to do.

Chapter Two
Handsome AND Patient

"Sorry about your foot," Ciara said to me backstage as she helped me wiggle my way out of my costume.

The wrestling match had gone fairly well. Ciara (or should I say Willy) and I circled menacingly around each other at first, each of us looking for the chance to pounce on the other. Willy (aka Ciara) was the first to strike, swooping in fast and engaging me in a clutch of death. As the crowd chanted "Willy! Willy! Willy!" over and over again, the two of us pushed each other around the ring, struggling to keep the upper hand.

I put up a good fight, but in the end, Willy was just too good for me. Soon he was tossing me around like a bouncy rag doll to the delight of the crowd below. But I wasn't ready to give up yet, and when Willy sent me rolling across the stage, I saw my chance. Seeing that he was off balance after shoving me so hard, I spun quickly around and bounced Willy down to the floor. Swept up in the moment, I leapt high into the air to execute a devastating body slam and win the match. But I had forgotten how bouncy our inflatable suits were, and instead of finishing Willy off with a decisive blow, I bounced right back up into the air again, flying off to one side, dazed and confused.

Seeing my confusion, Willy went for the kill and lumbered over to pin me to the mat, stepping painfully on my toes in the process. Thoroughly humiliated and defeated, I finally tapped out and conceded the match to Willy. The crowd went wild as Willy danced around the front of the stage in victory, leaving me to dust myself off and wobble onto my feet again.

"Don't worry," I told Ciara with a grin. "No harm done. Besides, I am pretty sure that traditional sumo wrestling doesn't involve things like body slams and other acrobatics."

The two of us laughed as Ciara pulled the last of the inflatable sumo suit off me and started to pull her costume on again.

"Aren't you getting undressed too?" I asked.

Ciara shook her head. "Willy has to make the rounds and take some photos with the kids," she said, pulling the enormous Willy body over her head once again. "See you out there!"

And with that she pushed her big head through the curtains and lumbered out into the crowd. I watched for a moment as kids swarmed around her, punching and grabbing at her costume as she waded through them.

Laughing to myself, I ducked into a changing cubicle to pull on a dry T-shirt and quickly slap on some deodorant. I was surprised at how sweaty the sumo costume had made me and decided to pull on a dry set of pants before I ventured out into the crowd after her.

Sumo wrestling had not only made me sweat but also surprisingly hungry as well. As I mingled with the crowd, I helped myself to maki rolls and nigiri sushi as servers with sample trays passed by every few minutes.

I couldn't believe how many people wanted to talk to me and wish me luck on my flight. I felt like some kind of celebrity as people asked me for my autograph and wanted to take photos with me standing next to them.

"You do realize that I'm not famous," I said as I posed with a young boy and his mother, making silly duck faces for the camera.

"You're probably right," the mother laughed. "But when we read in the newspaper that you were going to be here, my son immediately wanted to come down here to meet you and see your plane."

"Oh, I'm sorry," I replied, kneeling down to speak directly to her son. "My plane is parked up the coast somewhere. I had to take the train into the city this morning."

"That's okay," he replied, smiling shyly. "It was better seeing Wasabi Willy kick your butt."

"Hey!" I protested, feigning indignance as all of us laughed and some other people stepped forward to get their picture taken with me.

While all of this craziness was going on, I couldn't help but notice that the handsome young man in the dark suit was waiting patiently nearby for the crowd to thin out so that he could have a chance to talk to me as well.

I hope he wants to take a photo with me, I thought, grinning to myself as I signed the back of a Wasabi Willy take-out menu for a father and his two daughters. He was extremely handsome, tall, and athletic with dark hair and intense green eyes. He reminded of that *Batman* actor, Christian Bale. *In fact, maybe it IS Batman*, I thought, grinning to myself.

I looked over at him and smiled apologetically as I continued chatting with the various people who'd been waiting in line to meet me. "Don't worry," he mouthed back with a smile and a wave of his palm.

Handsome AND patient, I thought, and the mystery of who he was and what he wanted deepened.

Finally the crowd of well-wishers and photo-seekers thinned out and I found myself talking to the last group of people—a pair of teenaged girls and their mother.

"Do you really fly all by yourself?" one of the girls asked me as we lined up so their mother could take a photo. "I mean, you have a pilot's license, right?"

"Of course," I replied, nodding as I grabbed another piece of sushi from a passing tray.

"Where do you sleep at night?" the girl's friend asked.

I shrugged. "In hotels sometimes, or sometimes with people who my friends back home arrange for me to stay with. But most of the time I just sleep in the back of my plane on a mattress with a sleeping bag."

For some reason this seemed to impress them. "Do you ever get scared?" the first girl asked, eyes wide.

I leaned close to them as their mother prepared to take our picture. "Sometimes," I admitted, making us all laugh as their mother snapped the photo. "But don't tell anyone."

The two girls hugged me and thanked me before they headed off to find a few more sushi samples. That left only the handsome and mysterious stranger in the line of people waiting to see me.

"Hello," he said, smiling warmly as he stepped forward to shake my hand. "Kitty Hawk, I presume?"

"You presume correctly," I replied, blushing in spite of telling myself not to. At first, I couldn't quite place his accent. It was different from the lilting brogue I'd been getting used to ever since arriving in Ireland. His was more melodic and smooth, with rolling Rs and flowing syllables. He sounded like Shrek, just more authentic and less annoying—more like Sean Connery, actually.

Scottish, I realized. *He's from Scotland.*

"A pleasure to meet you, Kitty Hawk," he said. "My name is Andrew Murdoch, and I came here today because my family and I are interested in hiring you."

"Hiring *me*?!?" I asked, surprised. "To do what?"

"To solve a mystery," Andrew said. "One that's kept my family stumped for almost eighty years."

"Eighty years?!?" I replied, more surprised than ever. "After so much time, why on earth would you think that I could solve it if your family hasn't been able to?"

Andrew smiled. "I've heard a lot about your exploits in Florida and Iceland," he replied. "And I think you're just the kind of detective we need."

"A detective?!?" I replied, laughing at the thought of it. "I'm not a detective!"

Andrew raised his eyebrows and gave me a curious little smile. "I think you're more of a detective than you realize," he said. "You're a one-woman flying detective agency."

Chapter Three

A One-Woman Flying Detective Agency

A flying detective agency? The thought of it was enough to make me laugh, but I restrained myself because Andrew's offer was just too intriguing to ignore. I agreed to meet with him later that evening so that he could explain it all.

After wandering through Dublin's Temple Bar district past noisy pubs filled with Irish dancers and pints of Guinness, I finally found the tiny restaurant that I was looking for on a small side street off the main thoroughfare. Andrew was waiting for me in a booth near the back, and he stood up to greet me when he saw me crossing the room.

"Kitty, you made it," he said with a smile, taking my coat and hanging it on a coat hook at the end of the table.

"I was starting to wonder if I'd ever find it," I replied with a grin as I slid onto the bench directly across from him. "This neighborhood is like a loud, crazy maze of pubs and Irish music."

The waitress came over and we ordered some bottles of water and a couple bowls of Irish stew before Andrew got down to business. Pulling a plastic folder from his pocket, he extracted an old, yellowed envelope from inside and laid it on the table in front of me. It was addressed by hand to the Murdoch family in Dalbeattie, Scotland using long, flowing cursive writing.

"In 1937 my family received this envelope in the mail," he said, "with no return address and no indication whatsoever of where it came from except that the postmark was from London."

I leaned over to examine the stamp and postal mark at the corner of the envelope. I could see that it was indeed from London.

Andrew carefully opened the envelope, removed two items from inside, and placed them on the table so I could see them.

The first item was a news story torn out of an old newspaper.

TITANIC OWNER MAKES GENEROUS DONATION TO BRITISH MERCHANTMEN

London, January 2, 1931

In an effort to express his admiration for the heroic conduct of the officers and men of the British Mercantile Marine in weathering the storm of the Great War, Mr J. Bruce Ismay, former managing director of the White Star Line that owned Titanic and survivor of the disaster, has donated £25,000 to the Mercantile Marine Service Association. This munificent gift breaks all previous records for generosity, including those set by Ismay's late father, Thomas Henry Ismay, founder of the White Star Line, who once made a similar donation of £20,000 more than thirty years ago to the Liverpool Seamen's Pension Fund.

Following the sinking of the Titanic Mr. Ismay found himself the target of condemnation for having survived and failing to go down with his own ship. According to his own accounts he was on board the ship only in the capacity of an ordinary passenger and exerted no control or influence over the operation of the vessel itself. Ismay himself maintains that after the ship struck the iceberg he assisted in the loading of lifeboats and when there were no other women or children in sight as the last boat was finished loading he climbed in as it was being lowered away. However, in light of the fact that more than 1500 of his fellow passengers perished in the disaster Mr. Ismay was much criticised for his conduct.

The entire affair left Ismay a broken man and after resigning his chairmanship of the White Star Line in 1913 he became a virtual recluse and never again appeared at public functions or discussed the Titanic with anyone. As such he had no statement regarding his generous gift to the British Mercantile Marine but Harold Wilkes, the director of the organisation's Liverpool branch hoped that Mr. Ismay's gift will spawn a flood of similar donations to charitable organisations that benefit British seamen and their families.

"This horrific war has devastated our empire, drag on the institutions tasked with caring for those in need as well as their innocent widows and children. Our boys went through hell during the course of the war and whether their fate was to crawl resolutely through the Flanders mud or serve courageously upon the high seas, the treasure of our empire can only provide a limited degree of support to them and their families. The responsibility to safeguard their future lies with all citizens whose freedom these brave men defended. We must all do what we can to ensure that these brave men are not left hungry and destitute on the thoroughfares of our great cities. We British have a long history of rising to every challenge with heads held high. Whether slaying the dragons of our mythology or spilling the blood of our youth in defence of freedom, this generosity of spirit is but one of the many virtues that make us British. And as we have just witnessed during the course of this horrendous war, where there are those in need, whether within the borders of our own realm or off on some far distant foreign shore, it is our ancient duty to be as unyielding as stone as we stand shoulder to shoulder together against the onslaught like our fathers did before us. We must be ready and willing to sacrifice the many flowers of our generation to nip the plans of evil in the bud and defend our empire. Above all else, we must be British."

DAILY CROSSWORD JANUARY 2ND 1931

FAMED BALLERINA ANNA PAVLOVA FALLS ILL

Famed Russian ballerina Anna Pavlova has fallen ill with pneumonia after catching a chill during a train journey from the French Riviera to The Hague, Netherlands where she is scheduled to perform her legendary Dying Swan. Generally considered to be the greatest dancer of all time, Ms. Pavlova began her amazing career in her native Russia, later to debut on the London stage where audiences were instantly enthralled by her incomparable technique and unequalled grace. Since that time she has given hundreds of performances and travelled audiences all over the world. Just a few short weeks short of her 50th birthday the celebrated danseuse remains without an equal anywhere in the ballet world. Sources close to the dancer report that she is recuperating in the renowned Hotel Des Indes and hope that she will be back

The second was a postcard with a black and white photo of an enormous four-funneled steamship. According to the text at the bottom of the card, the ship was the *Titanic*.

Andrew neatly lined up everything on the table in front of us and looked at me with his dark, intense eyes.

R.M.S. TITANIC

"At the risk of seeming overly dramatic," he said overly dramatically, "perhaps a bit of background explanation is required before we go any further."

"Okay," I replied.

"What do you know about the *Titanic*?" he asked.

I thought about this for a moment, thinking about my only real source of knowledge on the topic, which was the *Titanic* movie. "I know a few things," I replied with a shrug. "I know that the *Titanic* was the largest ship in the world, and after it set off on its maiden voyage, it hit an iceberg and sank while hundreds of people were left behind and died because there weren't enough lifeboats."

Andrew nodded gravely. "Almost fifteen hundred people died," he said quietly, "making it one of the worst maritime disasters in history."

"Oh, and one other thing," I said, remembering another detail from the film. "The *Titanic* was supposed to be unsinkable."

Andrew nodded again. "That was what was believed, although some have argued that the owners and builders of the *Titanic* never actually claimed that the ship was unsinkable, but rather that she was *practically* unsinkable or *designed* to be unsinkable. It's just a matter of words at any rate, and the owners certainly didn't discourage the unsinkable myth, and most of the general public at that time considered it impossible for the ship to sink."

"But it did sink," I said, thinking about all those poor souls left behind after all the lifeboats had left. "And so many people paid for that with their lives."

"It could have been much worse, though," Andrew said. "When the *Titanic* sank, she had only slightly more than half the number of passengers that she was capable of accommodating."

"Really?" I asked, surprised. "Is that true?"

"Aye, it's a fact," Andrew replied. "Her total capacity for passengers and crew was more than three thousand five hundred, but at the time of the sinking she only had twenty two hundred people on board—more than a thousand less than she was capable of carrying."

"How much space was in the lifeboats for those people?" I asked, curious.

"One thousand, one hundred and seventy eight," Andrew replied.

I did the math in my head and was shocked. "That's only one third as many lifeboats as they needed," I replied. "I had no idea it was so few."

"That's the real tragedy of the *Titanic*," Andrew said, nodding in agreement.

"But why weren't there more lifeboats?" I asked. "Was it because the owners thought the ship was unsinkable and therefore didn't want to be bothered? What about government regulations and safety laws—didn't those force them to carry more lifeboats?"

Andrew shook his head. "Unfortunately, the laws of the time didn't require *Titanic* to have more lifeboats on board," he said. "In fact, the *Titanic* actually had four *more* lifeboats than the law required."

"How is that possible?!?" I asked, surprised. "Shouldn't the law be that a ship has enough lifeboats to hold every single person on board?"

Andrew shook his head again. "Back in those days this was unfortunately not the case," he replied. "Back then the rules calculating the number of lifeboats a ship needed was based on the ship's gross tonnage, not the number of passengers and crew. And to make things even worse, those regulations were terribly out-of-date considering how much larger the ships of the time were becoming. The figure for the number of lifeboats that *Titanic* was required to carry was based on a calculation for a ship weighing less than a quarter of her size."

I couldn't believe what Andrew was telling me. It was completely insane to calculate the number of lifeboats that way. Clearly, there were many things about the story of *Titanic* that I wasn't aware of.

"Maybe you should start at the beginning," I said as the waitress arrived with a pair of steaming bowls filled with Irish lamb stew. "Just give me the basics."

C h a p t e r   F o u r

If You Love Life Get Off This Ship At Cherboug

"Okay, the basics," Andrew said as I had my first taste of the deliciously thick Irish stew. I juggled a scalding hot chunk of potato on my tongue and listened while savoring the rich meaty stew flavored with a hint of Guinness.

"On the tenth of April, 1912, the *Titanic* set sail on its maiden voyage from Southampton, England," Andrew began. "She was the biggest ship in the world, although not by much since she was only a few inches longer and tons heavier than her sister ship, the *Olympic*, which had been launched the year before. Neither of them would remain the biggest for long since barely a month later the German Hamburg America line launched their newest ship, the *Imperator*, which was even larger."

"But at least the *Titanic* was the fastest ship in the world, right?" I asked.

Andrew shook his head. "Unfortunately, it wasn't," he replied. "At that time the fastest ship in the world was Cunard's *Mauretania*. But the thing that set the *Titanic* apart was how luxurious she was, far more so than the ships of rival companies and even more so than her own sister ship. She was the pride and joy of the White Star Line company as she steamed out of Southampton harbor that day on her way to Cherbourg, France.

"But then an unfortunate thing happened," Andrew said, pausing to have a spoonful of his stew. "After the tugboats maneuvered *Titanic* away from the dock, she began to make her way toward the English Channel under her own steam, passing by a pair of smaller ocean liners tied up nearby. As the passengers and crew watched in horror, these two ships were slowly pulled out on a collision course with *Titanic*.

"Now, don't forget that even though these two ships were small in comparison to the *Titanic*, they were enormous ocean liners nonetheless, each weighing more than ten thousand tons. The force of the suction from *Titanic*'s enormous propellers was too great for these ships to resist, and they were pulled away from the docks unexpectedly. With a series of cracks that sounded like rifle shots the three-inch-thick mooring lines of the closest ship snapped under the immense strain, leaving its back end to swing free into the river and toward *Titanic*'s stern.

"For a few tense moments the two ships swung closer and closer together and it looked like a collision was unavoidable. But thanks to some quick action by the captain of the *Titanic* and some maneuvering by a nearby tugboat, the disaster was averted and the ships missed each other with only a few feet to spare."

"That's unbelievable," I said as I watched Andrew lean forward to have another spoonful of stew. "But if the two ships *had* collided and the *Titanic* had been damaged, wouldn't they have been forced to cancel her maiden voyage?"

Andrew nodded. "And perhaps the lives of fifteen hundred people would've been saved," he said, "although one can never know for certain, of course."

"If only...." I said, my voice trailing off in mid-sentence as I imagined the history that could have been.

"But perhaps at least *one* life was saved as a result of the accident," Andrew commented. "Renee Harris, one of the survivors of *Titanic*, later told the story that after witnessing this near miss with the smaller ship, a stranger standing next to her turned and said, 'Do you love life?' Feeling a bit flustered at his question, she said, 'Of course I do.' The stranger nodded toward the smaller ship that *Titanic* had just missed by mere inches and said, 'That was a bad omen, so if you love life, then get off this ship at Cherbourg. That's what I'm going to do." Mrs. Harris laughed and dismissed his comments as ridiculous, but that man was true to his word; she never saw him again for the remainder of the voyage."

"Incredible," I said in amazement.

"He wasn't the only one who had a bad feeling about *Titanic*," Andrew continued. "After crossing the English Channel the ship anchored off of Cherbourg and prepared to take more passengers aboard. One of those passengers was Edith Russell who had visited an Arab fortune teller a few months earlier and been told that she would be involved in a very grave accident at sea. Despite this grim prediction, she booked passage on the *Titanic*, but as she approached the towering steel sides of the ship and the small passenger tender boat bumped and pounded against the great hull, her anxiety increased. She boarded the ship and immediately inquired about retrieving her luggage and returning to shore. She was told that she could leave, but that it would be impossible to locate her luggage in the ship's hold by that point. It would have to go on to New York without her. Since the contents of her luggage were very valuable, she asked about purchasing insurance if it went on without her. 'Ridiculous, this ship is unsinkable,' she was told, and so she reluctantly decided that it would be better if she stayed onboard rather than be separated from her belongings. But her feeling of unease persisted, and she went to her cabin to write a letter to her secretary in Paris saying that she wished the trip was already over because she could not get over her feelings of depression and foreboding."

"Wow," I said. "I can't believe it."

"She wasn't the only one to have such feelings of apprehension," Andrew added. "After all the passengers were aboard, the *Titanic* pulled up her anchors and sailed overnight to Queenstown, Ireland, where the ship made its last stop before heading across the Atlantic Ocean for New York City. As they loaded the last passengers and sacks of mail, a young stoker from the *Titanic*'s engine room named John Coffey was overwhelmed with a sense of fear, so he slipped off the ship and stowed away aboard one of the cargo tender boats that were heading back for dry land, thus saving his life.

"But even that wasn't the last of it. Another event soon occurred that people would later look back on as a bad omen, and it involved one of John Coffey's fellow stokers. As the ship prepared to steam out of Ireland, some of the passengers happened to glance up and noticed a black face peering down at them from out of the top of the ship's fourth funnel. To some he looked like the devil, grinning evilly down on them with a mischievous grin, but in reality he was merely one of the ship's engine room crew, his face black with coal dust, who had climbed up the inside of the funnel and stuck his head out as a joke. But joke or not, to some this was yet another sign that some kind of curse hung over the *Titanic*'s maiden voyage."

I was confused. "How could he climb up the inside of the funnel? Isn't that where all the smoke comes out?"

Andrew shook his head. "Not the fourth funnel. On the *Titanic*, the fourth funnel was a fake. It was built to make the ship seem larger and more impressive than it actually was."

I smiled and gave a cynical snort of laughter as Andrew continued his story.

"Despite this bad omen, the ship sailed out of Queenstown and into the open Atlantic without further incident," Andrew said. "She was headed for New York, and it was too late for anyone else to have second thoughts. But that didn't stop some passengers and crew from feeling uneasy despite the ship's steady progress. Down in Second Class was seven-year-old Eva Hart, who was travelling with her parents. Years after the disaster, Eva recalled that her mother had been very upset about sailing on the *Titanic* and was convinced that some sort of tragedy would occur. She had a premonition that it would happen at night, so she slept by day and spent her nights sitting up, fully awake and alert as she read or knitted. Even the *Titanic*'s own Chief Officer had his doubts about the ship. He wrote to his sister before leaving Queenstown that he didn't like the ship and that he had a queer feeling about it.

"But for most of the passengers on *Titanic*, there were no premonitions or thoughts of impending doom. To them the ship was a luxurious dream. In First Class, the well-to-do passengers enjoyed the same comforts and opulence that they were used to in hotels and restaurants back on land. Even down in Third Class, the passengers were enjoying a level of luxury that was unheard of on ships at the time—not that their small cabins or basic food was all that luxurious, of course, but compared to the wretched conditions on other ships of the period, the steerage passengers on *Titanic* lived like kings and queens.

"As the ship steamed westward, the passengers settled into the comfortable routine of shipboard life. For the next three days and nights, they ate and drank, relaxed and rested, read books, played cards, and enjoyed all of the amenities that their magnificent ship had to offer. For most passengers there was no reason to suspect that the crossing would be anything less than perfect.

"But all of that changed on the evening of the fourteenth of April," Andrew said, his face turning grim. "And that's where my family comes into the story, because at the moment that the *Titanic* struck the iceberg, the man who was the senior watch officer on the bridge was my great uncle, First Officer William McMaster Murdoch."

Chapter Five

A Mathematical Certainty

"Oh my god," I gasped in surprise. "Is it true?!? Your great uncle was on the *Titanic*?"

Andrew nodded. "It's true," he replied quietly.

"Did he...?" I struggled to find the right words.

"Survive?" Andrew suggested, reading my thoughts. "Unfortunately, he didn't. And because of that, my family has wondered ever since about his actions on that tragic night and how he died."

"His actions... what do you mean?" I asked.

Andrew took a final spoonful of stew and leaned back in his chair with a sigh.

"Let's just say that there are some differences of opinion regarding the actions of my great uncle that night," he said. "But what is absolutely known for certain is that on the night of Sunday, April 14th, 1912, he was on bridge of the *Titanic* as she steamed headlong toward the iceberg that would eventually sink her.

"Murdoch would have had a beautiful view from his position high up on the bridge, because the weather that night was remarkably clear. In fact, the North Atlantic was calmer and clearer than anyone could remembered it ever being, and as far as we know, it has never been like that since. There was no moon, and a million stars shone like diamonds through the pitch-blackness overhead, while the surface of the ocean lay as flat as a millpond.

"The temperature was bitterly cold. During the course of the evening, the air temperature had fallen to the freezing point, convincing passengers to head indoors to seek the inviting warmth of the ship's interior rooms. It was so cold that near the back of the ship Quartermaster George Rowe was standing on watch all alone on the docking bridge and noticed what he called 'whiskers 'round the light'— splinters of ice in the air giving off tiny rainbows of color as they passed close to the deck lights. This suggested to him that there were icebergs somewhere nearby.

"First class passenger Elizabeth Shutes also sensed the proximity of ice as she opened the porthole of her cabin to get a bit of fresh air. The air was biting cold and had a strange smell that she found familiar. She'd experienced the same odor in the air when she was in Switzerland visiting the ice caves of the Eiger glacier.

"The officers on the bridge also knew that they were approaching ice. The area they were sailing into typically had ice that time of year, and the crew had received a number of ice warnings throughout the day from other ships in the vicinity. Those warnings alerted them of an ice field somewhere on the *Titanic*'s course, and earlier in the evening, the captain had ordered a slight deviation farther south in the hope of avoiding the worst of it.

"But despite the warnings, the ship steamed on into the dark night. There was nothing unusual about this decision, even in such conditions, nor was it considered irresponsible by the standards of the time. Encountering ice on the North Atlantic was a regular occurrence, and instead of slowing down or stopping the accepted practice for avoiding a collision was to place lookouts overhead to spot any icebergs, and the ship was steered around them.

"Tragically, however, the weather conditions that night conspired against *Titanic*, and the normal accepted operating procedures failed to protect her most of passengers. The ship's second officer, Charles Lightoller, would later describe the conditions as being so rare that you would not see them even once in a hundred years. There was not a single cloud in the sky or the slightest breath of wind. The stars shone brightly, but there was no moon, and the ocean was a complete flat calm with no swell whatsoever. This meant that there were no waves to wash up against the base of an iceberg and make it easier to spot. Such conditions were unheard of, even to the experienced officers on the *Titanic*, but they were still no cause for alarm, so the ship steamed on.

"As the watch officer on duty at the time of the accident, my great uncle Murdoch would have been standing outside on the wings of the bridge, peering ahead into the darkness toward a dazzling sea of stars flickering at the horizon. Far above him in the crow's nest, two of the ship's lookouts, Frederick Fleet and Reginald Lee, were doing precisely the same, and just before twenty minutes to midnight, each of them saw a dark and ominous silhouette looming into view directly ahead of them, growing larger with every passing second.

"Lookout Fleet reached up to ring the crow's nest bell three times, a signal that there was an object directly ahead. He picked up the telephone connecting them to the bridge and waited for someone to answer. Down in the wheelhouse, Sixth Officer Moody answered the phone and asked them what they saw. 'Iceberg, right ahead!' Fleet responded.

"Murdoch probably spotted the iceberg as well and responded immediately, ordering the helm to be put 'hard-a-starboard' while he rushed over to the engine telegraphs to change the ship's speed. After he finished with that, he hurried to the panel that controlled the ship's watertight doors and activated the switch to close them. Within seconds, the enormous doors in the engine rooms began to close and sealed off the ship's individual watertight compartments. Having done everything he could to avoid a collision, there was nothing left to do but wait as they plowed on toward the enormous iceberg that loomed directly ahead of them, growing larger by the second.

"For the longest time the ship seemed to do nothing but continue on her course, driving straight for the towering iceberg. But then, slowly but surely, the bow of the ship swung to the left, almost swinging into the clear before striking the ice with a slight bump followed by a prolonged shudder and the faint noise of wrenching metal. The men on the bridge watched helplessly as the great tower of ice passed them by and scraped along the side of the ship. After a few moments, the grinding noise stopped, and from where they were standing, it looked like a close shave.

"Moments later, Captain Smith arrived on the bridge from his nearby cabin. Like many other passengers and crewmembers, he'd felt the jarring motion of the iceberg grinding along the side of the ship, and had rushed to the bridge to find out what was going on. 'It's an iceberg,' Murdoch informed him. 'I put us hard-a-starboard and tried to port 'round it, but she was too close, and we hit.'

"Fourth Officer Boxhall also arrived on the bridge to see what had happened and was ordered by the captain to go below and report back on the situation. Boxhall returned after a few minutes to report that several of the ship's forward compartments were flooding, and the captain sent for Thomas Andrews, *Titanic*'s chief designer, who was on board for the maiden voyage to evaluate the ship's performance.

"Other people soon arrived on the bridge to find out what was happening, including J. Bruce Ismay, the managing director of the White Star Line, the company that owned *Titanic*. Ismay asked whether the ship was seriously damaged. 'I'm afraid she is,' the captain replied.

"Already the *Titanic* was off kilter as a result of the flooding. Captain Smith checked the ship's instruments and determined that the ship was tilting two degrees at the bow from the weight of the water. 'My god,' he said quietly to himself before he and Thomas Andrews descended to the lower decks to assess the damage with their own eyes.

"What they found was not good. Firemen from the engine rooms were evacuating their berths at the front of the ship due to flooding. The forward cargo holds were flooded, and boiler rooms 6 and 5 were flooding fast. Postal clerks in the mailroom were in water up to their waists as they moved sacks of letters to higher ground to keep them dry, and even the ship's squash court was awash with water. The situation was grim, and Thomas Andrews knew immediately what it all meant. He gave the ship only an hour to live. It was a mathematical certainty. The *Titanic* would sink. And there were only enough lifeboats to save half the people on board."

C h a p t e r   S i x
Women And Children First

"What do you mean that it was a mathematical certainty that the *Titanic* would sink?" I asked after Andrew ordered us some after-dinner coffee.

Andrew reached down to grab the postcard of *Titanic* that we had been looking at earlier, and he put it on the table in front of me.

"Below the waterline, *Titanic*'s hull was divided into sixteen separate compartments," he explained, running a finger over the photograph to illustrate what he was talking about. "The *Titanic* was designed to stay afloat with any two of those compartments flooded, because at the time, this was considered the worst possible thing that could happen to a ship. In fact, depending on the location of the flooding, the *Titanic* could stay afloat with three or even four compartments flooded. But the collision with the iceberg on that cold April night had torn open three hundred feet of the hull and flooded five compartments, with more flooding taking place in a sixth. With so many compartments flooded there was no way around it—the *Titanic* was doomed."

"Thomas Andrews and Captain Smith quickly reached this conclusion as well and the captain soon gave the order for the lifeboats to be uncovered and swung out. The captain also visited the wireless room and told the operators to send a distress call to any nearby ships requesting their assistance. The situation was dire, and as the *Titanic* slowly dipped forward into the cold ocean, the captain gave the order to start putting people in the lifeboats and getting them off the ship, women and children first.

"My great uncle Murdoch started working on the lifeboats along the starboard side of the ship," Andrew said, "while Second Officer Lightoller looked after those on the port side. Both officers were concerned about how much weight the wooden boats and their lifeboat davits could handle. The boat deck on *Titanic* was sixty feet above the water, and since any kind of minor slip-up could have disastrous consequences, several of the first boats launched with significantly fewer people aboard than they were built to hold, some of them less than half full. The thinking was that once the lifeboats were safely in the water they could be filled from the hatches farther down along the side of the ship or by pulling swimmers from the water, but neither of those things happened.

"The situation was also made worse by the fact that people simply didn't want to get into the lifeboats. The ship was sinking slowly, but in the early moments, the *Titanic* seemed to be as solid as a rock, and the passengers believed it was far safer to stay on board than risk their lives on the open water in a lifeboat. As a result, nearly half of the available spaces in the lifeboats were left unfilled, and hundreds more people lost their lives."

"That's unbelievable," I said. "And there weren't even enough lifeboats to begin with."

Andrew nodded solemnly for a moment and then he continued his tale.

"One by one the boats were lowered," he said. "And gut-wrenching scenes played out all along both sides of the *Titanic*'s boat deck as husbands and fathers put their families into the lifeboats, kissed them goodbye, and melted into the crowd as they were lowered away. They probably said, 'Don't worry; I'll catch a later boat and see you in the morning.' But most of the men knew that there would be no later boats, and their chances of surviving were slim at best.

"As it turned out, a man's chances of survival also depended on which side of the ship he was on. On the port side Second Officer Lightoller was interpreting the age-old law of the sea, women and children first, as meaning no men were allowed in the boats until all the women and children were safely off the ship. Over on the starboard side, my great uncle Murdoch was interpreting this tenet a little more loosely and was allowing men into the boats when there were no women or children left on deck when each boat was ready to launch.

"The scene was completely surreal. All of this drama played out on the *Titanic*'s boat deck as the ship's band stood nearby playing light-hearted tunes in the frozen air to cheer the frightened passengers. High above them the stars shone brightly in a pitch-black sky pierced every few minutes by emergency rockets shrieking into the air.

"The rockets were being fired by Fourth Officer Joseph Boxhall and Quartermaster George Rowe from *Titanic*'s bridge. Together with the captain, they stared out across the black ocean in frustration toward the lights of a nearby ship on the horizon. The mysterious ship seemed to be tantalizingly close—only five or ten miles distant—which would make it the closest ship by far to *Titanic* and a god-send to the hopeless passengers and crew who would soon find themselves dying in the frozen waters of the North Atlantic. But no matter how hard Boxhall and Rowe tried to attract the ship's attention with rockets and signal lamps, there was no response.

"Nearby in the Marconi room the two wireless operators were busy tapping out distress calls over the radio waves to anyone who could hear them. They were in contact with several ships, the closest of which was the Cunard steamer *Carpathia*. It was fifty-eight miles away and coming hard toward them, but by the time that ship got to the *Titanic*, she had already sunk.

"The situation on the boat deck became increasingly desperate as each successive lifeboat left the ship and *Titanic's* bow sank deeper into the cold ocean. The officers loading the lifeboats met briefly in Murdoch's cabin where he issued a pistol to each of them just in case the crowds got out of control. A few of the officers had to use the weapons to fire shots into the air to keep people from rushing the lifeboats.

"All this time, running from place to place around the boat deck was J. Bruce Ismay, the head of the White Star Line, who was desperately trying to help load the lifeboats. His efforts were chaotic and sometimes unwelcome by the crewmembers tasked with preparing the boats, but he did whatever he could do to help before he eventually climbed into one of the last lifeboats to leave the ship—a decision that many people later considered cowardly and villainous.

"As the minutes ticked by, there was no longer any doubt that the *Titanic* was sinking, but the band played on, the sweet sound of their beautiful music floating out across the water. Soon the end was near, and the *Titanic* was sinking fast, leaving those left behind in a panic. Several men struggled to launch the remaining collapsible lifeboats from the roof of the officer's quarters. As the ship's stern slowly began to rise into the air, a wave washed over the boat deck and pushed the boats into the water.

"The stern continued to rise until it was standing almost vertically out of the water, lifting the ship's great propellers high in the air as *Titanic* prepared to take her final plunge. By then the band had stopped playing and had disappeared into the water, the instruments forever silenced.

"For a moment, the lights of the ship blazed brightly before flickering into darkness. A terrible roar arose from deep inside *Titanic* as the entire contents of the enormous ship broke free—everything from gigantic boilers to tiny teaspoons. High in the air the ship's stern seemed to hang motionless for an eternity before finally plummeting down into the icy black abyss.

"As the water closed over *Titanic's* aft railing, the great ship disappeared from sight, leaving only the horrific screams of the dying that would haunt the survivors for the rest of their lives. But slowly even those screams died out, leaving only an icy cold silence as the survivors waited in the darkness for rescue."

Chapter Seven
The Strangest-Looking Doodles I'd Ever Seen

"And that is the story of *Titanic*," Andrew said, leaning back in his chair and taking a sip of coffee.

"Incredible," I said, barely breathing as I contemplated his amazing story. After a few moments' pause, I asked, "So, what happened to your great uncle Murdoch? Did he drown along with everyone else who wasn't rescued?"

Andrew shook his head. "Actually, most people didn't drown; they died of hypothermia." he said.

"What do you mean?" I asked. "I thought most people drowned."

Andrew shook his head again. "Even though there weren't enough lifeboats, the one thing that *Titanic* had plenty of on board was life belts," he said. "So once people were in the water, most were able to stay afloat. But the problem was the temperature of the water. It was barely above the freezing point, and anyone who didn't drown or immediately die of shock wouldn't have lasted very long—half an hour, maybe a bit more."

"My god, I had no idea," I replied in amazement.

"But as for my great uncle, no one really knows for sure because his body was never recovered," Andrew said. "Some people think he was washed off of the ship by a wave, and either he drowned or died of exposure. But others swear that they saw him put a gun to his head and shoot himself."

I was stunned. Suddenly the memory of a scene from the *Titanic* movie came rushing back to me.

"That's in the movie, right?" I cried. "There's a scene showing that in the movie!"

Andrew nodded. "Exactly," he said. "And the possibility that Murdoch might have killed himself has bothered my family for a long time, along with other unresolved questions."

"Like what?" I asked, curious.

Andrew propped his elbows on the table and leaned toward me. "My family and I can't help but wonder what actions Murdoch took before and after the *Titanic* hit the iceberg. He was the watch officer on the bridge at the time, so a lot of critics and armchair sea captains over the last century have questioned his actions and passed judgment on him."

"That hardly seems fair," I protested. "They weren't there. How would they know what happened?"

Andrew shrugged. "No one really knows what happened," he said. "But the same doubt surrounds his so-called suicide—some of the survivors say one thing while others say something else entirely."

"But what exactly is it that they question about his actions?" I asked. "Do they think he did something wrong?"

"That's exactly what some people believe, yes," Andrew said. "It's a bit complicated sometimes, and I don't fully understand some of the crazier theories, but some people believe that the sinking of the *Titanic* was a direct result of improper actions taken by my great uncle."

I couldn't believe what I was hearing. "Like what?!?" I asked. "Give me an example."

Andrew sighed heavily. "Forgive me if I muck up the explanation," he said. "But the ship's engines are one example. By some accounts, after sighting the iceberg, Murdoch ordered the helm hard-a-starboard and then *reversed* the engines. The problem with this possibility is that the *Titanic* had three propellers, and only the first and third ones could be reversed. The center propeller, which was the one that had the primary effect on the ship's steering, could not be reversed. So if this is true, then Murdoch would have compromised the ship's ability to turn safely away from the iceberg."

I struggled to understand what Andrew was saying. "But what are the other options?" I asked. "What do other people think he did with the engines if he didn't reverse them?"

"Some survivors who'd been in *Titanic*'s engine room later testified that the engines were only set to stop the ship, not reverse it," Andrew said. "But there are controversies about this possibility as well, because if it's true, then this decision would also have compromised the *Titanic*'s steering. Some people say that without the flow of water from the center propeller, the ship's rudder would have been less effective, and this is why the *Titanic* was unable to turn away from the iceberg in time."

I stared at Andrew for a long moment, unsure of what to say.

"I told you it was complicated," he said, "and a little bit crazy."

"But what do these people expect Murdoch to have done?" I asked. "Keep going full steam straight into the iceberg?"

"Funny you should say that," Andrew said, laughing. "Because it's a well-known theory that if the *Titanic* had done exactly that—smashed straight into the iceberg—then she wouldn't have sunk."

"Huh?!?" I replied. "How is that possible?"

"It's simple," Andrew explained, leaning forward and pointing to the postcard of *Titanic* again. "Remember the watertight doors? Well, if *Titanic* had crashed headlong into the iceberg, the whole bow section of the ship would have been crushed and destroyed, right?"

"Right," I agreed, looking down at the photo.

"According to some people, at the absolute worst this would have breached only the first two of the ship's watertight compartments," Andrew said. "Not enough to have sunk her, in other words. Of course, people in the front sections would have been killed, and the rest would have been thrown around their cabins like rag dolls as a result of the impact, but the ship would have stayed afloat."

I thought this idea through for a few moments. In a way it sort of made sense, but that didn't make it any less crazy.

"But who would do that?" I asked. "Who would just let their ship drive straight into an iceberg when there was a chance that it could be avoided?"

Andrew leaned back and shrugged. "No one, I suppose," he replied. "But all these unanswered questions have disturbed my family for generations."

I picked up the postcard of *Titanic* from the table and tried to imagine it colliding headlong into a giant iceberg. With a thundering screech of metal, the sleek bow of the ship would have crumpled in on itself in a terrible crush of steel and ice. The damage would have been incredible, and the crash itself horrific, but as Andrew said, thanks to the system of watertight doors the ship might have stayed afloat, thus saving the lives of hundreds of people.

Still imagining this scene I flipped the postcard over to look at the back of it and was surprised by what I found there. Written in pencil were two neatly drawn rows of the strangest looking doodles I'd ever seen—circles and spirals and triangles and squiggly lines.

"What's this?" I asked, holding up the back of the card to show Andrew.

Andrew smiled weakly and paused to take a deep breath before he spoke. "I was hoping that you might be able to tell *me* the answer to that," he replied. "Finding the answer to that question is why I wanted to hire you."

Chapter Eight
The Storm That Breaks

"Hire me?" I asked in surprise, turning the card over again so I could take a second look at the series of strange doodles. "What makes you think that I have any idea what these are?"

Andrew smiled. "It's not that I think you already know what they are," he replied. "But I am hoping that you'll be able to help me figure it out."

I looked at Andrew in disbelief.

"Didn't you say that your family received this in the mail in 1937?" I asked.

Andrew nodded. "Correct," he said.

"Why didn't you try and figure it out before?" I asked in confusion.

"We did," Andrew replied. "Over the span of four generations my family has done hundreds of hours of research and consulted with all sorts of different kinds of experts, but unfortunately no one has yet been able to figure it out."

I could feel my eyebrows rising higher and higher in disbelief.

"And you think that I can?!?" I asked incredulously as I stared down again at the squiggles on the back of the postcard.

"I was hoping you might," Andrew admitted. "Based on your past experiences you seem to have a knack for finding hidden treasure."

"Treasure?" I asked. "I don't understand. Who said anything about treasure? What does any of this have to do with treasure?"

Andrew leaned forward to grab the old, yellowed envelope he'd shown me earlier, and he pulled out the newspaper clipping.

"There's more to it than just the postcard," Andrew reminded me as he slid the newspaper across the table toward me. It was a small square of newsprint that had been crudely torn from an old newspaper containing an article entitled *"TITANIC OWNER MAKES GENEROUS DONATION TO BRITISH MERCHANTMEN"* with the remnants of a half-finished crossword puzzle at the bottom.

TITANIC OWNER MAKES GENEROUS DONATION TO BRITISH MERCHANTMEN

London, January 2, 1931

In an effort to express his admiration for the heroic conduct of the officers and men of the British Mercantile Marine in weathering the storm of the Great War, Mr J. Bruce Ismay, former managing director of the White Star Line that owned Titanic and survivor of the disaster, has donated £25,000 to the Mercantile Marine Service Association. This munificent gift breaks all previous records for generosity, including those set by Ismay's own late father, Thomas Henry Ismay, founder of the White Star Line, who once made a similar donation of £20,000 more than thirty years ago to the Liverpool Seamen's Pension Fund.

Following the sinking of the Titanic Mr. Ismay found himself the target of condemnation for having survived and failing to go down with his own ship. According to his own accounts he was on board the ship only in the capacity of an ordinary passenger and exerted no control or influence over the operation of the vessel itself. Ismay himself maintains that after the ship struck the iceberg he assisted in the loading of lifeboats and when there were no other women or children in sight as the last boat was finished loading he climbed in as it was being lowered away. However, in light of the fact that more than 1500 of his fellow passengers perished in the disaster Mr. Ismay was much criticised for his conduct.

The entire affair left Ismay a broken man and after resigning his chairmanship of the White Star Line in 1913 he became a virtual recluse and never again appeared at public functions or discussed the Titanic with anyone. As such he had no statement regarding his generous gift to the British Mercantile Marine but Harold Wilkes, the director of the organisations Liverpool branch hoped that Mr. Ismay's gift will spawn a flood of similar donations to charitable organisations that benefit British seamen and their families.

"This horrific war has devastated our empire," said Mr. Wilkes. "And has created a crippling drag on the institutions tasked with caring for those in need as well as their innocent widows and children. Our boys went through hell during the course of the war and whether their fate was to crawl resolutely through the Flanders mud or serve courageously upon the high seas, the treasure of our empire can only provide a limited degree of support to them and their families. The responsibility to safeguard their future lies with all citizens whose freedom these brave men defended. We must all do what we can to ensure that these brave men are not left hungry and destitute on the thoroughfares of our great cities. We British have a long history of rising to every challenge with heads held high. Whether slaying the dragons of our mythology or spilling the blood of our youth in defence of freedom, this generosity of spirit is but one of the many virtues that make us British. And as we have just witnessed during the course of this horrendous war, where there are those in need, whether within the borders of our own realm or off on some far distant foreign shore, it is our ancient duty to be as unyielding as stone as we stand shoulder to shoulder together against the onslaught like our fathers did before us. We must be ready and willing to sacrifice the many flowers of our generation to nip the plans of evil in the bud and defend our empire. Above all else, we must be British."

DAILY CROSSWORD JANUARY 2ND 1931

FAMED BALLERINA ANNA PAVLOVA FALLS ILL

Famed Russian ballerina Anna Pavlova has fallen ill with pneumonia after catching a chill during a train journey from the French Riviera to The Hague, Netherlands where she is scheduled to perform her legendary Dying Swan. Generally considered to be the greatest dancer of all time, Ms. Pavlova began her amazing career in her native Russia, later to debut on the London stage where audiences were instantly enthralled by her incomparable technique and unequalled grace. Since that time she has given thousands of performances and travelled hundreds of thousands of miles to delight audiences all over the world. Just a few short weeks short of her 50th birthday the celebrated danseuse remains without an equal anywhere in the ballet world. Sources close to the dancer report that she is recuperating in the renowned Hotel Des Indes and hope that she will be back

I read the main article from top to bottom as Andrew waited patiently.

London, January 2, 1931

In an effort to express his admiration for the heroic conduct of the officers and men of the British Mercantile Marine in weathering the storm of the Great War, Mr. J. Bruce Ismay, former managing director of the White Star Line that owned Titanic and survivor of the disaster, has donated £25,000 to the Mercantile Marine Service Association. This munificent gift breaks all previous records for generosity, including those set by Ismay's own late father, Thomas Henry Ismay, founder of the White Star Line, who once made a similar donation of £20,000 more than thirty years ago to the Liverpool Seamen's Pension Fund.

Following the sinking of the Titanic Mr. Ismay found himself the target of condemnation for having survived and failing to go down with his own ship. According to his own accounts he was on board the ship only in the capacity of an ordinary passenger and exerted no control or influence over the operation of the vessel itself. Ismay himself maintains that <u>after</u> the ship struck the iceberg he assisted in the loading of lifeboats and when there were no other women or children in sight as the last boat was finished loading he climbed in as it was being lowered away. However, in light of the fact that more than 1500 of his fellow passengers perished in the disaster Mr. Ismay was much criticised for his conduct.

The entire affair left Ismay a broken man and after resigning his chairmanship of <u>the</u> White Star Line in 1913 he became a virtual recluse and never again appeared at public functions or discussed the Titanic with anyone. As such he had no statement regarding his generous gift to the British Mercantile Marine but Harold Wilkes, the director of the organisation's Liverpool branch hoped that Mr. Ismay's gift will spawn a <u>flood</u> of similar donations to charitable organisations that benefit British seamen and their families.

"This horrific war has devastated our empire," said Mr. Wilkes. "And has created a crippling <u>drag</u> on <u>the</u> institutions tasked with caring for those in need as well as their <u>innocent</u> widows and children. Our boys went <u>through</u> hell during <u>the</u> course of the war and whether their fate was to crawl resolutely through the Flanders <u>mud</u> or serve courageously upon <u>the</u> high seas, the <u>treasure</u> of our empire can only provide a limited degree of support to them and their families. The responsibility to safeguard their future <u>lies</u> with all citizens whose freedom these brave men defended. We must all do what we can to ensure that these brave men are <u>not</u> left hungry and destitute on the thoroughfares of our great cities. We British have a long history of rising to every challenge <u>with</u> heads held high. Whether slaying the <u>dragons</u> of our mythology or spilling the <u>blood</u> of our youth in defence of freedom, this generosity of spirit is <u>but</u> one of the many virtues that make us British. And as we have just witnessed during the course of this horrendous war, <u>where</u> there are those in need, whether within the borders of our own realm or off on some far distant foreign shore, it is our <u>ancient</u> duty to be as unyielding as <u>stone</u> as we stand shoulder to shoulder together against the onslaught <u>like</u> our fathers did before us. We must be ready and willing to sacrifice the many <u>flowers</u> of our generation to nip the plans of evil in the <u>bud</u> and defend our empire. Above all else, we must be British."

When I was finished reading, I looked up at Andrew with a confused expression on my face.

"I don't understand," I said, still unable to see what any of this had to do with hidden treasure or how I could possibly help him solve the mystery.

"Look closer," he replied, pointing to the various words that had been underlined in pencil.

I looked again and wrinkled my forehead as my eyes flicked from one underlined word to the next.

"The... storm... that... breaks...." I said under my breath as I read each underlined word in sequence. At first glance, the words seemed to be random, but taken together, they formed a kind of riddle.

I reached into my shoulder bag to pull out my Moleskine notebook and flipped it open to the first blank page where I transcribed each of the underlined words.

THE STORM THAT BREAKS AFTER THE FLOOD
DRAG THE INNOCENT THROUGH THE MUD
THE TREASURE LIES NOT WITH DRAGONS BLOOD
BUT WHERE ANCIENT STONE LIKE FLOWERS BUD

"The treasure," I said, breathless as I looked up to see Andrew smiling widely at me. "What treasure?"

Andrew leaned in closer and spoke in a low voice as he held up the old, yellowed envelope that the postcard and newspaper clipping had arrived in.

"My family believes that this envelope was sent to us by none other than J. Bruce Ismay himself, the former director of the White Star Line and so-called owner of the *Titanic*," he said, his voice growing with excitement as he recounted the reasons for his family's belief. "Look at the postmark on the envelope: London 1937. Ismay had a house in London where he spent much of his time in later life when he wasn't at his country estate in the west of Ireland. Ismay died in October 1937, shortly after this letter was posted, so perhaps he was trying to make some final resolutions to his life knowing that he didn't have long to live. Even the news story itself is about Ismay, and the first two lines of the riddle seem to also refer to him and the public shame he suffered for having survived the disaster."

"But what about the treasure?" I asked, confused about the last two lines of the riddle. "And what's this about dragon's blood and ancient stone?"

"My family has a theory about that as well," Andrew replied, nodding enthusiastically, and he leaned in even closer and spoke in a conspiratorial tone, "We think that the reference to dragon's blood is a clue that whatever the treasure was, it was being carried aboard the *Titanic* when she sank. Among the items on *Titanic*'s cargo manifest were seventy six cases of Dragon's Blood."

"Are you kidding me?!?" I asked in disbelief. "Dragon's blood?"

"Aye, that one fooled my family too," Andrew replied. "But as it turns out, it's not literally blood from dragons. It's a kind of powdered resin from a tree that grows in the Canary Islands. It's used as a dye or wood varnish, and is called dragon's blood because of its deep red color."

"Oh," I replied, somewhat disappointed.

"The important thing is that the riddle tells us that the treasure is *NOT* to be found with the Dragon's Blood," Andrew said. "And since the cases of Dragon's Blood went down with the ship, the treasure we are looking for must have been taken off the ship by one of the survivors when it sank."

I was starting to get a bit confused.

"But what treasure?" I asked. "What treasure do you think it's talking about?"

Andrew smiled a wide and excited smile as he leaned back from the table.

"The jewelled Rubaiyat of Omar Khayyam," he said simply. "My family believes that Ismay himself somehow smuggled the Rubaiyat off the *Titanic*, and all of these clues were sent to my family in order to help them find it."

Chapter Nine

For All He Knows I'm Terribly Disorganized

I looked across at Andrew with what must have been look of complete and utter bewilderment on my face.

"What the heck is the Rubaiyat of Omar Khayyam?" I asked as I watched the expression on Andrew's face slowly fade from a smile of excitement and pride to a look of pained sympathy for my confused state of mind.

"I'm sorry, I'm getting ahead of myself," he said. "The Rubaiyat is a book of poems written by the Persian astronomer Omar Khayyam about a thousand years ago."

"Is it valuable?" I asked, curious as to why such a book would be considered a treasure.

"The one on *Titanic* was," Andrew replied. "It was more than just a rare book of poems; its front and back covers were inlaid with a thousand precious gems set in pure gold."

That sounds more like treasure to me, I thought, grinning.

"The name Rubaiyat comes from the Persian word for four," Andrew explained, pointing to the lines of the riddle that I'd scribbled in my notebook. "A ruba'i is a four-lined poem, just like this one here, and the Rubaiyat itself is a collection of several four-lined poems."

"And that's why you think the treasure is the Rubaiyat?" I asked. "And that Ismay wanted your family to find it?"

"Well, yes," Andrew admitted, smiling sheepishly. "Or whatever else the treasure may be."

I carefully pondered all of this for a minute or two.

"What about the rest of the poem?" I asked, looking at my notebook. "The part about 'where ancient stone-like flowers bud'? This is where the treasure can be found, right?"

"That's what we believe, yes," he said, nodding.

"So where is it?" I asked, looking at Andrew with intense curiosity. "Where do ancient stone-like flowers bud?"

Andrew shook his head. "That's exactly what my family has wondered for generations now, but we haven't been able to figure it out."

I picked up the various bits of paper from the table and thumbed through them as Andrew looked on in silence. Everything Andrew had said made perfect sense. His family had apparently thought about this for a long time and had figured most of it out—all but the last line of the poem and the squiggly drawings on the back of the postcard. Unfortunately, those also seemed to be the most important pieces of information of all—the location of the treasure.

I looked down again at the series of squiggles on the back of the postcard. "Have you talked to any experts about these?" I asked. "You know, language experts, maybe?"

Andrew nodded. "Many times over the years," he replied. "Linguists, cryptographers, experts on ancient languages, everything my family could think of."

"And symbologists?" I asked. "Like that guy from *The Da Vinci Code*?"

Andrew laughed. "I'm not sure that's a real job," he said. "But yes, we've talked to experts like that as well."

I continued to examine the various clues, flipping quietly from one to the next. Finally, I put them down on the table and looked up at Andrew with a shrug.

"I'm sorry," I said quietly. "But I don't think I can help you with this. I have absolutely no idea about any of this, and I can't imagine that I could ever possibly have any ideas that you or your family haven't already thought of after so many years."

Andrew nodded slowly and gave me a thin smile. "My parents thought I was crazy to even come here," he said. "And of course I knew it was a long shot. But after so many years of stumbling around in the dark, I thought maybe a crazy long shot was exactly what my family needed to finally find the answer."

Andrew pulled a leather-bound checkbook and a pen from the inside pocket of his jacket and opened it on the table in front of him.

"No, no, Andrew, no," I said reaching over to stop him from filling out the check. "You don't have to, really. I am serious."

"A deal is a deal," he said, brushing my hand away to finish scribbling out the check, which he then slid across the table toward me.

"I won't cash it," I said stubbornly.

Andrew shrugged. "I can't force you to," he admitted as he carefully tucked the postcard and newspaper clipping back into the envelope and slid that across the table to me as well. "But please take it, and take the envelope; have a think about things overnight. Maybe something will come to you."

Andrew looked so sad and disappointed that somehow I couldn't refuse him. I picked up the envelope and stuck it into my shoulder bag. Andrew called the waitress over and paid our bill as I stared at the check lying face down on the table. *It can't hurt to look at it*, I thought, so I grabbed it and looked at the amount written there. Andrew was crazy if he thought I would take two hundred and fifty pounds for not actually doing anything.

"I really want you to keep the check," I told him in my firmest tone of voice as we made our way toward the exit. "We'll call it double or nothing. If I come up with anything that helps you, I'll take a check from you, no arguments. But I can't take all this money from you for just sitting here listening to all of these amazing stories and having a wonderful evening with you."

"I had a wonderful evening too," Andrew replied, smiling shyly. For a moment, he looked like he wanted to say something else, his dark eyes twinkling in the pub's dim candlelight.

"Let's do it again tomorrow," I suggested, surprising myself by being so forward. *What the hell*, I thought. *If he's not going to ask me out again, then I'll do it for him.*

Andrew smiled brightly. "I would love that," he replied as we stepped out into the noisy chaos of the streets of Temple Bar. We chatted and walked slowly together to my hotel overlooking the River Liffey that was just a few blocks away. I told him about my family and home in Canada, and he did the same, describing charming school break holidays at his family's home in southwestern Scotland. Before we knew it, we'd reached the entrance to my hotel, where we exchanged phone numbers and arranged to meet the next day for dinner.

"Tonight you had Irish lamb stew seasoned with Guinness beer," Andrew said. "Tomorrow we'll have Irish beef with a glaze made from Jameson's Irish whiskey."

"Mmmm...sounds amazing," I replied, my mouth nearly watering at the thought of it.

I promised him that I would look at the envelope and clues again overnight and let him know immediately if I thought of anything. He reached his hand out to shake mine goodbye, but I leaned forward on impulse and kissed him on the cheek, the left side of my lips brushing barely to the right of his mouth.

If that doesn't give him a clue, nothing will, I told myself as I pulled back again, blushing at my own brashness. I saw that Andrew was blushing too, and then he said goodnight and headed toward the river, crossing over using a picturesque footbridge and turning around at the top to smile brightly and wave goodbye.

I watched him until he disappeared from sight, and then I reluctantly climbed the stairs into the lobby of my hotel and rode the elevator to the top floor where my cozy little room was waiting.

Tossing my shoulder bag onto the night table, I went to have a quick shower before flopping down on the bed to check my e-mail. There was nothing interesting in my inbox, so I puttered around on the Internet for a while, checking news headlines and funny videos before switching my iPad off. I slid it into my shoulder bag, and when I saw the old envelope inside, I decided to be true to my word and have another look at everything.

These are the originals, I suddenly thought to myself. *Andrew is taking quite a risk leaving these with me.*

"Is he?" the little voice in my head asked. "Are you so untrustworthy?"

I shrugged to myself. *For all he knows I am terribly disorganized,* I replied. *And I'll lose them or something.*

I pulled the newspaper clipping and postcard from the envelope and laid all three items on the bed in front of me. I stared at them face up, and then I flipped them over. The backside of the news clipping was just some incomplete fragments of other news stories with no words underlined or anything else that seemed particularly interesting. Andrew's family would have gone over all of that with a fine-toothed comb anyway, I assumed. The good stuff was on the backside of the *Titanic* postcard where the handwritten scribbles were located.

I stared at them for what seemed like an eternity, but no matter how hard I tried, I couldn't think of anything that could possibly unravel the mystery of what the symbols meant.

Who am I kidding? I mused in frustration. *For nearly eighty years, Andrew's family has wondered about these markings. How am I possibly going to figure them out if his family and all those experts were unable to do it?*

I felt bad for Andrew. For whatever reason, he had pinned his hopes on me, and as crazy as that was, I wasn't looking forward to giving him the bad news that there was nothing I could do to help him. The only thing I was an expert on was flying planes. My knack for falling into situations involving lost treasure hardly qualified me to figure out mysterious cryptic clues such as this.

Feeling a bit dejected, I picked up the envelope and put everything away, flipping the postcard over to the photo on the front before tucking it away for the night.

R.M.S. TITANIC

And that's when I saw it.

Blinking my eyes hard in disbelief I took a closer look as my heart began to pound in my throat like a jackhammer. How was it possible that

I had noticed something that generations of Andrew's family and god knows how many other experts and hired consultants had missed?

But it was true and the proof was right there on the photograph in front of me.

Without wasting another precious second, I leapt across the room to grab my iPhone and sent Andrew a text message.

Chapter Ten
What Do You See?

Fifteen minutes later, Andrew was sitting across from me at the corner table of my hotel room. My message had arrived before he'd even reached his hotel, and he had immediately turned around and headed straight back, the both of us too excited about the discovery to wait until morning.

My mother (not to mention my father) would probably have something to say about me inviting a stranger up to my hotel room in the middle of the night, but that was the furthest thing from my mind as I held up the postcard with one hand so that Andrew could see it.

"What do you see?" I asked dramatically.

Andrew furrowed his brow and stared intently at the photograph, trying to see what I had discovered. I watched his dark eyes dart around from one place to the next as he searched the photo from top to bottom, but he wasn't seeing it.

"I don't understand," he finally said. "What am I supposed to be looking for?"

I grinned and savored my moment of triumph for a few seconds longer. It wasn't often that I was able to feel like the smartest person in the room, and I was planning to milk it for all it was worth.

"Did you know that *Titanic* was one of the first ships in history to ever send an SOS as a distress call?" I asked.

Andrew looked up, his eyes peering at me intently across the top of the postcard.

"Aye," he replied, nodding. "She wasn't the first ship to ever use it, but one of the first. Up to that point in time, most ships used the originally designated distress call of CQD. The *Titanic* sent that call as well, in addition to SOS."

"And do you know why they changed the standard distress call from CQD to SOS?" I asked, gloating.

Andrew's forehead wrinkled in thought for a moment. "It was easier to recognize," he replied. "In Morse code, SOS is so simple that even amateur radio operators would have recognized it: dot dot dot, dash dash dash, dot dot dot."

"Exactly," I said, leaning forward to hold the postcard closer to his face. "And with that in mind, look closer. What do you see now?"

Andrew furrowed his brow once more and examined the picture more closely.

His eyes flicked from place to place for a few more moments, but then he finally saw it. As I watched his reaction, his eyes snapped wide open in amazement, and he reached over to grab the postcard out of my hand. He leaned over and held it under the light of the nearby lamp for a better look.

"Oh my god," he said, his voice breathless and hoarse with emotion. "Oh my god, I can't believe it! I simply cannot believe it!"

I grinned and nodded in satisfaction as I watched the realization sink in. Andrew had finally seen what I had noticed just a half hour earlier. In the photograph, running along the starboard side of the ship in the white area just above the black hull, there was a row of portholes. Nothing unusual there, of course, but it was the seemingly random pattern of the different portholes that was unusual. In actuality, the pattern wasn't random at all. It was Morse code. Someone had airbrushed the photo to encode a secret message into it.

"What does it say?" Andrew asked, his voice rising in excitement. "Can I use your iPad to Google it?"

"Don't worry, I know Morse code," I replied. "When I was a kid, my dad and I used to drive my mom crazy at the dinner table by tapping out secret messages to each other."

"And?!?" Andrew asked in growing excitement. "What does it say?!? Does it tell us where the treasure is?"

I decided not to push my luck with Andrew's patience, so I put aside my gloating and told him what it said.

"The first three letters are SOS, which I think is just to get your attention," I said. "But the rest of the message reads *TURN YAMSIS TRAGEDY AROUND.*"

Andrew looked confused.

"Yamsis?" Andrew asked. "What does that mean?"

It was now my turn to furrow my brow in bewilderment. I had been hoping that Andrew already knew the answer to that question.

"I don't know," I said hesitantly. "It was such a strange word that I Googled a Morse Code chart to make double sure that I was decoding it correctly. But that's what it says: Yamsis."

Andrew stared intently at the photograph a bit longer.

"What about Googling the word yamsis," he suggested.

I grabbed my iPad and did as he suggested, flipping quickly through the result pages.

"Nothing that really makes any sense," I replied, tilting the screen in his direction so that he could see. "Wikipedia page about yams, article about yam production in Nigeria, how to cook yams, and so on."

Andrew thought about this some more.

"Try yamsis and *Titanic*," he suggested, sliding his chair over to my side of the table so that he could see what I was doing.

I tried that combination and scrolled through the results.

"No luck," I said, shaking my head. "That is even less helpful. There's just a bunch of stuff about yams."

I tried Googling the entire phrase and a few other combinations of the words while Andrew leaned over my shoulder to watch. I smiled to myself as I felt the warmth of his body radiating close to me and smelled the scent of his cologne. It was Aramis, if I wasn't mistaken. My dad had a bottle of it in my parents' bathroom at home.

We continued Googling everything we could think of to decipher the meaning of Yamsis, but no matter what we tried, nothing looked even remotely useful. I was completely stumped, and apparently so was Andrew. He moved his chair to the other side of the table and sat there for a long while, stroking his chin and staring silently at the *Titanic* photograph.

"I have absolutely no idea what this means," Andrew said finally, looking up at me from across the table. "But I have an idea who might know."

Chapter Eleven
Captain Lord And The Californian

Early the next morning, Andrew and I were driving north out of Dublin through the beautiful rolling green hills of Ireland. We were headed for Belfast where Andrew had a friend at the *Titanic* museum who he hoped would be able to help us with the new clue that I'd discovered the night before.

The drive was a reasonably short one, and just a couple of hours later we were winding our way through the streets of Belfast past painted murals and curbstones denoting which neighborhoods were Protestant and which were Catholic. We were headed for the waterfront past

shipyards and cargo docks with huge gantries and loading cranes towering overhead where Andrew's friend, Professor Patrick Flynn, had arranged to meet us.

We parked Andrew's car and walked down to the water's edge on foot, arriving at an enormous, long trench lined with brick that looked like a giant, empty swimming pool. Standing at the edge of the pit at the fence was a tall and generously proportioned man in a long, dark overcoat with a gray scarf wrapped snugly around his neck. His face was large and friendly, as if he were a giant himself, with dark gray hair and a close-cropped goatee.

The wind coming off the water was quite cool, even on such a sunny summer day. I pulled the collar of my jacket up to try and keep warm as we approached Andrew's friend.

"Master Murdoch!" Professor Flynn called out cheerily as he took a few steps toward us to clap Andrew in a big bearish hug.

"Professor Flynn, it's good to see you," Andrew replied, returning the hug before stepping out of it to introduce me. "This is my friend Kitty Hawk, visiting from Canada."

Professor Flynn smiled broadly and leaned over to shake my hand.

"You're probably wondering why I arranged to meet you all the way out here instead of in the warm museum," he said.

I glanced around us as gusts of cold wind whipped my hair from side to side. "I was actually wondering that a little bit," I admitted with a smile.

"I asked you here because this is a very special place," Professor Flynn said, wrapping his massive arms around the two of us and ushering us over to the side of the fence where we could peer down into the giant trench that yawned before us. "This is an almost sacred place, in fact, because it was right here in this little brick bathtub of ours that *Titanic* last sat on dry land. We call it *Titanic*'s footprint."

I turned my head to look down the length of the 'little brick bathtub.' *Of course*, I thought. *It's a dry dock.*

"Imagine the scene as *Titanic* stood here more than a century ago," Professor Flynn said with contagious enthusiasm as he gestured dramatically with his arms. "The dock would've been filled with frenetic activity as thousands of workers swarmed all over the *Titanic*, readying her for her maiden voyage. She was the largest moving object ever built—more than a hundred feet tall and nearly nine hundred feet long. Her bow would have towered above us, piercing the sky like a challenge to the gods."

"So this is where they built *Titanic*?" I asked, trying to imagine all of it as I leaned over the railing and peered down into the footprint.

Professor Flynn grinned excitedly. "Not entirely," he said, his booming voice echoing off the nearby buildings. "This is just where she was outfitted after her launch. The slipway where her hull was built is a bit farther up toward the museum. Come on, I'll show you!"

With that, Professor Flynn strode off, leaving Andrew and me scrambling to keep up with him. Despite being such a large and imposing man, he was a fast-walking ball of energy, and he moved with a quick and fluid grace that was almost poetic.

"So tell me, young Master Andrew," Professor Flynn said as we made our way through the harbor, "what urgent business is so important that it has brought you all the way here to Belfast—and me out of bed so early on a Sunday morning? It's not more nonsense about your great uncle, is it? Let me guess, someone published a new book claiming that alien beings from another dimension landed on *Titanic* and got First Officer Murdoch drunk so that he was passed out asleep when the ship hit the iceberg instead of standing on the bridge where he was supposed to be."

Professor Flynn didn't give Andrew a chance to answer but turned to me instead. "Has this young man been polluting your mind with all the ridiculous theories about his great uncle?" he asked.

I shrugged my shoulders. "He did mention a couple of things," I replied, "such as whether or not Murdoch reversed the engines, but nothing about aliens or Murdoch being drunk."

Professor Flynn raised his hands and shook his fists at the sky. "Oh blessed Lord, when will this boy ever learn?!" he cried melodramatically.

"Don't you listen to another word he tells you, young lady. His great uncle Murdoch was a fine man and an experienced officer who did everything he could to avoid hitting that iceberg. A lot of people who should know better have taken the liberty of disparaging his name over the last hundred years, but I can assure you that Murdoch wasn't drunk, nor did he make a steering error, and if you ask me, he didn't reverse those engines either. If these fools want to cast blame on anyone for the deaths of fifteen hundred people that night, they should cast it on bloody Captain Lord and the *Californian*."

Out of the corner of my eye, I saw Andrew smile and roll his eyes. "Here we go again," he muttered.

"Who's Captain Lord?" I asked. "And what's the *Californian*?"

Professor Flynn stopped dead in his tracks and looked over at Andrew in exaggerated astonishment. "You didn't tell her about the bloody *Californian*?" He turned to look me in the eyes and tell me the story. "Captain Lord was the commander of a steamship named the *Californian* that had stopped for the night at the edge of an ice field close to where *Titanic* would soon encounter the fatal iceberg. Officers on watch on *Californian* would later recount how they saw a large passenger ship coming up from behind them in the distance. They watched as the ship drew closer to their position, and then sometime past eleven thirty, she seemed to put her deck lights out and stop dead in the water. Around the same time, the *Californian*'s wireless operator climbed into bed for the night, switching off his set and leaving it unmanned until morning.

"The *Californian*'s watch officers kept an eye on the ship in the distance south of their position, and after some time, they saw her firing rockets. Rockets at sea mean distress, so the officers dutifully informed Captain Lord, who was having a nap in the chart room. Captain Lord didn't think much of it, however, and went back to sleep without even making the small effort of having the wireless operator woken up to check the airwaves for information.

"At the same time that this was happening, the *Titanic* was frantically sending out distress calls by wireless, and far to the south, another steamship, the *Carpathia*, heard the calls and was coming hard to their rescue. Meanwhile, on *Titanic*'s bridge they could see the lights of a much closer ship just to the north of them, maybe seven or ten miles away, and were desperately trying to get her attention with signal lamps and rockets, but there was no response, and *Titanic* sank deeper into the cold, black ocean.

"On the *Californian*, the bridge officers noticed that the ship to the south of them looked very strange somehow, with her lights turning queer as though something was wrong with her. They continued watching until it seemed as though the ship had steamed off in the opposite direction and disappeared. Captain Lord was then informed again of the situation, including the fact that the distressed ship had been firing rockets, and in response, he took no action and went back to sleep.

"By now the *Titanic* was long gone, and at four in the morning on the bridge of the *Californian*, a new watch officer was coming on duty. He was informed of the events of the night, and as he listened, he felt certain that something bad had happened. At four thirty, Captain Lord awoke and arrived on the bridge where he was informed about the mysterious ship that had been firing rockets overnight. The captain remained uninterested, so the watch officer eventually took it upon himself to awaken the wireless operator so that he could determine if there was any news. Of course, once the wireless set warmed up, they learned almost immediately that the *Titanic* had struck an iceberg and sunk to the bottom of the Atlantic.

"Finally, the *Californian* made its way to the location of the disaster, but instead of going straight there from their northerly position, the captain ordered the ship to steam west *through* the dangerous ice field before turning south and actually steaming *past* the position of *Carpathia*, which by that time had begun to rescue *Titanic* survivors from the lifeboats. Finally, the *Californian* turned northeast and approached *Carpathia*'s position from the south.

"All of this lollygagging about by the *Californian* seemed very suspicious, and it only served the purpose of making it look like she was arriving from a different direction than where she'd spent the night.

"By the time the *Californian* finally arrived on the scene, she could be of absolutely no assistance whatsoever, since by then all of *Titanic*'s lifeboats and survivors had been already rescued. The *Carpathia* signaled Captain Lord and asked him to search the area while she continued on to New York with the survivors. Captain Lord agreed, but he left the area shortly afterward, claiming that no survivors or bodies could be found, which was odd, since ships passing the area reported spotting bodies in the water for weeks afterward.

"Captain Lord was eventually called as a witness in both the US and British inquiries into the disaster, and he tried to explain his inaction on the night that *Titanic* sank. In a futile attempt to defend himself, he insisted that the ship that had been seen firing rockets could not have been *Titanic* because the *Californian* was too far away from the scene at the time. This explanation was rejected by both inquiries, but that didn't stop his supporters from trotting it out time and time again in his defense for the next hundred years.

"In fact, for every website full of ridiculous theories about Murdoch there are probably twenty more with ridiculous theories about the *Californian*," Professor Flynn said, nearing the end of his explanation. "But no matter how many people come forward with crazy ideas—the *Californian* was too far away to see anything, or the mysterious ship that the officers on *Titanic* could see in the distance was actually the planet Mars or whatever else they say—none of this changes the fact that according to *Californian*'s own officers and captain, they saw a ship in the distance firing distress rockets. Even if that ship *wasn't* the *Titanic*, the fact that the *Californian* did nothing to help a distressed ship within sight was unconscionable."

Chapter Twelve

It's Not A Word

"You can't be serious," I said, completely shocked by what Professor Flynn had just explained to us.

"Absolutely serious," he replied. "Every word of it is true."

The three of us had finished our walk through the harbor and had now reached the backside of the *Titanic* museum, a four-pointed star-shaped building with each point shaped to resemble the bow of the mighty ship, standing 126 feet high, the same height as *Titanic*'s hull. Around the front of the building, some visitors were milling around and lining up to go inside, but Professor Flynn ushered us in through a side entrance and into a service elevator to take us directly to the top floor where his office was located.

"But why weren't Captain Lord or any of the officers of *Californian* charged with a crime?" I asked angrily, still unable to comprehend that there was a ship just standing around doing nothing while a few miles away, the *Titanic* was on her way to the bottom of the ocean.

Professor Flynn stroked his salt-and-pepper goatee for a moment. "There was some consideration of it during the US and British inquiries into the disaster," he replied. "Both inquiries were harshly critical of Captain Lord's actions, but in the end, nothing was done about it."

"That just isn't fair," I protested, still angry and completely unsatisfied by how things had turned out.

"I agree," Professor Flynn said. "But if it's any consolation, as a result of all the criticism, Captain Lord was branded a coward by the general public and soon lost his job as captain of the *Californian*."

"At least that's something," I said.

"But, he did eventually find work again with another company," Professor Flynn continued as we left the elevator and made our way slowly down the hall to his office. "He became commander of one of their small cargo ships, which is a lot better than any of the surviving officers from *Titanic* did. None of *Titanic*'s officers ever went on to their own commands, despite the fact that most were well in line to do so before the disaster. Captain Lord also did a lot better than many of the *Titanic*'s surviving passengers. The trauma of the event was more than many of them could bear, even driving some to take their own lives."

"That's not making me feel better about it," I quipped, looking up at the professor with a rueful smile.

Professor Flynn shrugged his wide shoulders. "To be fair," he said earnestly, "there may not have been much that Captain Lord could have done, even if he had taken action. Sixty miles to the south of *Titanic*, the *Carpathia* and her commanding officer, Captain Rostron, immediately sprang into action when they received the first distress call. The captain swung his legs out of bed, instantly awake, and rather than waste precious time charting an exact course before starting out, he immediately ordered the ship to head in *Titanic*'s general direction. He knew that he could obtain a more precise heading as soon as it could be calculated. He then coolly rattled off a series of precise orders to get the ship ready for a rescue operation: prepare the dining rooms as makeshift medical centers; have hot coffee and soup available for the survivors; swing out the lifeboats; sling block and tackle with chair slings at each gangway for the sick and wounded; post extra lookouts to watch for ice; divert all non-essential steam to the engines for the highest possible speed. The list went on and on.

"Captain Rostron's impressive and meticulous reaction to the crisis was a damning contrast to the way that Captain Lord handled things. But even if Captain Lord had reacted similarly, at best the *Californian* would have arrived at the scene only as *Titanic* was preparing for her final plunge into the sea."

I was surprised by this. "Couldn't they have arrived earlier?" I asked. "Wouldn't the outcome have been different if they'd raced for the *Titanic* as soon as they spotted the rockets?"

Professor Flynn shook his head. "The first rocket was fired from *Titanic* at something like twelve forty-five in the morning," he replied. "This was already more than an hour after they'd struck the iceberg and about an hour and a half before the ship finally sank. Even if it were possible that *Californian* could have instantly steamed off after sighting the first rocket, it still would have taken them almost an hour to get to *Titanic*. By that time the last of the lifeboats were being put off, and the *Californian* couldn't have simply pulled up alongside and transferred the stranded passengers over. It would have been a dangerous and tricky rescue operation to pull survivors from the water. Not all of them would have made it, but many would have, and the people in the lifeboats would have been spared from hearing the nightmarish screams of the dying, which haunted them for the rest of their days. This is not what happened, however, and instead of earning the proud distinction of being the ship that saved the lives of the passengers of the *Titanic*, the *Californian* and her master stood idly by as the great ship went to her grave and took fifteen hundred souls with her."

I was stunned. "I really cannot believe all of this," I said. "Even if they couldn't have got there in time to save everyone, they still should have done *something*."

"I couldn't agree more, young lady," Professor Flynn said as he pulled out a set of keys from his pocket to unlock the door to his office. We stepped into a beautiful modern office with a long conference table off to one side and a large desk in front of a set of floor-to-ceiling windows on the other. Against the wall to the right was a huge model of the *Titanic* in a glass case buried under several stacks of papers, much as the rest of the room was.

Professor Flynn gestured for us to follow him over to the windows where a view out across a long, wide expanse of concrete and lawn stretched into the distance, sloping down toward the water as it went.

"As promised," the professor announced. "The slipways where *Titanic* and her sister the *Olympic* were built, or what's left of them anyway, which isn't much. But don't let the calm and quiet down there fool you; it was a circus a hundred years ago."

I put my face close to the window and peered down at the sparse area in front of me. Some spindly iron lamp standards lined the sides of the two slipways—faint reminders of the enormous latticework of steel gantries that would have once towered over the growing hulls of the two leviathans.

"The slipway at the left was where *Titanic* was born," Professor Flynn said, his voice turning quiet. "If you look carefully in the pavement, you can see that we've marked her outline."

I saw what the professor was talking about. Pointed like an arrow almost directly toward us, I could see the gigantic outline of the doomed ship gradually sloping away into the distance like a shadow.

"And once the hull was complete, they took her from here over to the dry dock to be completed?" I asked as I pulled out my iPhone to snap a picture of the view.

The professor nodded. "Exactly," he replied. "Just after noon on the 31st of May, 1911 more than one hundred thousand spectators watched as *Titanic*'s great hull slid gracefully down into the River Lagan, helped along by more than twenty tons of animal fat and soft soap to grease the slips, of course. From there they towed her over to the dry dock where she was fitted out."

The three of us stood silently at the window for a few moments longer, staring down at the slipways, lost in our thoughts. Professor Flynn was the first to break the spell as he stepped over to the far corner of the room where a Nespresso machine was perched on top of a cabinet.

"Coffee for everyone?" he asked as he opened a cabinet and found some clean cups and saucers.

I nodded yes to the coffee, and watched as Andrew stepped away from the window and followed the professor over to the large conference table on the other side of the room. The two of them began preparing a trio of coffees for us while I lingered at the window for a while longer. I was reluctant to leave the sight of the slipways with their enormous ship outlines. As the professor had said, there wasn't much left to remind people of the maelstrom of activity that had once taken place there, but it wasn't difficult to imagine *Titanic* standing proud and silent as thousands of workers swarmed like ants all over her.

The professor put the finishing touches on the final cup of coffee and gestured for Andrew and me to take a seat at the table across from him. I pulled myself away from the window and joined them.

"So, young master Andrew, it would seem that you're not here about your great uncle after all," Professor Flynn said as the three of us took our seats. "Which can only mean one thing: you're here about the bloody treasure again."

Andrew laughed and reached into his jacket and pulled out the faded yellow envelope with its mysterious contents. "As usual, you are quite right," he replied as he placed the envelope on the table and extracted the *Titanic* postcard from inside. He slid the card across the table to the professor.

"The infamous postcard with the funny writing again," the professor said, picking up the card and gazing at it laconically. It was obvious by his demeanor that he'd seen it many times before, but to appease Andrew, he casually flipped it over to glance at the back of it before putting it down again and looking across at Andrew as if to say, *Now what?*

"We've made a discovery about this card," Andrew said, answering the professor's unspoken challenge. "Or should I better say that Kitty here has made a discovery."

Professor Flynn raised his eyebrows and looked over at me, impressed. "Is that a fact?" He was clearly intrigued as he picked up the card again and flipped it over to study it more carefully as he asked, "She's deciphered the funny writing, has she?"

Andrew shook his head. "Not the writing," he said, taking the card from the professor's hands and flipping it over again. "She's discovered something about the photograph on the front."

Professor Flynn wrinkled his forehead and looked down at the photograph. "*Titanic* in Cork harbor," he said simply before lifting his eyes to stare intently across the table at Andrew, and then at me. "Probably the last photo ever taken of her, but I don't understand. What is there to discover about this?"

Andrew gestured to me. "It's only fair if Kitty tells you herself," he said. "She's the one who noticed it."

The professor looked me straight in the eyes, and the very serious expression on his face didn't escape my notice. For a second I felt rather nervous and pitied any of his students who might happen to get on his bad side.

"The portholes," I stammered, feeling silly and nervous under the professor's intense stare. "They spell out a message in Morse code."

The professor chuckled lightly in disbelief as he looked down at the photo again, but his laugh was quickly choked off when he realized the truth of what I was saying. His eyes went as wide as saucers, and he struggled to put on the half-glasses that were hanging around his neck on a string.

"Dear god in heaven, she's right," he bellowed in surprise and shock when he finally got his glasses on straight and had a good look at the photo. "My lord, my dear, I am sorry for laughing there for a moment. I thought you meant that the ship itself was built with a secret message in the portholes, not that this photograph had been altered."

"I understand," I replied.

"It was terrible of me," he said, "but I hope you can forgive me."

"Of course, professor," I replied, smiling at his sincere apology, which seemed funny after the comical struggle he'd had with his glasses. "There's nothing to forgive."

The professor stared down for a few seconds as I reached into my bag to pull out my Moleskine notepad so that I could show him the deciphered message.

"By god you're a bloody genius," the professor said as reached over with one hand to clap me heavily on the back in congratulations. "I can't believe that none of us noticed it before. We were so concerned with what was written on the back of the card that we didn't think to look more closely at the front."

I opened my notepad to the correct page and pushed it across the table for the professor to read as he ran his finger across the photo, decoding the message himself in his head.

"Turn Yamsis Tragedy around," he said, glancing down at my notepad and nodding in agreement. "What a bloody miracle this is. I am nearly speechless."

It was Andrew's turn to speak again. "We weren't sure about this word yamsis," he said. "It doesn't make any sense, but we tripled checked it, and it's definitely right."

"You better believe it is!" Professor Flynn roared as he banged the table triumphantly with his fist, his smiling face turning red in his excitement.

"You know what yamsis means?" I asked.

"There's no meaning to know," he replied, smiling the widest smile that I had ever seen. "It's not a word. It's a name. Yamsi is J. Bruce Ismay!"

Chapter Thirteen
Turn Yamsi's Tragedy Around

"Bruce Ismay?!?" Andrew and I cried in surprise as we leaned forward simultaneously to re-read the text, bonking our heads painfully together in the process.

"By god, yes!" Professor Flynn replied. "Yamsi is Ismay spelled backward."

The professor watched with a bemused smile as Andrew and I rubbed our injured foreheads and finally managed to place the notepad on the table between us.

"TURN YAMSIS TRAGEDY AROUND," I muttered as I read the coded message I'd written in my notebook.

I pulled a pencil from my bag and added an apostrophe.

"TURN YAMSI'S TRAGEDY AROUND," I said, correcting the pronunciation accordingly.

"I must be a complete fool," Andrew said in disbelief, leaning back and running his fingers through his hair as he stared blankly at my notebook. "Yamsi is Ismay backward."

While Andrew and I recovered from our shock, Professor Flynn got up from his chair and walked over to his bookshelf. He pulled down a thick book and took a seat across from us again. Flipping quickly through the pages he soon found the original of the altered photo from the postcard and spent a few moments comparing the two, chuckling in delight.

"Well, my dear, you've really done it," Professor Flynn said, pulling the glasses off his nose and letting them hang around his neck again. "My most sincere respect and admiration to you."

I nodded my thanks for the compliment. "It was nothing," I replied, blushing. "And congratulations to you too. You must be some kind of word wizard to have seen that Yamsi was Ismay backward."

The professor laughed a deep and hearty belly laugh. "Heavens, no, I'm no word wizard!" he cried. "It was Ismay himself who used the codename Yamsi."

The professor slid his glasses on his face again and flipped through the heavy book in front of him until he found what he was looking for.

"Look for yourself," he said, turning the book around so that it was facing me.

I looked down to see a picture of a telegram from the Marconi Wireless Telegraph Company of America with the date April 18, 1912 stamped at the top of the form. It contained a message from the steamship *Carpathia* to the White Star Line's New York Office:

Very important you should hold Cedric daylight Friday for Titanic crew reply

Yamsi

"While *Carpathia* was making its way to New York Ismay sent several 'Yamsi' messages like this back to his company's offices," Professor Flynn explained. "In this message he directed them to delay the sailing of one of their ships, the *Cedric*, to allow himself and the crew of *Titanic* to return to Britain as soon as possible."

I studied the picture for a moment, my brow wrinkled in confusion. "Okay," I said. "Now we know what Yamsi means, but what does the rest of the coded message mean?"

Andrew leaned forward on his elbows. "I was about to ask the same thing," he said. "Because the message almost makes *less* sense now than it did before. Turn Yamsi's tragedy around? Ismay's tragedy began with the sinking of the *Titanic* herself. How are we supposed to turn his tragedy around?"

"Build a time machine?" I suggested jokingly. "And go back to 1912 and prevent *Titanic* from hitting the iceberg?"

Andrew and I both laughed at my joke, but Professor Flynn reached for the thick book in front of me and began leafing through it as though he were searching for something.

"Don't tell me there's a blueprint for a time machine in there," Andrew said as the professor flipped from one page to the next until he found what he was looking for.

"Not a time machine, no..." Professor Flynn muttered as turned the book around and slid it across the table, "...but something even better."

Andrew and I both leaned forward to look, this time being careful not to smash our foreheads together. On the page in front of us was a black and white photo of an elderly gentleman with a wide handlebar moustache sitting in an overstuffed wing chair. The chair was next to a cozy fireplace in a dark-paneled sitting room with various photographs and paintings arranged on the walls.

Former White Star Line Chairman J. Bruce Ismay relaxes at his home at 15 Hill Street, London Mayfair, the caption read.

Andrew and I looked at each other in confusion before meeting the professor's eyes.

"I don't understand," Andrew said, looking over at me again for confirmation that he wasn't the only one missing the point. I shook my head. I had no idea either.

"Look a bit closer," Professor Flynn said, reaching across the table to point near the top of the photo with his thick index finger.

We both looked down again and saw what he was indicating. The photograph in the professor's book was quite small, so this pertinent detail was hard to make out at first glance, but above the fireplace hung a painting of the *Titanic* in her final throes, her stern rising high in the air in preparation for her final two-and-a-half-mile plunge to the bottom of the Atlantic.

"After the disaster, Ismay was a changed man," Professor Flynn said. "He turned inward on himself, seeking solitude and isolation. He kept mostly to himself, splitting his time between a beautiful home in the Mayfair district of London and a secluded lodge on the west coast of Ireland. His wife, Florence, knowing how the topic upset him, forbade even the mere mention of *Titanic* in his presence, but Ismay seemed bent on reliving the disaster repeatedly in his mind; he alternated between blaming himself and casting himself as a victim. He commissioned a painting that showed *Titanic*'s final moments in stark and horrific detail, and he would sit and stare at it for hours each night thinking his dark and lonely thoughts before retiring to bed."

Professor Flynn paused for a moment as he looked across the table at each of us directly in the eye before finishing his story.

"This is that painting," he said, tapping the photograph in the book with the tip of his index finger. "And the name of that painting is *Tragedy*."

Chapter Fourteen

Such A Tiny Hole Sank The Entire Ship?

"Turn Yamsi's *Tragedy* around," Andrew recited to himself as he stared blankly into the distance.

"We're supposed to turn what around? The painting?" I asked. "But why?"

Andrew leaned back with his hands clasped behind his head as he thought this through.

"There must be something on the back of the painting," he said, picking up the *Titanic* postcard and flipping it over to the handwritten squiggles on the back. "Something that can help us decipher this."

"But where *is* the painting?" I asked. "Does it even still exist?"

Andrew and I both looked at Professor Flynn, expecting him to know the answer. He seemed to know a lot of answers thus far, after all.

"Don't look at me," the professor replied. "I'm just an expert on *Titanic*. I have no idea where the painting might be nowadays; probably with the Ismay family somewhere."

"My mother might know," Andrew said as he reached into his inside jacket pocket and extracted a cell phone. "She's the one who got me hooked on this whole treasure hunt in the first place."

Andrew excused himself and wandered over to the corner of the room to make a phone call.

The professor and I watched Andrew go, and then he turned to ask me a question.

"I have to say that I am curious to know how you got caught up in all of this," he said.

I told him the short version of my backstory—about my flight around the world, complete with the Wasabi Willy promotional stop in Dublin and how Andrew had approached me there. All of it seemed so long ago, but in reality, it had hardly been more than twenty-four hours since I'd been sumo wrestling with the giant wasabi ball on Grafton Street.

The professor was surprised. "Andrew took a big chance coming to see you," he said. "His mother never would have done such a thing. And yet, look at all of this now. We have the first major breakthrough in the quest for more than seventy years thanks to you."

"I still can't believe that I was able to solve anything," I admitted, smiling a crooked little smile. "I don't know anything about *Titanic* at all. I hardly even know what she really looked like."

That gave me an idea, and I glanced across the room to where the large *Titanic* model was sitting in its glass case.

"Do you mind?" I asked politely, pointing over to the model. "Can I have a look at her?"

"Of course!" Professor Flynn replied, pulling himself to his feet and hurrying across the room to clear away the stacks of paper that were obscuring the view of the ship. "My apologies for the mess."

I leaned down for a better look and slowly ran my eyes over the hull and various decks of *Titanic*, trying to imagine the dramas that had played out on that dark, cold April night so long ago.

"And the damage from the iceberg?" I asked, looking up at the professor. "Where was the gash that the iceberg tore in the hull?"

Professor Flynn leaned down next to me. "From about here to here," he said, indicating a long stretch along the right side of the hull starting near the bow and continuing past the bridge. "But it wasn't a gash as much as it was three hundred feet of popped rivets and buckled hull plates."

I stood up straight and wrinkled my forehead in bewilderment. "What do you mean?" I asked. "Didn't the iceberg tear a gigantic hole in the ship's hull?"

The professor shook his head. "Not at all," he replied. "In fact, an enormous three–hundred-foot gash in the hull would have quickly overwhelmed the pumps and sunk *Titanic* much faster than she did. Experts at the inquiries following the disaster concluded that the area open to sea was only about twelve square feet—that's an area three feet by four feet, barely half the size of an average doorway. And once you spread that area over the entire long trail of damage caused by the iceberg, it averages out to a three-hundred-foot-long opening about half an inch wide."

"What?!?" I cried in surprise, drawing a quick glance from Andrew who was still in the corner talking on his cell phone. "Such a tiny hole sank the entire ship?!?"

"Well, that isn't exactly a tiny hole," the professor corrected. "It was three hundred feet long, after all, and breached five of the ship's compartments."

"Still," I replied. "I had no idea the damage was so small. It seems incredible that it could sink such a mighty ship as *Titanic*."

"True," the professor agreed. "But what has always bothered me is the portholes."

"I don't understand," I said.

"The portholes," he said again, pointing to the model and the hundreds of portholes lining *Titanic*'s hull. "A number of survivors reported seeing seawater pouring in through open portholes as they were lowered into the lifeboats and rowing for safety. The average porthole is almost a square foot in size."

I saw where he was going with this now. "And if twelve square feet of area was enough to sink the ship...." I said.

"Just imagine how much longer she could have stayed afloat if the captain or officers had thought to send someone down to close all the open portholes," Professor Flynn said, finishing my train of thought. "It wouldn't have been enough to keep them afloat until help arrived, but who knows, the little bit of extra time might have saved a few more lives."

"I wonder why they didn't think of closing the portholes!" I said, surprised.

"There were a lot of things they didn't think about that night," Andrew said, walking over to join us after finishing his phone call. "The idea that such a large-scale disaster could happen to a mighty ship like the *Titanic* just never occurred to anyone, not to the officers and crew, nor to anyone else. That's what makes her story such a tragic modern parable of mankind's hubris."

The professor and I nodded in agreement.

"So tell us, young master Murdoch," Professor Flynn finally said, breaking the silence. "What does your mother have to say about all of this?"

"Well, first of all, she sends her regards to you, Professor, and a warm greeting to Kitty as well. But most important of all, she thinks that Yamsi's *Tragedy* is still in the family, most likely in the family's London home."

"That's fabulous news!" the professor replied. "And...?"

Andrew grinned a triumphant grin—the kind that only someone closing in on the dream of a lifetime can grin. It was a grin I knew well; I'd been wearing a similar one during the past few months as the adventures of my 'round-the-world flight had unfolded in exciting and unforeseen ways.

"The best part is that she thinks she can arrange a meeting with Ismay's grandson in a couple days' time," Andrew added with a smile of eager anticipation.

Chapter Fifteen

Hitting The Highlights

Andrew's mother was as good as her word and successfully arranged a meeting for Andrew and me with Thomas J. Ismay at his home in London in two days' time. Meanwhile, Andrew would drive me back to Dublin and continue by ferry to his parents' home in Scotland before meeting me in London for the meeting. The wait seemed almost unbearable in my excitement to find out what the back of the painting would tell us; I couldn't even imagine how Andrew was feeling. But there

was nothing we could do in the meantime but wait, so I decided to make the best use of the interlude and head directly to London to do some sightseeing.

The flight across the Irish Sea was a quick one, but once I was over the United Kingdom, the route was complicated by the maze of controlled airspace that covered the country. As I was handed off from one control tower to the next, circling far around greater London to the east side, I almost questioned my decision to fly into the city on my own, but I knew I would have to get used this kind of thing if I expected to fly across the rest of Europe. It wasn't the barren wilderness of Alaska, after all. In these parts, I had to share the skies with hundreds of other aircraft.

Eventually I went in for a smooth landing at a nice long strip of water running parallel to London's city airport and left my plane moored at a nearby private marina. From there it was a quick ride by light rail and the underground into the heart of the city to see the sights.

Of course, London has far more to see and do than can be accomplished in just a few days, and I already had more time scheduled in the city, including the opening of a couple of Wasabi Willy restaurants in the coming weeks, but to start off, I hit the basic tourist highlights: Big Ben, Trafalgar Square, Buckingham Palace, Piccadilly Circus, and St.

Paul's Cathedral. All of those places were great, of course, but I have to say that my favorite stop on my first day in London was something that Professor Flynn had suggested—Shakespeare's *Globe* theatre.

Situated on the banks of the River Thames, the modern-day reconstruction of Shakespeare's theatre is located just a couple of hundred meters from the site of the original theatre, the remains of which are now buried under a housing development and the Southwark Bridge. I joined a tour of the theatre and listened intently as the quirky guide explained the histories of both the original and modern versions of the theatre before taking us for a look at the inside.

The interior of the theatre was absolutely breathtaking. Three levels of tiered seating curled in a tight ring around a large area open to the sky with a wide rectangular stage at one end. I felt like I had been instantly transported in time back to Elizabethan London in the 1500s.

The guide explained that the entire building was constructed using only the methods and materials available to the builders of the original theatre, including traditional handmade Tudor bricks, white plaster made with goat's hair, and of course hundreds of English oak trees. The beautiful red marble columns holding the roof over the stage were made from oak painted to look like stone. Even the roof of the seating galleries was made in its original fashion, and is the only thatch roof that has been allowed in London since half the city burned in the Great Fire of 1666.

But the thing that fascinated me the most about the Globe was something that the guide explained to us as he showed some photographs of recent performances at the theatre. Many of the plays performed there are done in the traditional style that Shakespeare and his players would have used. This means that there are no sets and very few props with the actors dressing in appropriate clothes to identify who and what they are. A lavishly dressed actress wearing extravagant and expensive dresses might be a queen or princess while a man in military uniform is clearly a soldier. To the theatregoers of the sixteenth and seventeenth centuries the different outfits would clearly identify the lifestyle and professions of the various characters in a play. In modern times, however, the meanings of these different Elizabethan costumes would be lost on the audience, and so the plays are staged using their modern equivalents—a soldier in a modern military uniform or a wealthy banker in an expensive business suit.

After the tour ended, I headed for the nearest tube station to catch an underground train to the north of London to make a stop that I'd promised my dad I would make. Just a couple of blocks from the St. John's Wood underground station is one of the most famous streets in the entire world, and probably the most famous crosswalk.

In the late 1960s, four very famous young musicians took a break from recording in the EMI studios nearby, and they did a photo shoot with the four of them walking across the street. The photograph they took that day later became the cover of their band's final album, and the name of the road became the album's title—*Abbey Road*.

The band, of course, was The Beatles, and my father insisted that I take a picture of the famous crosswalk and send it to him. I was worried that I would feel a bit stupid taking a picture of a crosswalk, but as it turned out, I wasn't the only one. Nearly a dozen other tourists of different shapes and sizes were busy striding over the crosswalk while their partners stood at a marked spot in the middle of the road to take their pictures.

"Do you want me to snap one of you there, love?" a middle-aged woman carrying two bulging bags of groceries asked me as she was walking past.

"No, thank you," I replied, not wanting my iPhone to get stolen on my first day in London, but I quickly had seconds thoughts. "Actually, I'm sorry—I would like that very much, if you don't mind."

"Not at all, love," she replied. "Happens all the time, believe me."

And with that I handed her my precious iPhone and watched as she dodged some taxis to take her position right in the middle of the busy street. Swinging my arms and doing my best Paul McCartney impersonation, I strode across the street and back a couple of times until the lady gave me a thumbs-up and called me over to show me the photos and to hand my phone to me.

"Perfect," I said with a huge smile as I touched the screen and scrolled through the photos she'd taken. "Thank you so much."

"No worries," she replied, picking up her bags and heading off down the street again. "Don't forget dear, all you need is love."

I smiled and watched her walk away, disappearing into one of the row houses farther down the street before I realized that I hadn't even asked her name.

How rude of me, I thought and headed toward the underground station where I caught a train into central London.

Twenty minutes later, I found myself in Trafalgar Square, sitting on the base of the Nelson Column near one of the imposing lion statues and watching the last rays of sun disappearing from the sky. All around me the city swirled with activity, and for a long while, I just sat there above it all, savoring a crisp, delicious apple as I watched the people rushing past. I wondered about the stories of their lives.

It had been an absolutely perfect day, but I was looking forward to the next because Andrew and I were scheduled to meet with Bruce Ismay's grandson Thomas at his home in nearby Mayfair. I was hardly able to contain my excitement, so I couldn't begin to imagine how excited Andrew must be to finally get some answers to the riddles he'd been trying to solve for so many years.

I had agreed to meet up with Andrew at the tube station closest to Ismay's house just before our appointment at three o'clock. Before that, I had some other plans that had been arranged for me by the gracious Professor Flynn.

"When in London, it is a moral imperative that you see the greatest museum in the world," the professor had told me in Belfast. "And what better way to see the British Museum than your own private tour by a dear friend of mine who is one of the curators there?"

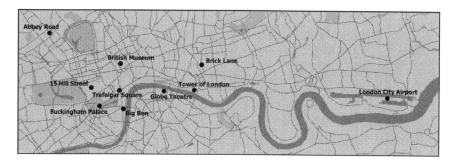

Chapter Sixteen

The 'Rock' Star Of The British Museum

Professor Flynn's curator friend at the British Museum was a woman named Katherine Briggs-Wallace. He'd arranged for me to meet her in front of the museum at ten o'clock in the morning. I arrived a bit early and walked through the iron gates and up to the front entrance. It was quite awe-inspiring, like approaching some ancient Greek temple with fluted Ionic columns lining its covered portico.

Don't I sound clever? Okay, I admit it; before we went into the museum, Katherine gave me an explanation of the various types of columns used in ancient architecture. Doric, Ionic, Corinthian, Tuscan, Greek, Roman, bases, capitals—she talked so fast that I found my brain struggling to keep up with her. By the time she started with an analogy of the various orders of classical architecture as expressions of music and philosophy, I was totally lost.

Katherine was an absolutely stunning middle-aged woman in her late forties who looked nothing like I would have expected the curator of a history museum to look like (that will teach me to believe in stereotypes). When she first came down the stairs, taking long confident strides with her long blonde hair flowing gracefully behind her, I felt like I was in one of those movies where the film suddenly goes into slow motion as a particularly dramatic character enters the scene.

"Hello, Kitty, I'm Katherine," she said, gracefully extending her hand as she instantly picked me out of the crowd of people mingling around the entrance. Even the way she spoke was stately and elegant, her accent and the timbre of her voice lending an air of sophistication to her words.

"It's a pleasure to meet you, Ms. Briggs-Wallace," I replied, shaking her hand. "Thank you for taking time to meet with me today."

Katherine raised her index finger and pretended to scold me. "Call me Katherine," she said, tsk-tsking me. "Or Kate, even. If we're about to share an adventure together exploring the halls of ancient history, then we should certainly be on a first name basis. Don't you agree?"

"I do," I agreed, grinning.

"Excellent," she replied. "Then where shall we begin? Why not right here in the beginning in the wonderful colonnaded portico of our great museum?"

From there she launched into an energetic and fast-paced impromptu lecture on classical architecture in which she spanned centuries of history, music, and philosophy, all in the space of just a few minutes. She had even brought with her a flipbook of diagrams and photos to illustrate what she was talking about. By the time she was finished, I felt like I had personally travelled the long, dusty roads of the Greek and Roman empires, grinning the whole time at the sheer wonder of it.

"But of course these ancient columns here are all fakes; they're not even two hundred years old," she said, gesturing at the forest of columns just up the steps from us. "The only thing ancient about them is the committee of stuffy old men who drew up the plans for a bigger museum to house all the artifacts they'd plundered from the far reaches of the British Empire."

Fakes or not, I took out my iPhone and snapped a photo of Katherine standing like a Greek goddess in front of the museum's front steps.

"What do you say we go see some *real* ancient history?" she asked. "What type of things interest you the most?"

I thought about this for a moment.

"Egyptian history," I replied, thinking ahead to my eventual stop in Egypt on my around-the-world flight. "Mummies, pharaohs, their gods and beliefs—you know, that kind of thing—oh, and of course hieroglyphics."

Katherine smiled widely. "Well, you've come to the right place for that," she said excitedly, grabbing me by the hand. "Come on! Let's go!"

As Katherine led me like a bewildered child up the steps into the grand halls of the museum, I could see why she and Professor Flynn were such good friends.They were both incredibly energetic and passionate about their work and fields of expertise. Katherine's field of expertise, it turned out, was pretty much everything that was built, written, thought, or believed from the very dawn of civilization to the moment she met me in front of the museum. The complete whole of human history, she called it.

"The word museum comes from the word *muse*," Katherine explained as we breezed across the spectacular glass-domed inner courtyard. "The ancient Greeks believed that the muses were the nine daughters of Zeus and the Titan Mnemosyne, descendant of Earth and Sky and the embodiment of memory. The muses themselves were the Earthly personifications of knowledge, music, dance, literature, and science. The ancient Greek cult of the muses built a shrine to them that they called a museum. That's how I like to think of our own little museum here—as a shrine to knowledge."

Katherine led me through an arched doorway at the far end of the great court where we confronted the unmistakably unique face of an Easter Island statue staring blindly into the distance.

"Let's start here at the farthest reaches of the earth," Katherine said, looking at me with a wild grin on her face. "And circle back to the birthplaces of civilization."

"Sounds good," I replied, putting myself completely at her mercy.

"Then let's get on with it, shall we?" she cried, and with that we were off on a whirlwind odyssey through the Far East, North America, the

Middle East, Ancient Greece, Assyria, and finally to what I'd been waiting for—Ancient Egypt.

We made our way through the mummies and sarcophagi to the great hall where enormous statues of gods and pharaohs looked down on us from an abyss that spanned thousands of years.

"The British Museum is home to the largest collection of ancient Egyptian artifacts in the world outside of Egypt itself," Katherine explained.

"Why is that?" I asked, surprised that so many important objects were not in Egypt.

"Some of it was sheer plunder," Katherine admitted, "taken as spoils of war or just simply carted away by pompous colonial masters who wanted a souvenir of Egypt to put in their backyards. Some of these arrogant men justified the theft on the grounds that the artefacts were better off in their hands than left to the Egyptians themselves. But as racist and bigoted as this kind of thinking was, there was also quite an unfortunate truth about it. When most of these objects were brought to England, the Egyptians were busy selling off the mummified corpses of humans and animals by the ton to be ground up and used as fertilizer or medicine. Even the eternal pyramids weren't safe since the governor of Egypt at the time, Muhammad Ali Pasha, suggested tearing them down and using the stones to build a dam on the Nile. This plan would have been put into effect had not the chief engineer, a Frenchman, concocted a falsified financial report demonstrating that it would be cheaper to quarry new stone for the dam.

"But that wouldn't be the last time that a project to build a dam on the Nile would threaten ancient sites. In the 1960s, a dam flooded thousands of years of history. Before the project was completed, UNESCO was able to successfully move the Temple of Ramses II at Abu Simbel and the Sanctuary of Isis at Philae to higher ground, one stone at a time, but hundreds of other temples and unknown thousands of historical treasures are now lying at the bottom of the manmade Lake Nasser."

"That's unbelievable!" I exclaimed in disbelief. "How could they do that?"

Katherine shrugged. "Indifference to the importance of history, I suppose," she said.

"But knocking down the pyramids?!?" I replied in exasperation.

"It's important to remember that Egypt was ruled by the Ottoman Turks during that period," Katherine said. "They were not Egyptians and therefore had no personal connection to these sites of antiquity."

"Unbelievable," I muttered as Katherine and I arrived at a tall glass case surrounded by dozens of people taking photographs. Inside was a large rectangular black stone, damaged and broken at several corners, with a series of writings etched onto its surface on one polished face.

"Which brings us to the last stop on our tour today," Katherine said, gesturing toward the glass case with understated flourish. "But I know it's something that you've been waiting to see because if you want to know about Egyptian hieroglyphics, this is the place where it all started."

"What is it?" I asked, standing on my tiptoes and trying to see over the crowd of people.

"This little fellow is the real rock star of the British Museum," Katherine said, the crowd parting as if on cue to give me an unobstructed view for a moment. "This is the Rosetta stone."

Chapter Seventeen
The Symbol For Life

"The Rosetta stone... of course!" I said as I took my iPhone from my pocket to snap a quick photo before the crowd spoiled my view again. "I've heard of that, although I have no idea why."

"It's very famous, as you can see," Katherine said, nodding toward the continuous crowd of people surrounding it. "And it is arguably the most important object in our museum, depending on who you talk to. But certainly when it comes to the history of deciphering Egyptian hieroglyphics, it is of incomparable significance."

Katherine and I stepped to the side and found a quiet corner where we could see the stone but she had space to pull out her flipbook and explain things to me.

"The ancient Egyptian writing that we know as hieroglyphs was used in Egypt for literally thousands of years," Katherine said. "But as the Egyptian empire began to decline, and Egypt was conquered by the Greeks and Romans, the use of hieroglyphs slowly diminished, and they slipped completely out of use by about 400 AD. After that, it didn't take long for the understanding of the hieroglyphs to fade from historical memory, and a thousand years later when the Europeans started to take interest in all things Egyptian, there was no one left who had the slightest clue how to read them. Many different scholars tried and failed to unravel the mystery of the hieroglyphs, but none of them came close.

"But all of that began to change one day in 1799 when a French soldier from Napoleon's invasion force was digging near the town of Rosetta. Napoleon had come to conquer Egypt by military force, and so he'd obviously brought many soldiers and weapons with him, but because he also understood the importance of knowledge, he had brought a number of different scholars and experts with him as well. He'd brought nerds, in other words!"

Katherine smiled as I chuckled at her choice of words, and then she continued.

"But when that soldier unearthed a large stone with writing on it, these nerdy scholars were able to instantly appreciate the immense value of what had just been discovered. The British immediately recognized the value of the stone and made sure to seize it as a spoil of war when their forces returned to reconquer Egypt a few years later, a fact that history can never forget because they helpfully carved proof of the stone's new ownership on the side of it where it reads, *Captured in Egypt by the British Army in 1801*."

Katherine rolled her eyes and made me laugh while she flipped through her book to a page showing the original ancient inscriptions on the front face of the Rosetta stone.

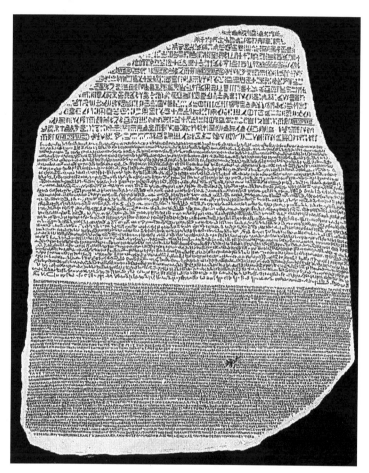

"The key to its mystery was the discovery that the stone contained writing in three different languages," Katherine said, indicating each as she explained. "Egyptian hieroglyphs at the top, Egyptian Demotic script in the middle and Greek at the bottom. The hieroglyphs were a complete mystery, and the Demotic script was a written form of the Egyptian language largely unfamiliar to the Frenchmen, but to these nerdy scholars, the Greek was as familiar as their own native tongue. They had no problem reading what it said. It was a decree issued by the high priests of Memphis on the first anniversary of the coronation of Ptolemy V, ruler of Egypt:

"*On the fourth day of the ninth year of the reign of Ptolemy, a child who has risen as king in the place of his father*... blah blah blah blah... Ptolemy... blah blah blah... Ptolemy again... blah blah blah... Ptolemy did a bunch of great stuff... blah blah blah and on and on and on," Katherine said, making me laugh by rolling her eyes at the longwinded bureaucratic language. "It's a lot of boilerplate wording, but what *really* got these nerd's hearts racing was the last line of the decree, which read, *this decree shall be written on a stela of hard stone in sacred writing, native writing, and in Greek writing.* In other words, just like a No Smoking sign in an international airport, the Rosetta stone contained *three* different versions of the same text written in three different languages: in Greek because that was the official language of the Greek empire, of which Egypt was a part at the time; in Demotic script because that was the written form of the spoke Egyptian language; and in hieroglyphs because that was the sacred writing used by the priests of the temples from which the decree was issued."

I nearly gasped at the significance of this. If they could read one or even two of those languages, then deciphering the third one, the hieroglyphs, should be easy.

"I see your eyes getting wide," Katherine said with a laugh. "But it's a bit more complicated than you might expect."

"It always is," I replied, laughing along with her.

Katherine turned to the next page that showed a close-up of the hieroglyphs etched onto the Rosetta stone.

"The hieroglyphs were considered to be a sacred language," Katherine explained. "But the exact nature of that language was unknown. The assumption was that it must be similar to Chinese—a written language where each picture represented a word or an idea. But if that were true, it seemed as though there were too many individual hieroglyphs at the top of the stone to represent the five hundred or so Greek words written at the bottom. And there was also the question of these oval boxes drawn around some of the hieroglyphs. Because of their shape, the French soldiers called them *cartouches*, which was the name for the oblong paper and gunpowder cartridges that were used in rifles at the time."

"But why did the ancient Egyptians circle certain combinations of symbols?" Katherine asked, grinning as she pointed to one of the cartouches on her flipbook. "And why was this particular combination repeated several times throughout the hieroglyphic section?"

"And what about this other one?" Katherine asked, sliding her finger along the page to another cartouche.

"This one is shorter," she continued. "But it's identical to the right half of the longer cartouche. Could it be that these combinations of symbols had some meaning? Why would the ancient Egyptians draw attention to these particular symbols? Could they have some special importance? Why were they repeated so many times?"

Katherine paused and looked at me expectantly, waiting for me to make the connection. My mind raced to find the answer but came up with nothing. My face had just begun to flush in embarrassment when I remembered what she'd said when translating the decree for me—the name that she'd repeated over and over again.

"Ptolemy!" I cried out, my voice echoing off the hard stone ceiling and walls of the great hall and drawing looks from the nearby crowd.

"Exactly!" Katherine replied. "The ancient Egyptians had the very helpful habit of circling combinations of symbols that were important, and what could be more important than the name of the king?"

"But why is one longer than the other?" I asked.

"This one is simply his name, Ptolemy," Katherine replied, pointing to the shorter of the two cartouches. "The other is his name plus his title: *Ptolemy, the ever-living, beloved of Ptah*, a flowery designation included in the Greek and Demotic sections of the stone. Reading right to left it spells P—T—O—L—M—I—S, which is a form of the Greek *Ptolemaios*."

S I   M L   O   TP

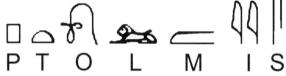

P   T   O   L   M   I S

Katherine flipped to the next page in her book, which showed a symbol-by-symbol breakdown of the letters in the name Ptolemy—one reading right to left the other left to right.

"The direction in which you read the symbols is determined by which way the animals or humans in the sentence face," Katherine explained, pointing to the lion symbol representing the L in Ptolemy. "If they're facing left, you read from the left and vice versa."

I leaned forward to examine the two groups of symbols more closely, noticing that the name Ptolemy took up almost half of the space in the longer cartouche.

"Why does it take so many symbols to spell Ptolemy and so few to spell out the rest of his title?"

"Aha!" Katherine cried. "That is a very good question, and one that reveals the delightfully complex and intricate nature of the hieroglyphs."

"Oh no," I said with a grin, bracing myself for another of Katherine's whirlwind explanations. "Am I gonna regret asking this?"

"You might," Katherine joked as she pointed again to the lion symbol in Ptolemy. "What makes the written language of the hieroglyphs so amazing is that not only do some symbols represent phonetic sounds such as the lion for L, but some symbols *also* represent entire words or ideas or things. For instance, the lion symbol here also represents a lion."

"Okay, easy enough so far," I said.

"This partly explains why there are so many thousands of different symbols used in Egyptian hieroglyphics," Katherine continued. "Another reason is because instead of just having twenty or thirty letters in their alphabet to represent each of the phonetic sounds of their spoken language, they also used different symbols for combinations of phonetic sounds, and sometimes they used two or three or four together, like this one, which I am sure you know...."

Katherine flipped some more pages and showed me a symbol I knew well.

"Ankh," I said aloud as Katherine pointed to the symbol.

"Exactly," she replied. "This symbol represents the phonetic combination of nkh. It is also the symbol for *life*. But even this doesn't explain why so many symbols are used in hieroglyphics. Another reason is that the Egyptians sometimes had more than one symbol to represent the same phonetic sounds."

"Yikes," I said. "That's complicated."

"It gets worse," Katherine continued. "Many of these same symbols were also used as what they call determinatives, which means that even though they might have a phonetic value or literal meaning in some circumstances, in others they don't, and they simply determine the meaning of the other symbols that surround them. Like the hieroglyph of a tree branch which represents the phonetic sound 'ht.' It also has a literal meaning of 'wood.' But it can also be used as a determinative in combination with other symbols to indicate that something is made of wood, like the word 'wooden.'"

Katherine was beginning to lose me again and the blank look on my face must have exposed my bewilderment.

"Oh dear, I'm sorry," Katherine apologized. "I keep going on and on about this."

"No, no," I replied. "Don't be sorry. I am completely fascinated by all of this."

"How about one last thing about hieroglyphics and then we call it day and get some lunch?" Katherine suggested.

"Perfect," I replied, realizing that I was starting to get quite hungry after hours of exploring the museum.

Katherine nodded and flipped through her book a few pages further until she found what she was looking for.

"The Egyptians believed that as long as their name was written down somewhere before they died then they would not just simply disappear at the moment of death but instead would move on to the afterlife," Katherine explained, holding up her flipbook for me to see. "This cartouche was inscribed on a number of items that were contained within a previously unknown and untouched tomb that was discovered in the Valley of the Kings in Egypt in 1922."

"Now that you know some of the phonetic symbols used in hieroglyphics, maybe you can decipher this one," Katherine said. "I'll make it easier by telling you what the top and bottom lines mean. The bottom line is symbolic and gives the king's title as Ruler of Heliopolis of Upper Egypt. The top line is the last part of the name, which is the god Amun, but in Egyptian, the name of a god was always written first out of respect, even though it was pronounced at the end of the king's name. Keeping in mind that the bird symbol represents a U sound in this context, see if you can sound out the rest."

I leaned close and examined the picture carefully.

"Okay," I said, thinking things through as I spoke aloud. "The bird is looking to the right, so I have to read it right to left. The little half circles on either side of the bird are the same as the second letter in Ptolemy, so that must be T. And the last symbol is the ankh."

I blinked hard, shocked speechless for a moment when I suddenly put it all together.

"Tutankhamun!" I cried, looking over at Katherine in amazement. "It's Tutankhamun!"

"Yes!" Katherine exclaimed in delight. "Tutankhamun—whose name literally means 'the living image of Amun.'"

"And it's the living image because the ankh represents life, right?!" I cried out again, very proud of myself.

"Yes, exactly!" Katherine replied.

"There was an ankh in Ptolemy's official title, too," I continued, my mind racing to remember how she'd translated it. "And the ankh must represent life in that title as well, because you said he was the ever living, beloved of...someone."

"Not just someone, actually, but Ptah, the god of architecture,"

Katherine replied. "But yes, there was an ankh in Ptolemy's title representing life. By god, we'll make an Egyptologist out of you yet!"

"Thank you so much," I said, rushing over in my excitement to give Katherine a hug. "Really, thank you for everything you've done for me today."

"It was a pleasure, Kitty, believe me," Katherine replied, taken slightly aback by my sudden display of affection. "And I don't know about you, but I am feeling quite hungry now after all of this talk of ancient civilizations."

"Me too," I agreed, listening to my stomach growl impatiently.

"Perhaps some cuisine from another of the world's most ancient civilizations will cap off this excursion perfectly," Katherine suggested.

"Everything is good with me," I replied.

"Then it's decided," Katherine said. "To the underground!"

Chapter Eighteen
No Turning Back Now

A quick journey on the underground brought us to a rather dodgy-looking street in East London called Brick Lane. I think it wasn't *actually* dodgy, in all honesty, but the incessant come-ons from restaurant owners standing in front of their eateries gave the area a slight air of disrepute. Katherine breezed efficiently past all of them without even making eye contact, ignoring their offers of free drinks and discounts until we arrived at the restaurant she'd had in mind from the beginning.

As promised, lunch consisted of food from another of the world's great civilizations—India. I have to admit that I hadn't eaten much Indian food back home in Canada, as there aren't many Indian restaurants in my hometown of Tofino, and I have to admit that I have always been a little scared of how spicy the food might be. But as it turns out, there are many curry options for the spice averse, including a dish that Katherine suggested for me, a sweet curry with mango and almonds called Chicken Korma. Katherine was more adventurous and took a much more fiery Vindaloo lamb curry that I was so afraid of that she couldn't even tempt me to taste a tiny spoonful of it. Maybe I'm a coward, but I like to actually *taste* the flavors of the foods I eat, not be overpowered by them.

Katherine was as fascinating a lunch partner as she was a tour guide, and she kept me spellbound and laughing throughout the entire meal with stories from behind the scenes of the British Museum. After we had eaten the last of the naan bread and the pappadums, I tried to pay the bill for both of us, but she insisted on treating me. I protested in earnest, but she stubbornly waved my money away.

We left the restaurant and leisurely made our way toward the underground station. This time as we ran the gauntlet of the various barkers standing in front of every restaurant, they left us alone for some reason. Did they somehow know that we'd already eaten and there was no point propositioning us? I wondered.

The two of us took a train as far as Holburn station where we got off near the British Museum so that Katherine could return to work. From there I would continue on to Green Park station to meet up with Andrew. Katherine and I said farewell on the platform, and then I hopped into the next arriving train and rode off into the depths of the London underworld.

As the train carriage clacked and shuddered its way through the subterranean darkness, I could feel my excitement growing in anticipation of the meeting with Thomas Ismay. I couldn't wait to see Andrew. He would be a hundred times more excited than I was.

"The next station is Green Park," a voice announced as the train approached the station. "Alight here for Green Park and Buckingham Palace. This is a Piccadilly Line train for London Heathrow."

I jumped up from my seat and waited as the train slowed down to a complete stop.

"Mind the gap," another announcement reminded everyone as the doors opened, and I stepped off the train onto the platform, taking care to do exactly that as I disembarked.

I looked up to see which direction the way out was. I was getting pretty good at finding my way through the maze of underground tunnels and stations, and soon spotted the familiar black and yellow sign. I'd learned that just following the crowd wasn't always the best idea since many people were heading for another platform to change trains rather than making their way to the outside world. Besides, I'd also learned the hard way that there are almost as many clueless tourists on the underground as there are knowledgeable locals, and after haplessly following a group of clueless people the day before who I *thought* knew what they were doing, I decided I was better off relying on my own wits rather than those of other people.

I shuffled along with the crowd exiting the underground, climbing the stairs and escalators until finally emerging into the world of sunshine and fresh air once again. I wasn't quite sure which exit I was supposed to use, and had learned that for the uninitiated it always took a bit of guesswork and hoping for the best when making your up-to-street level. I came out on the park side of the street, which was a good thing, because I needed to be on that side of the street anyway. Andrew had told me to meet him at the corner of the Hotel Ritz, and with just a quick look around, I spotted a lighted sign hanging over an arched walkway; the sign read *THE RITZ.*

Ooh la la, fancy, I thought to myself with a grin as I made my way over to the sign and Andrew, who was already waiting for me beneath it. As usual he was wearing a beautiful dark suit and tie, and looked every inch the respectable gentleman.

"Kitty! Hello!" Andrew said brightly when he saw me approaching. He was smiling from ear to ear, and as I approached, he reached out his hand to shake mine. Ignoring his outstretched hand, I gave him a big hug and kissed him on the cheek.

"Are you ready?" I asked happily, noting with pleasure that my self-assured greeting had put a delightful blush in his cheeks .

"As ready as ever," he replied, gesturing for me to walk with him to a crosswalk .

"I can't believe how excited I am," I told him. "You must be hardly able to control yourself."

Andrew grinned and nodded. "Don't be fooled by my calm and cool exterior," he said. "My stomach has been doing somersaults all day and night since we planned this meeting."

We crossed the street and made our way down a maze of quieter side streets until we reached a long open square with tall trees and benches lining a wide pathway through the grassy lawn. Circling around to the other side of the park, we walked up to another quiet side street running perpendicular away from the park.

HILL STREET W1
CITY OF WESTMINSTER

"This is it," Andrew said, looking a bit more nervous now. "It's just a short way down this street."

We walked together down the street past one brown brick row house after another until we reached the right address. It was a tall house, the same as most of the others on the street, and through the tall front windows, I could see a comfortable sitting room perfectly illuminated by a dazzling crystal chandelier.

"There's no turning back now," Andrew said as he raised his finger to press the door buzzer. Holding his finger just an inch away from the button, he hesitated and looked at me for a moment. I smiled and patted him on the shoulder in reassurance. He smiled and looked forward again to press the buzzer. Inside the house, we heard the muffled sounds of a rattling electric bell and footsteps approaching the door. Andrew and I heard the loud clunk of a deadbolt, and the door opened to reveal a tall, regal-looking man who looked to be in his mid-eighties and was the spitting image of Christopher Plummer, the actor.

Chapter Nineteen

Grandfather, Have You Ever Been Shipwrecked?

"Good afternoon," the man greeted us with a thin smile. "You are Mr. Andrew Murdoch, I presume."

Andrew nodded and reached out to shake the old man's hand. "You presume correctly, sir," Andrew said. "And may I introduce my colleague, Ms. Kitty Hawk."

Colleague? I thought, and I glanced at Andrew in amusement. *I like the sound of that somehow. It gives the impression that we are in this together, like a team.*

"A pleasure to meet you both," the old man said with a polite smile, "especially you, Ms. Hawk. I am Thomas Ismay, as you know. Please come in, and we'll take a seat in the drawing room."

Mr. Ismay led us into his home and down a long hallway to another door where he shepherded us into his sitting room. Despite his advanced age, he moved with a deliberate grace and power that I found almost hypnotic, almost threatening, like a panther ready to pounce or perhaps a cobra coiled up and ready to strike.

"Please make yourselves comfortable," Ismay said, gesturing to a trio of soft armchairs circled around the fireplace. "I have brewed some fresh tea that should just now be ready."

Andrew tapped me on the elbow and nodded silently toward the back of the room where a familiar painting was hanging on the wall alongside various others. The dark silhouette of *Titanic*'s sloping decks angling into the ocean was unmistakable. It was the *Tragedy*.

"Do you take milk and sugar?" Ismay asked as he poured the tea into a set of beautiful antique china cups and saucers decorated with a colorful floral motif.

"Milk for me, thank you, sir," Andrew responded.

"For me as well, thank you," I said, and I watched Ismay prepare our teas and place them on a polished silver tray alongside some pastries.

"I had some cranberry scones delivered this morning for the occasion, and I've reheated them a bit in the oven," Ismay said as he carried the tray over and placed it on the low table between us. "There's strawberry jam and cream as well, so please help yourself."

I felt so sophisticated sipping tea from an antique cup and taking dainty bites of a deliciously warm scone. It felt as though I was having tea with a member of the royal family, but of course, I knew that I was just a barbaric hillbilly when it came to the English ritual of afternoon tea.

"So tell me, Mr. Murdoch, what exactly is it that brings you here this afternoon?" Ismay said as he took his seat across from us. "I am sure you know that I spoke with your mother many years ago about this letter that your family received just before my grandfather's death. I have absolutely no knowledge of anything that might shed some light on the matter. In fact, as you may already know, I am not at all convinced that the letter came from my grandfather in the first place."

I was surprised to hear him get right to the point in such a direct manner as this.

"May I ask why that is, sir?" I said, opening my big mouth before realizing that I was sticking my foot in it. "About the letter, I mean. Why do you think it was written by someone other than your grandfather?"

Mr. Ismay turned and stared at me across the room with his piercing blue eyes. I felt like I was back in school and he was one of the more demanding teachers, scrutinizing me and sizing me up.

"It's a question of motive, really," he said. "Why *would* my grandfather send such a letter to Mr. Murdoch's family? And why all the subterfuge? Why all these riddles and nonsense about treasures? If the letter is indeed from my grandfather, then why wouldn't he just come straight out and say what he wanted to say?"

I nodded in understanding. *There is some sense to that, I suppose*, I thought.

"My grandfather was raked over the coals for having the audacity to survive *Titanic*," Ismay continued, a hint of emotion and frustration creeping into his voice. "The newspapers and general public on both sides of the Atlantic crucified him for not going down with the ship, but there was no reason why he should have done so. There was no moral obligation for him, a mere passenger on the ship, to sacrifice his own life. He spent most of the night helping passengers into the lifeboats, and when he saw one of the last ones being lowered into the water, he decided to jump into it since there was no one else left."

"No one else?!?" I interrupted, not sure I'd heard him correctly. I could almost feel Andrew tensing up at my bold outburst.

"Yes, of course," Ismay replied calmly, unnerved. "It was a big ship, and most of the people had already moved aft to get as far away from the water as possible. The bow of the ship was completely submerged, and my grandfather jumped into what he thought was the last lifeboat to leave the ship. He helped row the boat to safety, and as the ship made her final plunge, he refused to watch because he could not bear to witness her demise.

"All night they rowed, and were picked up the next morning by the *Carpathia*, who had steamed through the night to come to their rescue. My grandfather was a complete wreck and isolated himself in the doctor's cabin for the entire voyage to New York. His hair had gone from black to gray almost overnight, and he was distraught to learn that women had perished in the disaster even as he and other men had survived. Those who visited him in the doctor's cabin saw a broken man staring blankly into space and shaking like a leaf as he muttered repeatedly that he should have gone down with the ship.

"A few days later, when the *Carpathia* finally arrived in New York, things went from bad to worse for my grandfather. The United States Senate had convened a special inquiry into the *Titanic* disaster and ordered my grandfather to be its first witness the next morning. He complied with this summons, of course, and in an extraordinary feat of composure, he gave the inquiry his testimony calmly and methodically.

"Meanwhile, the newspapers and public were calling for his head," Mr. Ismay continued, his voice rising almost imperceptibly with every word he spoke. "Following the testimony of one of the *Titanic's* surviving officers, Fifth Officer Lowe, an uproar broke out in the media. On the night of the disaster, when Lowe was frantically rushing around the deck shepherding people into lifeboats, my grandfather shouted, 'Lower away, lower away!' Lowe didn't appreciate being ordered around by someone he thought was just another passenger, and he shouted back, 'If you get the hell out of here, I might be able to do something.' The press had a field day with this and encouraged the small towns of Ismay, Texas, and Ismay, Montana, to change their names to Lowe in remembrance of the only man who had the guts to tell off the cowardly Bruce Ismay. Throughout this onslaught, my grandfather stayed strong and weathered the storms that swirled around him in the wake of the loss of his beloved *Titanic*.

"A few weeks later, on his return to England my grandfather was forced to endure yet another inquiry, a British one this time. Once again, he maintained his poise and dignity in the face of public scrutiny, but at least the British inquiry and public were more understanding than the Americans had been, and Lord Mersey, the Wreck Commissioner overseeing the hearings, said that he did not agree with the belief that my grandfather should have gone down with the ship. Mersey said that as there were no other passengers in need of rescue, and there was room in the lifeboat as it was being lowered into the water, had my grandfather not jumped, he would have added one more life, his own, to those who were lost."

Mr. Ismay paused for a moment to take a deep breath and a sip of tea. Clearly, the memories of his grandfather and the ordeals he had suffered were a very emotional topic for him. I had more questions but kept my mouth shut, as did Andrew, who was sitting quietly nearby, listening respectfully as Mr. Ismay continued.

"My grandfather loved ships so much, but after the loss of the *Titanic*, he never cared to see another ship again as long as he lived," Ismay said quietly as he stroked his chin and gazed out the windows to the street outside. "For most of his entire adult life he combed through every newspaper for any mention of himself or his ships, cutting the relevant articles out and carefully pasting them in enormous leather-bound scrapbooks."

I glanced at Andrew, my look saying what we were both thinking. *He cut articles out of newspapers—like the one your family got in the mail!* Andrew gave me an almost imperceptible nod and we continued listening.

"After *Titanic*, my grandfather was never the same," Ismay continued quietly, his voice calm once again. "He was shunned even by his friends. He woke everyone in the house with his screams as he relived the tragedy in his nightmares. He decided that he needed to live somewhere far away from everything so that he could rest and relax, so he bought a country lodge in Ireland where he pursued his passion for fishing, spending countless hours angling for salmon and trout in the cold Irish rivers.

"Do you know what his Irish neighbors sometimes called him behind his back?" Ismay said with a grim, tight-lipped expression as he leaned close to me.

I shook my head and cleared my throat nervously. "No, sir," I replied.

Ismay leaned back again, folding his hands across his chest. "His name—Bruce Ismay—sounds very similar to the Gaelic *Brú síos mé*, which means *lower me down* in the Irish language—a cruel pun on his having been lowered away to safety on one of *Titanic*'s lifeboats."

I raised my eyebrows slightly. *A cruel pun, indeed,* I thought.

Ismay shook his head in remorse as he gazed distantly out the windows. "My grandfather did his best to keep going, but he was a changed man, and the easiest way for him to cope was to isolate himself from the rest of the world," he said. "When he traveled by train, he always booked an entire first class compartment for himself, and he traveled by night if he could, drawing the shades so he wouldn't be seen. Whenever he was here in London, he wandered through the parks, feeding the pigeons and talking to the homeless and forgotten souls as though they were the only people who could understand him. Sometimes he would go to the cinema or attend afternoon music concerts by himself, always buying two seats—one for him and the other for his coat and hat."

For a long moment, the three of us sat in silence as Ismay stared vacantly out of the windows, tears welling in his eyes. I decided to lighten the mood.

"Do you remember your grandfather from when you were a child?" I asked quietly. "You must have been very young at the time."

Ismay turned toward me and nodded slowly. "I was," he said, his eyes shining, "but I have many fond memories of him, most of them taking place right here in this very house."

Ismay looked around the room for a few moments, smiling brightly at the memories.

"He was a wonderful, kind, and generous man who was capable of great love, even in his state of isolation," Ismay said. "My only regret from all the time I spent with him was something stupid that I said as the family sat down for Christmas dinner one year when I was six or seven years old."

"What was that?" I asked compassionately.

Ismay leaned close to me again and looked me in the eyes.

"You must understand that we grandchildren knew nothing of my grandfather's connection to *Titanic*," Ismay said, his voice low. "The topic was never mentioned in our family, and we didn't learn of it until long after his death."

I nodded. "I understand," I said.

"We were all sitting around the table," Ismay continued, "talking and laughing and celebrating when someone mentioned something about Grandfather's involvement in shipping companies. This caught my attention, because at the time, I couldn't get enough of stories of shipwrecks and buried treasure, and I was even hoping that I would get a wooden pirate ship as a present for Christmas that year. Fascinated to hear that my grandfather was once involved with ships, I turned to him and asked, 'Grandfather, have you ever been shipwrecked?'

"You can imagine the silence that fell over the room like a heavy curtain."

Ismay paused for dramatic emphasis, his eyes narrowing and his mouth tightening into a thin line.

"Complete and utter silence descended as everyone waited for his response!" he exclaimed, pounding the arm of his chair for emphasis. Even stoic Andrew jumped involuntarily at Ismay's raised voice.

"Every eye at the dinner table turned to look at my grandfather," Ismay continued. "He cleared his throat and dabbed the sides of his mouth with a napkin. 'Yes,' he told me simply. 'I was once on a ship that was believed to be unsinkable.'"

Chapter Twenty
Who Would Be Calling Me At This Time Of Night?

Mr. Ismay picked up his teacup and took another sip as he settled back into his chair to let the impact of his story sink in. For a few long moments, the three of us sat there saying nothing with only the occasional clinking of china to break the silence.

Andrew put his teacup down and leaned forward in his chair, his hands clasped in a polite and imploring gesture.

"Thank you very much for the tea and information, Mr. Ismay," he said. "I don't want to occupy too much more of your valuable time, so I will get to the point of what brings us here to see you today."

"Are you not here to discuss these riddles and treasure nonsense?" Ismay asked. "I understood from your mother that this was the reason you wanted to speak with me. But as I've already told you, I'm afraid there's nothing I can do to help you."

Andrew nodded. "That *is* why we are here," he said. "But we've just recently come across some new information that leads me to believe that there *is* something you can do for us. I believe it will resolve everything and provide the solution to all these riddles and nonsense."

Ismay blinked and looked perplexed. "I'm afraid I don't understand," he said. "I don't know anything more than what I told your mother many years ago."

"It's not information from you that we're after," Andrew said, "but something that is in your possession."

Andrew pulled the yellowed envelope from his pocket and showed Ismay the postcard of *Titanic* with its hidden message in Morse code.

"Turn Yamsi's Tragedy around, it says," Andrew explained. "When we realized that Yamsi is Ismay spelled backward, and when we learned that the painting depicted in this postcard is titled *Tragedy*—the very same painting displayed there, on your wall—we felt certain that there must be some information hidden on the back of it. We just had no idea that we would see this painting today, in person, here in your house...."

Andrew ran out of words, and he simply lifted his hand to point to the dimly lit corner of the room where the *Tragedy* was hanging. Ismay looked in the direction that Andrew was indicating.

"That old thing? That belonged to my grandfather," Ismay said in complete bewilderment. "I'm sorry, but can you explain again why on earth you think there's something hidden on the back of this particular painting?"

Andrew held up the *Titanic* postcard for Ismay to get a good look at it.

"Hidden in this photograph that was sent to my family almost eighty years ago is a secret message in Morse code," Andrew explained, speaking slowly and deliberately, "you know—the message that reads 'Turn Yamsi's Tragedy Around.' Yamsi which is Ismay backward, is a codename that was used by your grandfather in wireless communications, and *Tragedy* is the name of that painting hanging right over there. 'Turn Yamsi's Tragedy Around' seems to imply that there is something on the back of that painting that whoever sent this photograph to my family wanted us to see."

Ismay was speechless at Andrew's calm, calculated explanation, and for a long moment, Andrew and I simply sat in awkward silence waiting for him to speak.

"That is preposterous," Ismay sputtered, his thin lips pressed tightly together as though he'd just eaten something sour.

"Perhaps," Andrew conceded. "But you have to admit that after so many years of dead ends and confusing leads, it is quite remarkable for us to make a breakthrough like this."

Ismay continued staring at us with a dour expression on his face. He turned to look back at the painting again for a moment then glared at us with spiteful eyes.

"Impossible!" he said, his voice rising, sputtering and uncertain. "It's simply not possible!"

Andrew smiled calmly and held up the *Titanic* postcard yet again so that Ismay could see it.

"I can understand your reluctance to believe," Andrew said. "But I assure you, we have checked it numerous times. If you'll just look, you will see the hidden message for yourself."

Ismay was not interested and dismissed Andrew and the postcard with a brisk wave of his hand. He was growing increasingly agitated by the second, and I wondered how Andrew was going to convince him.

"I am telling you, it is impossible," Ismay repeated stubbornly. "I have seen the back of this painting with my own two eyes, and I can tell you with absolute certainty that there are no hidden messages written there."

"It may be hidden, sir," Andrew replied. "Or it may not even be a message at all. It may be something else entirely—something that one might not even recognize as being of significance."

"There are no messages there!" Ismay shouted. "No markings of any kind! I have seen it with my own two eyes!"

"With all due respect, sir," Andrew said, struggling to keep his voice even and calm. "Whatever reason you had for looking at the back of the painting, I doubt very much that it was to find a hidden message or anything of the sort. You simply may not have seen what is there for what it really is."

Ismay sat in silence, glaring across at Andrew and me, his eyes narrow and lips stretched tightly into a thin line across his teeth.

"The painting is right there, sir," Andrew continued, his voice low and thoroughly calm. "It would be a simple matter to allow us access to it so that we could see for ourselves and be absolutely certain."

"You listen here, young man!" Ismay hissed as he leaned forward suddenly, startling us both with his unexpected ferocity. "I have given you my answer! There is nothing whatsoever on the back of that painting. You can either accept what I am telling you or not. I do not give a damn either way. But under no circumstances will I allow you or your friend here to have access to it so you can desecrate one of my grandfather's most cherished possessions simply to cater to your family's endlessly whimsical theories and speculations! Now if you don't mind I would ask you to please leave immediately."

Andrew and I sat in stunned silence as Ismay's powerful voice echoed from every surface of the house. A clock on the mantle ticked incessantly, counting off every excruciating second of the unbearably uncomfortable silence.

"You are quite right, Mr Ismay," Andrew said quietly, smiling weakly as he spoke. "My apologies for pressing the issue, but I hope you can understand that we had to try."

Andrew collected his things and slowly got to his feet. I was still stunned but managed to quickly pull myself together and follow his lead. Mr. Ismay also rose to his feet and gave Andrew a curt nod as was made our way back down the hall to the front door.

"Thank you again for your time today, sir," Andrew said, extending his hand to Mr. Ismay.

Ismay looked down at Andrew's outstretched hand with a stern look on his face, and for a moment, I thought he would refuse to shake it, but after a few long seconds he finally did and gave the two of us another thin-lipped smile.

"It was a pleasure to meet you both," Ismay said, reaching over to shake my hand as well. I felt a twinge of revulsion as his cold and bony palm clasped over mine, but I managed to find the strength to smile and thank him for the tea and scones.

Ismay closed the door behind us and left us standing speechless on the sidewalk in front of his house. When we'd first arrived, the sun had been shining brightly overhead in a nearly cloudless sky, but now the day had turned dark and overcast with a cold wind whipping visciously down the narrow side street.

"There's a storm coming," I said, smelling the air and feeling the change in the weather deep down in my bones.

Andrew nodded and stared blankly up at the roiling gray clouds overhead.

"What will you do now?" I asked, putting my hand on Andrew's shoulder. He looked down at me and shrugged his shoulders.

"I have no idea," he said sadly, and the two of us walked wordlessly together back to the underground station.

As we reached the top of the stairs for the Green Park station, I turned to Andrew, who still seemed lost in thought. "Do you want to get something to eat?" I asked. "Or something?"

Andrew looked at me, smiling faintly.

"If you don't mind, I think I'll just go back to my hotel and try to figure things out," he said. "I'm sorry."

"No, no, please don't worry," I said dismissing his concerns with a wave of my hand. "I understand completely."

"I'll give you a call and we can meet for breakfast tomorrow morning, okay?" he said, giving me a quick hug and starting down the steps into the underground.

"Perfect," I replied and watched him disappear around the corner with a wave.

I ducked into a nearby Starbucks and got a coffee before venturing across the street and taking a leisurely stroll through Green Park, stopping frequently to sit on benches and just relax. The weather wasn't ideal, with a cold wind that occasionally swirled into a frenzy and thrashed at the corners of my jacket, but at least it wasn't raining. Not yet, anyway, and the Londoners didn't seem to mind. All around me the city buzzed and churned with life and activity.

I continued down through Green Park and sat for a while on the Victoria Memorial in front of Buckingham Palace, watching the tall-hatted guards in red coats standing guard out front. Mostly they did nothing but stare straight ahead, alert and unflappable, but every now and then they would come to life and pace back and forth in front of the entrance to the palace. I admired them for their vigilance and concentration and was willing to bet that they were glad for the sudden change in the weather. It can't be easy to keep cool underneath those giant fur hats in summertime, after all.

From the palace, I wandered through St. James Park down to the edge of the river and the parliament buildings. It was a few minutes before seven, so I hung around waiting for Big Ben to strike the hour before I continued up Whitehall to Trafalgar Square and the towering Nelson Column.

For the second evening in a row, I climbed up to the base of the column and simply enjoyed watching the world pass me by. The streets below were an endless stream of taxicabs and double-decker busses with tourists swarming all around, undeterred by the wind and cold.

As the evening really began to set in, however, the weather eventually got the better of me, and I decided to head for the underground and back to my hotel. I grabbed a sandwich at the train station and took it back to my room to eat while I did a bit of reading. It had been a long and tiring day, and soon I feel asleep mid-sentence with my book propped against my face.

The next thing I knew I was being woken up by the jarring ring of my cell phone. I pushed the book off my face, completely disoriented, and took a moment to figure out where I was.

It must be Andrew, I thought, scrambling to reach for my iPhone. *I must have overslept.*

With my phone ringing incessantly I struggled to dig through my shoulder bag and finally found my phone buried under a notebook, but by the time I pulled it free, it had stopped ringing.

The clock on my phone read *2:37 a.m.*

What the hell?!? I asked myself. *Who would be calling me at this time of night?!?*

I didn't have to wait long to find out; within seconds the phone rang again, and Andrew's name popped up on the screen.

I answered the call and held the phone up to my ear.

"Andrew?!? What's going on? It's the middle of the night."

"I know, I know," he replied, his voice distant and muffled by a lot of noise on his end of the line. "And I'm sorry. But can you meet me outside in front of your hotel in five minutes?"

"Five minutes?" I replied, thinking quickly. "Yes of course, I can. But why? What's going on?"

"I'll explain when I see you," Andrew said. "Just make sure to be out in front in five minutes, and don't be late."

Chapter Twenty-One
It Wasn't A Lion, Exactly

I jumped out of bed and quickly threw on some clothes, keeping a close eye on my watch to make sure I didn't keep Andrew waiting. *Five minutes*, he'd said. *Why the rush, and why five minutes?*

I pulled on a jacket and headed down the steps to the ground floor and then out the front door. The narrow side street running in front of my hotel was dark and deserted, but in the distance I could hear some busses and traffic on one of the busier roads a couple of streets over.

I looked at my watch. I had made it on time, with a minute to spare in fact, but as the seconds ticked past, Andrew's five-minute deadline came and went. Soon it was six minutes, then seven and eight.

I began to get a bit uneasy standing out there in the dark night when I finally heard the sound of screeching tires coming around the corner to my right. I looked up to see a black London cab racing down the narrow street toward me. The car was speeding like crazy, and I was surprised when it came squealing to an abrupt halt right in front of me.

"Get in, get in!" I heard a familiar voice shouting at me through the open window of the front seat.

"Andrew?!?" I replied, totally confused.

"Get in, get in quick!" Andrew repeated. He sounded desperate.

I rushed out into the street, yanked open the back door of the cab, and piled inside. Andrew didn't even wait for the door to close behind me before he hit the gas again and sped off down the street, sending me tumbling into the seats at the back of the taxi.

"What in the world is going on, Andrew?!?" I asked as I pulled myself upright again and grasped the sides and roof of the taxi as he screeched around another corner. "Why are you driving a taxi?"

"I borrowed it from a friend of mine," Andrew called back to me over his shoulder as he continued to negotiate the side streets of London like a professional race car driver.

"But why?" I asked. "And why are you driving like such a crazy maniac?"

"I think I'm being followed," Andrew replied, glancing nervously into his rear-view mirror.

I turned around to look out of the back window of the cab. Andrew had turned back onto a busier street and there were a few sets of headlights behind us, including those from an imposing black Audi sedan.

"Are you sure?" I asked, turning to face forward again.

"Pretty sure, yes," Andrew replied.

"But why would someone be following you?"

Andrew glanced back at me with a guilty expression on his face.

"This is why," he said, lifting up a flat black nylon bag that was lying on the seat next to him. The bag was about three feet by two feet with a handle on top.

"What is that?" I asked, already guessing the answer.

"It's the painting," Andrew said.

"The painting?!?" I replied.

"The painting," Andrew said again. "The *Tragedy*."

"How did you get it?!?" I asked, but once again, I had already guessed the answer.

Andrew glanced back at me over his shoulder. "I stole it."

"Oh my god, Andrew," I gasped. "Are you crazy?!? I can't believe it!"

But I actually *could* believe it. In fact, part of me was quite overjoyed to hear that Andrew had stolen it. There was something about Thomas Ismay's blunt and stubborn refusal to let us examine the painting that had really made me angry—and suspicious that he was definitely hiding something. Earlier in the day, I hadn't been able to understand how Andrew could remain so calm in the face of such obstinacy, but I realized now that he had probably started plotting this little heist from the moment it became clear that Ismay wasn't going to let us look at the back of the painting.

"I know, I know," Andrew said, taking another corner at high speed, tires squealing and the entire car shuddering sideways. "And I'm sorry to drag you into this, but I just didn't know where else to turn."

"How did you get it?" I asked, pushing myself upright once the car straightened out again.

"Probably the less you know, the better," Andrew said. "But it wasn't my intention to steal it unless I had to. I just wanted to take a look at it and put it back, but I heard burglar alarms going off and lights coming on everywhere, so I just grabbed it and ran."

"And the taxicab?" I asked. "What is the point of this?"

"Camouflage," Andrew replied. "In case we get caught and have to make a run for it. What better way to lose ourselves on the streets of London than in a black London cab?"

"Good thinking," I said, looking back at the headlights of the Audi tailing us. "Except that you don't seem to be having much luck losing the guy who's following you. But I'm willing to bet that's where I come into the story, right?"

Andrew glanced at me in the mirror, a somber expression on his face. "Kitty, I know I never should have picked you up and dragged you into this," he said. "But you do realize that if you help me, it will make you an accessory to a crime."

"Pffft!" I replied dismissively. "It wouldn't be the first time."

Andrew gave me a funny look. "No, I suppose it wouldn't be," he said.

"Just tell me what I need to do, Andrew. And don't worry about me. I can take care of myself."

Andrew glanced at me one last time then nodded and reached into the pocket of his jacket. He pulled out a strange, round key on a coiled rubber lead with a clip at the end. It was a magnetic key of some kind, and somehow it looked very familiar to me.

"Take this," he said, handing the key to me through an opening in the Plexiglas separating us. "In about two minutes I am going to come around a sharp corner and go under a railway bridge. I'll stop the car for a second, and when I do, you need to jump out and grab the painting from the front seat. On the other side of the road, you will see some statues along the side of the river that you can hide behind. Just duck behind something and get out of sight as quickly as possible."

"Okay, I can do that," I said. "And what about you?"

"I'm going to keep on driving," Andrew said, "and try to lead whoever is following us as far away from you as possible."

"What if they don't fall for that?" I asked.

Andrew nodded toward the key in my hand. "That's what the key is for," he said. "I'll try to distract them, but if I fail, then just down the steps from where I'm dropping you there's a Jet Ski tied up at the side of the river. If our friends in the black Audi aren't fooled, then get on that, and there's no way they'll be able to follow you."

Now I understood why the key looked so familiar. It was a key for a Jet Ski.

"You do know how to drive a Jet Ski, right?" Andrew asked with a worried expression.

I grinned. "You bet I do," I replied. "I grew up by the ocean, remember?"

"Okay. Good. Then just insert the key and wait a couple of seconds before hitting the starter," Andrew instructed. "Then give it some gas and get the hell out of there."

I nodded and leaned forward to get ready.

"Only use the Jet Ski if you absolutely have to," Andrew cautioned. "With any luck our friends in the Audi will keep following me, and then you just need to wait five or ten minutes before taking a taxi back to your hotel. There's no use risking your neck racing about on the river in the middle of the night for no reason."

"Understood," I replied.

Andrew made a quick series of sudden turns, weaving in and out of small streets to confuse the driver of the Audi. He squealed around one last corner, taking it as fast as he dared to, and we turned onto a road running parallel to the Thames. He floored the accelerator, racing faster and faster to give me as much time as possible to disappear before the black Audi caught up and came around the corner behind us.

"Okay, get ready," Andrew said. "Now!!"

Andrew slammed on the brakes, and the taxicab screeched to a halt next to a towering spire and some lion statues standing at the side of the river. I pulled open my door and grabbed the painting as Andrew handed it to me from the front seat. In an instant, he was off again, his door slamming shut as he stepped down hard on the gas pedal. As he peeled off, I ran as fast I could across the street and jumped out of sight behind the retaining wall of one of the two lion statues flanking the towering column overlooking the river.

The seconds ticked slowly until finally I heard the sound of another car coming up fast on the road behind me—but I almost didn't hear it. I was too busy staring mesmerized at the inscriptions on the front of the lion statue. To be accurate, it wasn't a lion, exactly. It was a sphinx. And carved on the front of it just above my head was some writing in Egyptian hieroglyphics.

Chapter Twenty-Two
Like A Horror Movie Or Something

With the sound of the approaching car growing stronger with every passing millisecond, I leaned the painting against the retaining wall and pulled myself up to get a better look at the hieroglyphics etched into the front of the sphinx statue. The pedestal on which the statue was mounted was almost as tall as I was, but with a bit of effort I was able to crawl partway up the retaining wall to look over the sphinx's paws and see what was written there.

I couldn't read the hieroglyphs, obviously, but I have to admit that my heart skipped a beat when I recognized a couple of the symbols from Katherine's lesson in hieroglyphics the day before. The one that really got my mind racing was the ankh symbol—the symbol for life—and I actually reached forward in awe for half a second to trace the embossed symbol with my fingers.

"Umm, that car is coming up pretty fast," the little voice in my head reminded me nervously. "Shouldn't you be out of sight when it goes past?"

I know, I know, I replied. *Stop worrying so much.*

I lowered myself down the retaining wall, and as my feet touched the ground, I happened to look up at the column towering high above me between the two sphinx statues. I was surprised to see that it wasn't a column at all—it was an Egyptian obelisk. And if I thought that the six or seven hieroglyphs I'd just seen on the sphinx statues were exciting, then my heart really began to race when I saw by the dim light of the street lamps that the entire obelisk was covered from top to bottom with more of the ancient Egyptian writing. Literally hundreds of hieroglyphs were carved into every face of the four-sided obelisk, including dozens of examples of characters circled and grouped together by so-called *cartouches.*

What was it that Katherine said? I asked myself. *Oh yeah, I remember now: the ancient Egyptians had a very helpful habit of circling combinations of symbols that were important.*

I stared up at the obelisk with my mind racing at three hundred miles an hour, wondering what each circled group of symbols meant and why they were so important to the ancient Egyptians who had carved them. It also occurred to me that there was a *cartouche* on the front of the sphinx statue as well. But what did the symbols mean? Why were these groups of symbols so important?

"Can we please not forget about the approaching car," the little voice in my head whined, reminding me to get my butt behind the wall again.

Yeah, yeah, yeah, I told myself, sliding down out of sight with plenty of time to spare.

I crouched behind the pedestal and watched as the headlights flickered through the trees casting eerie shadows on the strange ancient writings I'd been gazing at moments prior. I was expecting the car to continue accelerating and roar right past me, but as I watched the changing angles of the beams of light, I became nervous. It looked like the car was starting to slow down as it approached my position.

Oh no, that's bad, I thought. I looked anxiously to my right where a flight of steps descended into the river. In the late evening gloom, I was relieved to see the back end of a Jet Ski floating there, riding the gentle ripples and waves of the river.

I pulled the magnetic key out of my pocket and nervously fingered it as I watched the Audi's headlights getting closer. There was no doubt about it; the car was definitely slowing down. My heart pounded faster and faster as I watched the approaching headlights. Just as the car reached the far side of the sphinx statues, a sudden burst of lighting ripped the sky open and made me nearly jump out of my skin as the world around me was instantly revealed in a brief flash of stark electric light.

Oh my god, I thought, startled out of my wits. *As if this wasn't scary enough already, now it's like a horror movie or something.*

The peal of thunder following the flash came quickly and rolled over the sleeping city like a tidal wave. The noise drowned out the sound of the car engine that was somewhere behind me, but as the thunder slowly grumbled into silence again, I heard the distinct and familiar sound of brakes screeching to a halt.

That does it. I have to get out of here—now! I pivoted forward onto one knee as I grabbed the handle of the painting portfolio with my left hand.

"I told you not to stick your head out to read the hieroglyphics," the little voice in my head, said but I knew it was wrong. There was no possible way that I could have been spotted that way. The driver of the black Audi must have seen me when I ran across the street, or maybe he simply saw Andrew driving off and guessed correctly that someone had jumped from the car.

With my senses on high alert, I quickly crawled to my feet and climbed over the railing of the nearby steps. I had just started down them, heading toward the water, when I heard a car door open from somewhere close above me. In the distance beyond, I could also hear the sound of a car engine roaring as it accelerated toward us from up the street.

I hope that isn't Andrew coming back to save me, I thought as I tucked the painting portfolio under my arm and clambered down the steps. *I'll end up escaping, and he'll just get caught for nothing.*

I reached water level and saw that the Jet Ski was tied to the railing with a series of chaotic knots. Andrew was clearly not a sailor, and in an attempt to make the knot secure, he had just tied a bunch of granny knots, one after another, until the line was just a big mess.

"You've got to be kidding me," I muttered under my breath as I struggled to untie the unruly series of knots.

As I worked, I glanced up the stairs to keep an eye on what was happening. So far, there was nothing, but I could see the beam of a flashlight weaving in and out through the trees and statues.

Somebody was searching for me.

I finally finished untying the last knot as another flash of lightning tore across the sky and bathed the river in a blinding and gruesome light. The deafening hammer of thunder came soon thereafter, followed almost immediately by another flash of lightning. As soon as I placed the painting securely on the runners of the Jet Ski and grabbed the handlebars to pull myself onboard, the heavens fizzled and crackled with electrostatic as if some mad scientist was out there trying to bring Frankenstein to life.

I inserted the key but didn't start the engine. The noise would instantly draw the attention of whoever was looking for me, so I hesitated for a moment as I kicked off the cement wall and drifted a few feet into the river. I was hoping in vain for some other way out of this situation.

The beam of the flashlight wove and turned as whoever was up there continued their search. My finger was hovering uncertainly over the starter switch when I heard another squeal of car brakes.

"Hey!" I heard a familiar voice shouting from above. It was Andrew.

Stupid, stupid, stupid! Why did you come back? I cursed as I finally pushed the starter switch and the engine rumbled to life. As far as I could see, the best thing I could do for Andrew now was to get the hell out of there with the painting as quickly as possible.

As soon as I raced the engine, giving it some gas before taking off, the beam of the flashlight appeared over the top of the stairs and pointed directly down at me, blinding me with its pale blue light. I shielded my eyes and tried to see who was behind it, but as anyone who's ever had a flashlight pointed right at them knows, it's completely impossible to see anything.

Just then, Mother Nature came to my assistance. A cold blast of wind whipped across the river, and the first few heavy drops of a soon-coming deluge fell from the sky.

My breath caught in my throat as I twisted my wrist to give the Jet Ski its final burst of gas, and as I made a quick curling turn before firing out toward the middle of the river, I saw the tall, slender form of an older man standing at the top of the stairs, his thin white hair blowing maniacally in the sudden gusts of wind. It was Thomas Ismay.

Chapter Twenty-Three
The Answer Was Obvious

The instant I poured on the gas the Jet Ski sprang into life beneath me and I roared out into the River Thames leaving Thomas Ismay (and unfortunately also Andrew) far behind me. I was still in shock from the discovery that it was Ismay who was chasing after us, and as I pulled away from the riverbank, I was stunned to see him moving with the speed and dexterity of a much younger man. The day before I had watched the deliberate and graceful way in which he'd moved, and it had reminded me of a panther or a cobra. Suddenly that comparison felt all too dangerously accurate as I watched him quickly scramble along the edge of the concrete wall, keeping his eyes on me the whole time.

Up at street level and beyond I could see the outline of a black London taxicab stopped in the middle of the road. I could also see the dim silhouette of a figure next to the cab, standing halfway in and halfway out of the open driver's door. It was Andrew.

"Come on, Andrew!" I said to myself as I raced out into the middle of the river. "Get the hell out of there!"

Andrew couldn't possibly have heard me, but he certainly got the point and ducked into the cab, hitting the gas pedal to roar off down the street in the opposite direction from where I was heading.

Ismay heard him take off and quickly dashed toward his car, disappearing out of my line of sight between the statues and trees as I pulled farther away from the scene. A few moments later, when I was a safe distance from shore, I idled the engine and watched his black Audi spin around in the middle of the street and speed off in pursuit of Andrew. I watched him for as long as I could.

It was dark out on the river, but thanks to the bright glow of the city all around me and the increasingly frequent flashes of lightning, I was able to see fairly well when I gunned the engine and sped off again. Behind me to my left, I could see the familiar shape of Big Ben and the houses of parliament beyond the nearest bridge. Towering over those on the opposite side of the river stood the London Eye—the enormous Ferris wheel built for the turn of the millennium. All of that helped me to orient myself as I throttled downriver in the opposite direction, heading east to the marina where my plane was tied up. I considered simply finding somewhere to tie up again and taking a taxi back to my hotel, but I had no idea where Ismay was anymore or if he could somehow find a way to follow me from a distance on one of the roads or bridges with a view on the river. For the moment, I felt safe in the middle of the river, and my plane seemed an obvious place to go. It was quite far away, so I would be able to put as much distance between me and Ismay as possible. Plus, I could tie up the Jet Ski there and spend the rest of the night sleeping in the back of my plane—if I could even fall back asleep, that is. I would probably be too anxious and full of adrenaline to sleep a wink.

I continued downriver, navigating across the black water under bridges and weaving in and out through various barges that were moored along the river. Even in the middle of the night, the river was full of all sorts of tricky obstacles, and as I struggled to peer into the darkness, I repeatedly wished that I had a little bit more light.

Why don't they make these things with a pair of headlights? I asked myself as I zipped past another set of boats tied up in the middle of the river. The answer was obvious—you weren't supposed to drive around in the middle of the night on a Jet Ski, so why would they build them with headlights? Besides, even if I had them, the lights would only draw attention to me and make it that much easier for Ismay to spot me. Call me crazy, but I felt a lot safer racing around in the dark than I would have with a big pair of bright headlights lighting my way and announcing my presence to the world.

The bridges were the worst, though, I have to admit. Out on the open river, the brilliant lights of the big city lining both sides of the river reflected off the water, and that was enough to see by. But every time I passed under a bridge—and as I was quickly learning that central London has a *lot* of bridges—I had to ease off the gas and slow down to make the passage through the inky blackness that seemed to cling like a dense fog to the support pillars underneath. Once safely through to the other side and back into the glow of the city, I felt confident enough to run the engine at full throttle and continue my escape.

The imposing dome of St. Paul's Cathedral rose up out of the city amid a forest of modern office towers. To my right the Shard skyscraper towered above the landscape like a jagged splinter of crystal piercing the sky and looming ever closer as I continued downriver. Passing under another bridge, the Tower of London and the famous Tower Bridge came into view up ahead. I still had a long way to go.

With this realization, I questioned the wisdom of my decision to ride all the way out to where my plane was parked. It really was a long way to go, and with the wind picking up and the rain falling more heavily, it was getting a bit rough out on the river. But I decided to stick to the plan, because if I remembered correctly from my maps and charts, the Tower Bridge was the last bridge over the river, and past that, things should thin out, which would allow me to go a bit faster.

Another burst of lightning flashed across the sky as the Tower of London glided past and I approached the bridge with its fancy spires and gothic towers illuminated by various floodlights all around. I was driving straight up the middle of the river, directly between the bridge's two impressive main towers. I couldn't help but look up in awe as I passed underneath, and as I did, another flash of lightning forked across the sky and lit up the bridge in a blinding series of flickering white lights.

As the lighting flashes sizzled across the sky, I had one of the biggest and most frightening shocks of my entire life. Standing right at the midpoint of the bridge almost directly over my head was the gaunt and white-haired figure of Thomas Ismay leaning over the decorative iron railing, glowering fiercely down at me and watching my every move as I disappeared out of sight beneath him.

Chapter Twenty-Four
That's When Things Always Go Really Wrong

Seeing Ismay standing there above me on the bridge was like seeing a ghost—it was shocking and utterly terrifying. With my face completely white and my heart pounding in my chest, I instantly let go of the throttle and cranked the Jet Ski into a quick turn so that I would remain out of sight under the bridge instead of continuing to the other side. I slowly pulled up alongside one of the bridge's enormous pylons to keep out of the wind and rain as much as possible, my eyes darting around as I desperately searched for a glimpse of Ismay.

What am I going to do? What am I going to DO?!? He's right there—right above me!

"Just be cool," I muttered to myself, "and think this through."

For the moment, I was safe enough. Ismay might have been just thirty feet above me on the bridge, but unless he had a boat, I was perfectly safe on the river below him. In fact, even if he *had* a boat, I would still see him coming from a mile away, and on my Jet Ski, I would be able to outrun him easily. That was the most important thing, I quickly realized. I had the advantage of speed.

How fast can a Jet Ski go? I asked myself, quickly thinking back to all the times at home in Canada when we'd tried to run them as fast as they would go. I'd never had the guts to take one all the way to its top speed. It was just too fast for me, and I got nervous after a certain point, but I'd certainly taken some of them faster than sixty miles an hour, and that is really quite fast in such a small craft.

I reassured myself that unless Ismay had some super turbo racing boat nearby or another high performance Jet Ski like the one I was on, it was pretty safe to assume that no matter what he did or how hard he tried to keep up with me, I would easily be able to outrun him.

"And this is the last bridge over the river," I reminded myself. "East of here there's nothing but open water. I'll be able to really crank it up from here on out."

The solution was simple. All I had to do was run the Jet Ski as fast as it would go and watch Ismay fade into the distance in my rear-view mirror. There was nothing he could do to catch me. Of course, he could *try* to keep up with me by car as I raced downriver, but that was highly unlikely, considering that he'd be driving on city streets with traffic lights and twists and turns and cross streets to contend with. The more I thought about it, the more I realized there was simply no way he would be able to keep up with me.

Full of confidence that I now firmly held the upper hand in the situation, I twisted the throttle and puttered out from under the bridge and back on the upriver side where I'd first spotted Ismay looking down at me from above. Before I started my dash downriver, I wanted to be sure that I knew exactly where he was.

With the rain pouring down around me and a brisk wind ripping at my collar, I scanned the railings of the bridge for a glimpse of him. Lightning crackled across the sky, giving the entire scene a completely surreal glow, but there was no sight of him.

Dammit, I thought. *What if he's already gone on ahead of me? Or who knows where?*

Then I spotted him, moving along the pedestrian walkway at the side of the bridge, and soon he was rushing over to where I was floating idly down the river just below where he was.

"You there!" he called out angrily as he hurried along the railing, gripping it with his long bony fingers, one hand after the other as though he were climbing it. "You down there on the river! You have my painting, and I want it back! You're going to regret the day you crossed me, young lady! When I get my hands on you, I'm going to tear you into little pieces and scatter them into the wind! I am going to make you wish you had...."

Ismay was really agitated. Before this tirade, I might have been inclined to feel a bit sorry for him. I mean, after all, he was right. We did steal his painting. But once he started beaking at me and threatening me, I have to say that I'd had just about enough of him for one night.

"Hey!!!" I yelled, shrieking hysterically and cutting him off in mid-threat.

Ismay was taken aback by my sudden outburst and pulled his head back in a comical expression of disbelief. I looked Ismay straight in the eye and slowly shook my head in disapproval.

"You should have just let us look at the painting," I said simply, shrugging my shoulders defiantly before I reached down to crank the throttle on the Jet Ski.

"You're going to regret this!" Ismay bellowed down to me, his fingers wrapped around the railing of the bridge so tightly that all the blood had left them and they looked just like the bones of a bleached white skeleton.

That final threat was the last thing I heard from Ismay before the roar of my engine drowned him out completely. I watched Ismay fuming and pacing powerlessly above me as I accelerated out of sight beneath him.

Another burst of lightning flashed across the sky as I passed underneath the bridge and shot through to the other side, twisting open the throttle even more, almost as far as it would go. I was really flying across the water now and didn't even bother to look back as I rocketed down the river away from Ismay.

By the dim lights of the city, I watched the speedometer creeping higher and higher as I willed myself to go faster: thirty miles an hour, then thirty-five, forty, forty-five, then fifty.

I hesitated. I was getting a bit nervous, but I reminded myself that the faster I got away, the safer I would be, and the safer I would feel once I got where I was going. I opened the throttle up even more, and as I negotiated my way through the various small waves and currents of the river, I tried to keep myself as close to sixty miles an hour as I could.

I was making much better time now, following the contours of the river as it meandered back and forth toward the Millennium Dome. I knew that once I was past that unmistakable landmark, I was home free. My plane was parked in a marina only a short distance beyond it.

From time to time I looked over my shoulder as I blazed along the water. I don't know what I expected to see, but it made me feel better to know that I was quickly putting a lot of distance between Ismay and me, and I felt calmer with every passing minute.

As I rounded one of the last curves of the river and the great white Millennium Dome finally came into view, another flash of lightning ripped through the clouds, and suddenly the wind picked up speed. The wind was so bad, in fact, that I had to ease back on the throttle as I made my way up and around the last bend in the river.

I was almost there—but that's always when things go really wrong, isn't it?

Chapter Twenty-Five
Weather You Would Almost Wish For

Suddenly the wind really began to blow like a hurricane, whipping the surface of the river into a frenzy of whitecaps and flying spray. The rain soon followed and began to pour so hard that it was like a solid sheet of water plummeting from the heavens, soaking my clothes completely to the skin.

I hope that painting portfolio is waterproof, I thought, forgetting about Ismay as I slowed to almost a complete stop and struggled to see through the cascade of water that was obscuring my vision. I could hardly see a thing, but of course that also meant that even if Ismay was out there somewhere watching me, then he wouldn't be able to see me either. And that could only work to my advantage.

The worst of the deluge lasted only a few minutes before easing off a bit, and I was able to continue on my way, pushing the Jet Ski as fast as I dared. By now, the waves were quite choppy, and I found myself plunging down nose first from one crest to the next, slicing the waves in two, and sending buckets of water splashing all over.

Well, this is fun, isn't it? I thought cynically as I kept one foot solidly anchored against the painting bag and my left hand on its handle so I wouldn't lose it as I crashed through the waves. Actually, it *was* kind of fun. It was the kind of weather that you would almost wish for if you were out at the lake in the summertime with your friends, racing around on your Jet Skis just for the fun of it. After all, there's nothing better than smashing through big waves and sending water splashing everywhere, right? I guess it's a bit less fun in the middle of the night during a thunderstorm when you're trying to escape with a stolen painting from a maniacal old man.

From one crest into the next, I rode the Jet Ski over every oncoming wave. I hoped that no one on shore was watching me. I don't mean Ismay. I was confident that he was far behind me, but if anyone was out there watching they would think I was a complete lunatic and might call the police. The last thing I needed was to have to explain to the police why I was cruising down the river in the middle of the night during a storm.

My muscles were sore from keeping such a tight grip on the painting bag with one hand while I kept the Jet Ski steady with the other. For a moment, I lost my grip and had to twist myself to keep from losing the painting. I caught it just in time, but in the process, I released my grip on the throttle, which made me crash down much harder into the next crest than I'd expected to, smacking into it with a teeth-jarring crack. A surge of water came up and pounded me in the face and went straight into my mouth, making me choke and sputter.

Salt water? I thought to myself, spitting the brackish, salty river water out of my mouth. I would have expected the water to be fresh, but then I remembered that the Thames is a tidal river, with salt water from the ocean mixing with the fresh water of the river as the tides came in and out.

I cursed myself for not remembering this sooner and not being more careful when I was racing down the river. For all I knew it was low tide and there were all sorts of treacherous hidden dangers lurking just beneath the surface.

I had another problem as well. The marina where my plane was tied up was connected to the river, but that was only possible when the tide was high and it required going through a system of locks. That meant that there was no way I could just drive up to where my plane was. I would have to wait until the tides were right and there was someone on duty to operate the lock doors.

I shook my head angrily, furious with my own stupidity. I slowed down as I pulled up alongside the entrance channel to the marina and checked things out. Just as I expected, the lock doors were closed. No one would be around to open them for hours.

The rain and wind slacked off a bit, and it looked as if some light was coming into the sky in the east. I considered just floating in the middle of the river until the sun came up, but quickly discarded that idea. I had no idea where Ismay was by that point, and besides which, a teenaged girl sitting on a Jet Ski in the middle of the river would attract far too much attention and questions.

Well, Andrew, I don't know if this is your Jet Ski or if it belongs to a friend of yours, but I'm going to have to take a risk and beach it, and come back for it later.

Because the Thames is a tidal river, it has beaches in many spots. It seems crazy to imagine it, but right in the heart of the city of London, there are actually people who regularly comb the beaches of the Thames at low tide looking for interesting artifacts and treasures—the remnants of a clay pipe, perhaps, or fragments of pottery or shards of an old hand-blown glass beer bottle. It was supposed to be great fun, but the most important thing about those beaches at that moment was that I find somewhere to drive the Jet Ski onto the riverbank and leave it there until daybreak.

I drove in close and cruised back and forth along the shoreline, looking for somewhere suitable to pull in. I was relieved to see quite a few good spots where I could run the Jet Ski aground and hide it for a few hours. In fact, I was surprised to see that there was even an actual boat ramp sloping down into the river from a street close to the marina where my plane was docked. I could hardly believe my eyes. It was tucked away next to a small stretch of beach and a few houses. Tied up there, the Jet Ski would blend in, but more importantly, it would be almost invisible to Ismay, who might be looking for it. It was perfect.

I slowly idled toward the shoreline, shutting down my engine as I got close to avoid sucking mud or rocks into the water jets, and then I just let the forward momentum carry me over to a set of posts that were sticking out of the water. When the nose of the Jet Ski scraped bottom and rode up onto the muddy beach, I jumped off with the mooring line in my hand to tie it securely to a nearby post.

"Perfect," I murmured, and I grabbed the painting bag and splashed up to dry land. I had a bit of a hike ahead of me through the rain to get to the marina but it was all on solid city streets and sidewalks, so I didn't mind. The rain helped wash the mud off my shoes anyway.

I hope the Jet Ski is still there when I come back, I thought as I made my way through a sleepy residential neighborhood to my plane. *It should be. I hope it will be, anyway. I hope.*

But to be honest, I didn't really care at that point. I was soaking wet and miserable, and I wanted to get to my plane where I would be safe and warm again. Fifteen minutes later, I got my wish and pulled myself up onto one of the pontoons of my trusty De Havilland Beaver. I sat under the wing and peeled off my dirty shoes and wet socks. When I was done, I slid the painting portfolio into the back seat of my plane and crawled inside, closing the door behind me. I dug around through my equipment bags until I found a towel and some dry clothes then quickly dried off and changed before pulling a sleeping bag around me for warmth.

Finally I was dry again and warming up a bit. I was exhausted and felt like I had just been through a very long night, but in fact it had only been a few hours since Andrew had called and woken me from my peaceful slumber in my hotel room.

I glanced over at the painting portfolio leaning up on the passenger seat, slowly dripping on the towel I had folded and placed underneath it.

All that trouble for a stupid painting, I thought bitterly, but I knew that it wasn't just a stupid painting, and now that I was safe and warm and dry, there was no reason to be bitter—just the opposite, in fact.

"Turn Yamsi's Tragedy Around," the coded message read. And now, after so much time and trouble, Yamsi's *Tragedy* was sitting just a few feet away from me—and so were all the answers.

Chapter Twenty-Six
Don't Forget You've Stolen It Now Too

I reached over to grab my iPhone out of the inside pocket of my jacket. I was dying of curiosity to find out what was on the back of that painting, but first things first, I had to call Andrew and see if he was all right. I flipped through my address book and dialed his number, tapping my fingers impatiently on the back of the seat while I waited for him to answer.

The phone rang repeatedly, but no one picked up. Finally, I heard a click, and my breath caught in my throat in anticipation, but it was just his voice mail message kicking in. I ended the call and dialed again, but as before, all I got was his voice mail message.

I set the phone down and leaned back to think things through. *Where could he be?* I wondered. *Oh god, I hope he's okay.*

A sudden noise from somewhere outside on the dock startled me, and I spun around to see what it was. I switched off the small cabin light and peered out through the windows. *Is someone out there? Is ISMAY out there?!??*

With my breath getting faster and shallower, I searched all around the dock and my plane as my eyes adjusted to the dim light. There was no one out there as far as I could see, but my plane was rocking gently in the wind and rain, occasionally bumping against the rubber fenders lining the dock.

It was just the wind, I told myself. *Don't start getting paranoid. How would Ismay get into the marina without the security code for the gates?*

"Maybe you're not paranoid enough," the little voice in my head commented as my eyes darted around my plane before I dialed Andrew's number again.

Ring-ring, ring-ring, ring-ring—then voice mail again.

Why isn't he answering?! I ended the call and put the phone down again. *Where in the world could he be?!*

I nearly jumped out of my skin when I suddenly heard the noise again—a sort of wet metallic smacking sound coming from just outside the plane. I crawled over the passenger bench to the cargo door window on the right side of the plane and carefully raised my head to look outside. There was nothing there—nothing and no one.

But what is making that noise?! I thought to myself, panicking at the thought of Thomas Ismay sneaking around the marina at night, stalking me...hunting me.

"Don't be ridiculous," the little voice in my head scolded. "It's not Thomas Ismay out there. He's eighty years old!"

I'm not being ridiculous! I replied. *You saw how he was moving along the riverbank—like a dangerous jungle cat. I wish I were half as fast and limber as that.*

I peered nervously out the window and heard the noise again. This time I was better able to judge where it was coming from, and glanced up to the underside of the wing to see what was making it.

"Oh my god," I said aloud in relieved but annoyed frustration. "I am so stupid."

When I'd taken my shoes and socks off outside, I'd hung my socks up to dry on the support strut underneath the plane's wing. The wet metallic smacking sound was my wet sock flapping in the wind against the underside of the wing.

With a heavy melodramatic sigh, I leaned back in the seat again, shaking my head and laughing at my own stupidity as I dialed Andrew's number for the fourth time.

Ring-ring, ring-ring, ring-ring, voice mail.

I was starting to get quite worried about Andrew. Every time his voice mail clicked in, I half expected to hear the low, thin voice of Thomas Ismay on the other end of the line answering the phone and telling me to bring the painting to him if I ever wanted to see Andrew alive again.

It was ridiculous to think this, I know. Ismay wasn't a cartoon villain from some old black and white silent movie. He didn't have Andrew tied up on the railroad tracks somewhere, twirling his thin handlebar moustache and laughing wickedly as a speeding locomotive bore down on him. He was just a regular old man who was angry that Andrew stole his painting.

"And you too, don't forget," the little voice in my head reminded me. "You've stolen it now too."

"And me too," I said aloud, nodding to myself as I looked up at the black portfolio bag leaning against the seats in the cockpit. "And since Andrew isn't answering his phone, I am finally going to have a look at what's on the back of that painting."

I switched on the cabin light and leaned forward, carefully unzipping the top of the bag with a towel at the ready to catch any extra water that might drip out as I opened it. I reached inside with my palm to see how wet it was and was relieved to feel that it was actually almost completely dry on the inside. The zipper had let in a bit of water along the top, but the rest of the case was bone dry on the inside.

Gripping the edge of the picture frame I gently slid the painting out of the bag and twisted it around so that I could maneuver it onto the passenger seat next to me. The painting showed the scene of a dark and freezing night on the North Atlantic as the *Titanic* neared her final death plunge to the bottom of the ocean. The sea was flat calm, like glass, with towering icebergs dotting the horizon and a million brilliant shining stars overhead. In the foreground, the desperately cold passengers crowded into several lifeboats watched as *Titanic*'s stern rose up out of the water at a forty-five degree angle, her lights burning brightly. The painting also depicted passengers frantically making their way up the steep slope of the deck, clinging to just a few more moments of life before the ship went down. It was a horrible scene, but it was merely a glimpse of the true horror that occurred on that frigid April night so long ago.

Why would Bruce Ismay commission such a painting? I wondered as I stared at the scene, shivering at just the mere thought of being plunged to my death in that ice-cold water. *Why would he torture himself by hanging a painting like this in his home where he would see it every day for the rest of his life?*

"Because he felt responsible," I said aloud, answering my own question. "Because he felt he needed to torture himself. That was his punishment. He needed to cast himself as a victim, because deep down he believed he was the one to blame for all of that death and suffering. And he felt guilty for surviving when others had not."

I stared at the scene for a few minutes longer, feeling sad and lonely, as though I could somehow feel Bruce Ismay's pain by simply seeing the painting through his eyes. I could almost feel him reaching out across the chasm of time and space—and I suppose in a way he was, because somewhere on the back of that painting was something that he wanted certain people, like Andrew's family, to see.

Thinking of Andrew again made me reach over for my phone to try calling him one more time, but just as I picked it up, I nearly dropped it again as it burst into life in my hands, vibrating and lighting up suddenly and scaring the crap out of me.

I juggled the phone in my hands for a second, turning it over to see who was calling, and somehow managing not to drop it in the process. I breathed a sigh of relief when I saw the caller ID on the front screen. It was Andrew finally returning my calls.

Chapter Twenty-Seven
This Is Complete Gibberish To Me

"Andrew! Is that you?!" I said anxiously after pressing the call button and putting the phone to my ear. I was terrified that I would hear Thomas Ismay's cold, hard patrician tone at the other end of the line instead of Andrew's soft Scottish lilt.

"Kitty, yes, it's me," Andrew answered, his voice distant and breathless. "Where are you?"

"I'm safe, don't worry," I replied. "What about you? Where are you?"

"I'm safe too," he said. "I'm in a hotel somewhere in north London. After I made a run for it last night, I wasn't sure whether I'd lost Ismay and his goons, so I pulled into this hotel's underground parking garage and took an elevator straight up into the lobby and checked in."

"Ismay and his goons?!" I asked, confused.

"Yes," Andrew replied. "There was at least one other person with him driving the car, and who knows who else was with him."

I thought this over for a second.

"Well, whoever was following you, it couldn't have been Ismay," I explained. "Because when I was running downriver I spotted Ismay standing on the Tower Bridge. If he was there, he couldn't have been following you."

"Oh my god," Andrew replied. "Did he see you?"

I laughed. "You could say that, yes," I replied. "But don't worry; he couldn't possibly have kept up with me after that."

Andrew was quiet for a second as though he was trying to decide whether to believe me or not.

"Okay," he said hesitantly. "If you're sure that you're safe."

"I am," I assured him. "Trust me."

Andrew fell silent again for a few more moments as he thought things through.

"You need to open up the painting and take a look at the back of it," he said finally.

"What?! Without you?"

"I think I'm safe as long as I stay in my room," he replied, speaking quickly and nervously. "But I have no idea who might be out there watching for me. And you might be safe wherever you are for the moment, but we have no idea what's going to happen next...."

Andrew's voice trailed off.

"And?" I asked. "What if Ismay somehow finds us and we lose the painting?"

"Exactly," Andrew replied. "That's why you have to open it right away to look at the back and see what's written there. Take pictures of it and send them to me. That way if anything goes wrong...."

"Then all of this won't have been for nothing," I said, finishing his sentence.

"Exactly," he said.

"Okay," I said. "Let me see what I can do."

"Call me back as soon as you can," Andrew replied, and we said goodbye.

I pulled the painting all the way out of its case and laid it as flat as I could to see the back. Whoever had framed the painting had gone to a lot of trouble to secure it in the frame as tightly as possible.

"I'm going to need my tools," I muttered, and I crawled over the seat into the back of my plane and pulled my tool chest out from its storage compartment. I glanced out the windows and noted that the storm had blown over and the sky was beginning to clear, brightening in the east as dawn quickly approached. The extra light was helpful for my little project with the painting, and it gave me a better view of the surroundings outside of my plane. I breathed a bit easier as the sinister darkness of the night slowly gave way to the day.

With a pair of screwdrivers in my hand I went to work on the painting and struggled to loosen the wooden bracket attached to the back of the picture frame. It was old and looked like no one had touched it for decades, which was probably true. In fact, the last person to set eyes on the inside of that picture frame was probably Bruce Ismay himself.

I wiggled the flat head of my screwdriver back and forth to ease the bracket loose, taking care not to break anything.

I gently lifted the bracket and laid it to the side so that I could see the back of the painting. I blinked hard when I finally saw what was written there.

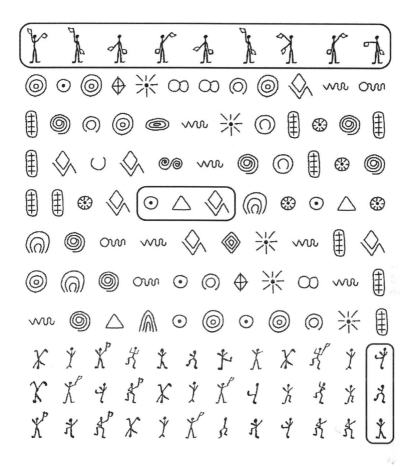

Covering the entire back of the painting was row upon row of various cryptic characters and symbols similar to the ones on the back of the *Titanic* postcard that Andrew's family had received in the mail. Above and below that strange writing there were rows and rows of little drawings of stick figures in various poses.

I suddenly wished that Andrew were there with me. Our theory was right. There *was* a hidden message on the back of the painting. But as I sat there staring at the rows of enigmatic writing, I couldn't help but wrinkle my forehead in bewilderment.

"What in the world *is* all this?" I asked in confusion as I reached for my iPhone to take some photos.

I snapped a few pictures then quickly forwarded them to Andrew before dialing his number and waiting for him to answer.

Ring-ring, ring-ring, ring-ring.

Oh god, what if he doesn't answer?

I breathed a sigh of relief when I heard a click at the other end of the line.

"Andrew?" I said as the call connected.

"I'm here, Kitty," he replied, his voice sounding distant and perplexed.

"Did you get the photos?" I asked.

"I did," Andrew replied slowly. "I'm looking at them now."

"And?" I asked expectantly. "Does any of it make any sense to you?"

Andrew hesitated, and I could almost hear him shaking his head in complete incomprehension.

"No," he said finally. "This is complete gibberish to me."

I was disappointed and utterly speechless. After everything that we'd been through, it was unbelievable to think that instead of finally getting some answers, we were left with more questions.

"So what do we do now?" I asked, feeling completely frustrated and discouraged.

"We have to go see a friend of mine," Andrew said. "And let's hope that he can help us."

Chapter Twenty-Eight

Jdaeadieb?!?

Andrew told me that he'd get back in touch with me later in the day after making some arrangements with his friend. Until then, I just planned to lay low and hide out.

After we said goodbye and I hung up the phone, I switched off the cabin lights inside my plane and leaned back to try and get comfortable on the passenger seats. Outside the skies were clearing and the sun was well on its way toward sunrise, so I propped the painting against the bench and stared at it in the soft light of dawn until I grew sleepy and dozed off.

What in the world is all of this supposed to mean? I wondered as I drifted in and out of consciousness.

I couldn't make any sense out of it at all. Obviously, the three circled sets of characters scrawled on the back of the painting were important, but I could not figure out why. Clearly, they were inspired by the oval-shaped *cartouches* used in Egyptian hieroglyphics, but if the rest of the writing was even half as complicated as hieroglyphs, then there was no hope that I could *ever* solve it...but I still had to try.

Fully awake now, I sat there watching the sun come up and realized I had nothing better to do.

Is it some kind of alphabet? Does it read from left to right or right to left?

I remembered what Katherine had told me about hieroglyphic writing and how the direction to read it depended on which way the animals and humans in the pictograms were looking. The stick figures on the back of the painting were definitely human, but they were so rudimentary that there was no way to tell if they were looking left or right.

The stick figures look a bit like that system of flag signals that ships use to communicate with each other, I thought, looking more closely at the line of characters at the top. *The one where each flag signal is a separate letter of the alphabet. What's that called again?*

I pulled myself upright and grabbed my iPhone to use the Internet.

"Semaphore... right," I mumbled to myself as I found the answer I was looking for on Google. I clicked on a chart of the semaphore alphabet to enlarge it, but it was difficult to read it on such a small screen.

What is that first character? Is it J?!? I struggled to decode the message letter by letter. *Is the next one D?!?*

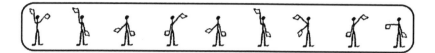

J—D—A—E—A—D—I—E—B, the message read.

"Jdaeadieb?!?" I said aloud. "What is that supposed to mean?!?"

It was gibberish. Clearly, the characters weren't supposed to be semaphore after all, which meant that the one and only part of the message that even looked remotely familiar to me wasn't what I thought it was. It was hopeless. I was definitely out of my league.

"I hope your friend can figure this out, Andrew," I said to myself as I looked out the window and leaned back again to watch a family just down the dock from me untie their sailboat and push it out into the open water to sail off toward the river.

I sat bolt upright.

The locks leading to the Thames must be open, I thought as I reached to pull on a jacket. *If that family is sailing out to the river, then that means I'll be able to come in with the Jet Ski.*

I pulled on some dry sneakers and hopped down onto the dock to check things out. I wasn't keen on leaving the safety of my plane—I had no idea whether Ismay was out there somewhere still searching for me—but I knew I couldn't leave the Jet Ski where I'd left it, so I walked down the dock and talked to the owners of the marina who explained to me how to come in from the river through the locks.

I thanked them and walked down the road through the rows of houses to where I'd left the Jet Ski tied up a few hours earlier. It was only a short walk, but it seemed to last forever as I turned every corner expecting to see Thomas Ismay jumping out to grab me. But I was just being paranoid. Ismay was nowhere to be seen. In fact, there was hardly anyone on the streets at all as the city slowly waking up and coming to life.

I reached the boat ramp and was surprised to see how much higher the water level was than when I'd last been there. The Jet Ski was still securely tied up to the post where I'd left it, but instead of being beached up on the riverbank, it was now floating free and surrounded by water.

I looked down at my dry shoes and wished that I'd worn the wet ones instead—I didn't have an endless supply of dry footwear, after all. Obviously I wasn't going to walk all the way back to my plane to change shoes, so I just gritted my teeth and splashed out into the river, hoping that I wouldn't get too wet and muddy.

Fortunately, the water wasn't very deep close to the shoreline, and I was able to climb onto the Jet Ski without getting wet any higher than my knees. I untied from the post and gently pushed myself out into deeper water before I started the engine and headed downriver along the shoreline to the entrance to the locks.

My timing was perfect. I arrived just as the family and their sailboat were coming out into the Thames, and as soon as they were clear, I idled my way into the lock and watched in fascination as it slowly filled to carry me up to the water level of the marina beyond.

The whole operation was over in just a few minutes, and I gave the operator a wave as I headed out the open doors on the other side and went straight for my plane to tie up again. It occurred to me that I should keep the Jet Ski as much out of sight as I could, just in case Ismay came looking for it, so I pulled up underneath the fuselage of my plane and tied it almost completely out of sight.

I scrambled onto the pontoons and stripped off my wet shoes so that I could leave them drying in the sun next to the other pair. With that done, I climbed into the back of my plane again to change into a dry pair of sweatpants. Everything was just as I'd left it. Thomas Ismay hadn't shown up while I was away.

I wrapped myself in my sleeping bag again and leaned back on the passenger seats to get comfortable. I was hoping to get a bit of sleep, but my plans were interrupted by an electronic chirp from under my seat where I'd hidden my iPhone. I had a new text message from Andrew.

Meet me at the tower hill underground station at 7pm. Next to the old Roman city walls. My friend will meet us there.

Chapter Twenty-Nine
Am I Paranoid Enough?

As soon as I saw the message from Andrew, I decided that since we weren't meeting up until later that evening, I was finally going to get some sleep. After all the excitement of the night, I was ready to climb into bed somewhere; the only question was where?

I could stay and sleep in my plane, of course. I had everything I needed, including a sleeping bag and an air mattress, but in the city, I had a warm and comfortable bed waiting for me in a hotel room, and it would be stupid to let that go to waste.

Should I risk it? I asked myself, uncertain whether I was safer staying right where I was. *God only knows where Ismay is.*

"He's probably out there looking for you right now," the little voice in my head observed. "And since he has absolutely no idea where your hotel room is, he's probably looking for a Jet Ski parked somewhere down river from the Tower Bridge where he last saw you."

There was no arguing with that logic. And with the added temptation of being able to sleep in a real bed thrown into the equation, I was convinced that I was better off in my hotel room.

I quickly packed a few things and slid the painting into the carrying bag before heading up the dock to the marina office. Just to be absolutely sure that I wouldn't accidentally bump into Ismay or any of his goons, I asked the manager to call me a taxi so I could get dropped off right at the front door of my hotel.

I thanked the manager and went out to wait for the taxi at the entrance gate to the marina. I felt very nervous and exposed standing out there in the open, but the taxi arrived in just a few minutes, and I was soon on my way.

Sitting in the back of the cab and watching the city zip past outside the windows, I had to smile at the thought of the painting and me ending up in another taxi together. Hopefully things would turn out a little less exciting this time—and drier, since I was down to my last pair of dry shoes.

When the taxi pulled up to the hotel, I paid the driver, ducked out of the cab, and went straight through the front door of my hotel and immediately up the narrow stairs to my room.

Locking the door behind me, I breathed a sigh of relief and was able to relax for the first time since I'd left the marina. There were thousands of hotels in the city of London, and unless Ismay called every single one of them asking for me, he'd never be able to find me.

He wouldn't do that, would he? I was suddenly concerned when I remembered that Andrew had introduced me to Ismay by name. *He couldn't possibly phone every hotel in London asking for Kitty Hawk, right?*

I was being ridiculous. Of course he couldn't do that. But I couldn't shake the feeling of unease as I climbed into the bed that I'd hastily abandoned the night before after Andrew's unexpected phone call. It took me a long while to fall asleep, but eventually my exhaustion got the best of me and I drifted off.

I woke again several hours later and cursed myself for not setting an alarm. It was already well past five o'clock, and if I was going to meet up with Andrew at seven, I needed to get moving. I had a quick shower and changed into some clean clothes before grabbing the awkwardly large painting and its carrying case, and headed out the door.

Leaving the safety of my hotel room made me a bit nervous, and I found myself constantly looking over my shoulder as I walked down the street toward the nearest underground station. I considered taking a taxi to where I was meeting Andrew, but from where I was near Victoria there was a direct train connection to the Tower Hill station, so I decided I was better off sticking to the underground. Besides, it was the end of the working day, and once I reached Victoria Station there were thousands of people swarming all around me at all times. *Ismay would have to be a fool to try something among all these witnesses*, I mused, feeling overly confident.

"You seem to forget," the little voice in my head reminded me, "that Ismay's not the criminal here. You are. The only thing these people would witness would be the police slapping some handcuffs on you and dragging you off to jail."

Good point, I said to myself, pulling my baseball cap over my eyes as I passed by a policeman standing on duty near the top of the stairs leading down to the underground station. It was easy to forget that Andrew and I had broken the law by stealing Ismay's painting, and no matter how fearsome he was in his pursuit of us, he was still only just trying to recover what was rightfully his in the first place.

Down in the station I bought a ticket from one of the machines and headed through the turnstiles to the escalators that led to the train platforms. From my short time in London, I'd already learned that the secret to finding a seat on the Tube trains was to stand at the ends of the platforms while waiting to get on because the cars at the ends of the trains tended to be emptier. A few extra steps down the platform before the train arrived generally made the difference between being squished in a crush of people in one of the middle cars or sitting in your own seat with plenty of space around you in one of the end cars.

An escalating blast of air announced the approach of the next train, and I waited to get on as it rushed past me and ground slowly to a halt. I boarded the train and took a seat at the end of the car where I was close to the doors and had a good view of everyone. As the doors closed and the train prepared to leave the station, I took a quick inventory of all my fellow passengers to see if any of them looked particularly suspicious. Ismay was nowhere in sight; that much was certain. I'd been keeping an eye out for him ever since I'd left the hotel. But maybe one of his goons, as Andrew had called them, was on the train watching me. The word goons instantly brought to mind an image of large and menacing-looking men in dark suits and sunglasses. There was no one on the train like that, at least, but who knew which of the innocent-looking people around me might be one of Ismay's spies. So as the train pulled away from the station with a bump, grudgingly picking up speed, I kept a close eye on my fellow passengers to see if anyone was watching me.

This is ridiculous, I thought as I carefully scrutinized each person's face. *They're all just minding their own business like normal people usually do.*

"When did you get so paranoid?" the little voice in my head asked me.

When everyone started plotting against me, I replied, quoting from a movie that I'd once watched with my dad as my eyes darted from face to face. *But the real question isn't whether or not I'm paranoid,* I thought, continuing with the theme of quoting from movies that my father had made me watch with him. *The question is am I paranoid ENOUGH.*

Chapter Thirty
The Most Notorious Serial Killer Of All Time

Paranoid or not, I actually didn't have anything to worry about, but that didn't keep me from keeping a careful tally of everyone who got on and off the train at its various stops. I soon realized that the only people left onboard who'd originally gotten on with me at Victoria station were a young father and his preschool-aged daughter, and a goth girl who looked like she was an art student, because she was scribbling furiously in a notebook during the entire train ride.

Maybe I look like an art student too, I thought as I kept one hand balanced on the top of the painting portfolio that was resting on the floor in front of me. *That might explain why Goth Girl keeps looking over at me.*

"Maybe she's one of Ismay's spies," the little voice in my head teased.

She's probably just freaked out that I keep staring at her, I thought, turning my eyes away and deciding that I'd better tone down my surveillance of my fellow passengers before some of *them* started to get a bit paranoid as well.

At the next stop, the father and daughter got off the train, and as we rattled on to the next station, Goth Girl started to collect her things and prepared to leave as well. So much for paranoia.

"You're very pretty," Goth Girl said, and when the train doors opened, she quickly tore a page out of her notebook and handed it to me. I took the paper from her and was shocked to see that it was a sketch of me sitting across from her on the train. Apparently, I was right: she was an art student—or something.

I looked up to thank her, but she was already gone, quickly disappearing into the river of people pouring down the train platform. I struggled to catch sight of her again, but the train doors closed and we rattled off into the dark subterranean tunnels.

As the train rumbled toward its next stop, I stared down in amazement at the sketch. I couldn't take my eyes off it. I couldn't believe what a perfect likeness it was and that a complete stranger had just given it to me.

The train conductor announced the next stop, Tower Hill, and I forced myself to stop staring at the sketch and put it away safely in my shoulder bag. I quickly dragged the painting over to the doors and stepped off the train onto the platform. As the doors closed behind me I moved off to the side to wait for the crowd to thin out a bit before I headed for the exit. I nervously scanned the faces swarming around me for any sign of Thomas Ismay. I couldn't see him anywhere, but the Tower Hill station was a busy one, and he could easily be hiding in plain sight somewhere among the sea of faces surrounding me.

Why would Andrew pick such a busy place to meet? I wondered as I made my way toward the exit. I immediately realized that it was probably precisely because this station was so busy that Andrew had chosen it. The anonymity of the crowds worked as much to our advantage as it did to Ismay's. Even if he somehow managed to find us here, the crowd of potential witnesses all around us would keep him from trying anything funny. This reasoning should have made me feel better, but I have to admit that I couldn't stop looking around nervously as I joined the crowds making their way up to street level.

Andrew had said to meet him next to the old Roman city walls, and as I stepped out into the fresh air, it didn't take long to figure out what he'd meant by that. Straight ahead as I passed through the exit was a long section of ancient brick wall looming forty feet above me. The wall was in a state of ruin and had obviously been built and rebuilt for centuries before finally falling into disuse and disrepair. It was clearly very old, but even though most of the bricks and mortar seemed a lot newer than Roman times, the base of the wall seemed very ancient indeed, and I was sure it dated back to the days when London was part of the Roman Empire.

If I'd had any further doubt as to the wall's Roman origins, there was a statue of a Roman emperor standing right in front of the exit to prove that point. His hand was raised in greeting, and someone had stuck a Starbucks cup into it as a joke. I grinned as I passed him by and almost felt sorry for the poor guy. At one time, he had been the powerful ruler of most of the Western world, and had now been reduced to toasting hoards of arriving tourists with a cup of overpriced coffee.

I climbed the stairs to a higher level and found a space to sit on a ledge near the wall. Crowds of people were milling around, snapping pictures of the Tower of London just across the street. It suddenly occurred to me that earlier that morning I had been racing through the darkness down the River Thames just on the opposite side of the Tower's fortifications from where I was currently sitting.

A shiver went down my spine when I also realized that just out of sight beyond the Tower of London was the Tower Bridge where I'd last seen Thomas Ismay—and he'd last seen me.

Oh my god, Andrew, I thought to myself. *Why did you choose to meet me here, of all places?*

But there was no turning back now, and besides, it was ridiculous to think that I might bump into Ismay just because I'd seen him somewhere nearby more than fifteen hours earlier. I laughed nervously to myself, trying to bolster my courage, but it didn't help much.

"Come on, Andrew. Where are you?" I muttered under my breath as I watched a large group of tourists gathering nearby for some kind of walking tour. The guide was busy taking money from each of them, dozens upon dozens in total, until he must have collected more than five hundred pounds in cash. Probably even more than that, in fact, judging by how much money was changing hands.

That's not a bad way to make a living, I thought as I continued to look around anxiously, scanning the crowd and hoping to catch a glimpse of Andrew. He was nowhere to be seen, and it was already quarter past seven. I could only hope that nothing had happened to him, but I was getting more worried with every passing minute.

"Thank you for your patience everyone. We'll start the tour in just one moment," the guide announced loudly as he took payment from some final customers. He gave them some change and stuffed his handful of cash into the inside pocket of his jacket before excusing himself through the gathered crowd of people and walking directly toward me.

Why is he walking over toward me?!? I asked myself, panicking as I quickly looked around for an escape route in case I had to make a run for it.

"You're Andrew's friend, right?" the tour guide asked in a low voice as he got closer.

I nodded. "Yes," I said, my panic quickly turning to concern. "Is he okay? Has something happened?"

"No, no, don't worry, he's fine," the tour guide said, smiling and shaking his head. "He's just a bit delayed, and asked me to look after you until he can join us."

I breathed a sigh of relief. "Join us?" I asked, confused.

He pointed over his shoulder at the crowd of people who were waiting behind him. "You know, duty calls," he said with a grin. "I've got a tour to do, as you can see. But Andrew's going to catch up with us along the way, so why don't you just tag along with us until then?"

"Oh," I replied in surprise. "Okay."

"I'm Richard, by the way," the tour guide said, extending his elbow toward me so I could grab hold of it.

"Kitty Hawk," I replied and threaded my arm around his as we walked toward his tour group.

"It's a pleasure to meet you," Richard said quickly under his breath before turning to his group and speaking to them in a loud, clear voice to be heard over the noise of the busy crowds milling about. "Ladies and gentleman, welcome to London. Welcome to our tour. My name is Richard, and if you could please follow me down this side street here where it's a bit quieter, we can get started on tonight's hunt for the most notorious serial killer of all time—Jack the Ripper!"

Chapter Thirty-One
Dear Boss

I felt like I was in some kind of crazy dream as I fell in with the rest of the group following Richard like a flock of sheep through the backstreets of London. As promised, Richard led us down a side street and into a small quiet recess so we could all gather around him. I felt a bit safer among the crowd of people but that didn't keep me from looking over my shoulder every few minutes.

"On the seventh of August, 1888," Richard began, dramatically setting the scene as he hopped up onto some nearby stairs to address the group, "the body of a thirty-nine-year old prostitute named Martha Tabram was found in the stairwell of a building about a mile from here at George Yard. Her body was discovered by one of the building's tenants at about four forty-five a.m. as he was leaving to go to work. The police were immediately notified, and a doctor soon arrived to examine the body.

"The doctor concluded that Martha had been ferociously stabbed to death in the stairwell. A total of thirty-nine separate knife wounds penetrated her throat and body. And yet the residents of the building had heard nothing unusual that night, except for one woman who had heard a cry of 'murder!' sometime in the night, but thought nothing of it since such cries were commonplace in the dismal and violent slums of London's East End.

"Was Martha Tabram the first victim of Jack the Ripper?" Richard asked. "Within weeks the Ripper would begin his reign of terror, striking fear into the hearts of all Londoners as he methodically stalked and killed the prostitutes of the East End. The police and the public considered Martha to be a Ripper victim, but many modern experts disagree. The nature of her wounds and the manner in which she was killed are not consistent with the later murders. Martha's throat was stabbed, not slashed open. Her body likewise suffered no extensive mutilations other than the stabbing wounds. Her body was not extensively mutilated, nor were her innards ripped out as were those of later victims.

"Are the experts right?" Richard asked, leaning forward and lowering his voice almost to a whisper to maximize the suspense.

"Are the experts ever right?" an anonymous voice in the crowd called out, making everyone laugh.

"Sometimes, maybe," Richard replied, laughing along with the rest of us. "But if you ask me, this time they were not. I think Martha Tabram's wounds were different because the Ripper had not yet found the distinctive *modus operandi* that would characterize the later murders. I think when the Ripper murdered Martha Tabram he was new at his chosen trade and was just getting started."

Richard fell silent, letting his words sink in for a few moments before gesturing for us to follow him to the next stop on the walking tour. He led us up the road a short distance and then bundled us into another quiet recess overlooking a busy street.

"If you were to walk straight down this street to the right," Richard began, "you would walk straight through the heart of London's Whitechapel district and within a few hundred meters of the sites where all of Jack the Ripper's victims were found. The farthest away from where we're standing right now is the spot where the Ripper's first official victim was found at three forty a.m. on the morning of the 31st of August, 1888. Her name was Polly Nichols, and her body was found in front of the entrance to a stable on a street less than a mile from here called Buck's Row. Her throat was slashed open, and there were several deep cuts and mutilations to the area around her stomach. She was dead but she clearly hadn't been for long, since one of the men who found her believed that he could still feel her breathing faintly before he rushed off to find a policeman.

"Like Martha Tabram, Polly Nichols was a prostitute, and as I said earlier, because the slashing cuts and mutilations to her body were different from the stab wounds suffered by Martha three weeks earlier, it is generally accepted that Polly was the Ripper's first victim. But this of course ignores the fact that however gruesome the injuries to Polly might have been, they were nowhere near as grisly as those that the Ripper's *next* victim would suffer.

"Just one week after Polly Nichols' body was found, the body of yet another East End prostitute, Annie Chapman, was discovered in the backyard of a house on Hanbury Street, which is just off the famous Brick Lane where I am sure many of you have sat down for some curry at some point in your holidays.

"Little did you know how close to the Ripper you were!" Richard cackled in glee. "But I hope none of you went for curry just before you came on this tour, because when I tell you what the Ripper did to the body of Annie Chapman, it will turn your stomach inside out. Like the previous victim, Annie's throat was slashed open, almost separating the head from the body. Her abdomen was likewise slashed open, and she had been disemboweled, her intestines thrown over her shoulders and some of her organs removed.

"It was a real mess, let me tell you," Richard said. "Much more violent and horrific than the two previous murders. In fact, one could argue that the degree of horror and violence inflicted on each of the Ripper's victims increased with every new body found. As I said before, the Ripper was just getting started. And so are we. Off to the next stop on our tour!"

Richard lifted his walking stick into the air as a signal for us to follow, and he led us across the road like a slow-motion cavalry charge. From there he ducked down a small side street and into a parking lot where he stopped and waited for the rest of us to catch up with him.

"Gather 'round, gather 'round, my friends," Richard said, stepping up onto a ledge near some benches at the corner of the lot. "Come close so you can hear what I have to say, because now the hunt for the Ripper truly begins."

Richard waited patiently as we all shuffled in closer, laughing and joking with some people in the front row, and then started with his next explanation.

"Before we discuss the Ripper's next victims," Richard began, "we must first discuss where the name 'Jack the Ripper' originated, because up 'til now in our story, the murderer was simply referred to as 'the Whitechapel Murderer,' which is a perfectly accurate description, of course, but not particularly catchy. As we all know, any serial killer worth his salt has to have a memorable name, and in the same way that the Ripper's crimes gave rise to the idea of the modern serial killer, his unforgettable *nom de guerre* likewise became synonymous throughout the world with brutal and ghastly murder.

"But was the name one that the killer himself dreamed up? Or was it one that was thrust upon him from elsewhere? This is an important question, because the name itself comes from a letter that was received by the police just two and a half weeks after the murder of Annie Chapman. The letter read something like this:

Dear boss. I keep hearing the police have caught me but they won't fix me just yet. Grand work the last job was. I gave the lady no time to squeal. How can they catch me now? I love my work and want to start again. You will soon hear of me with my funny little games. Good luck. Yours truly, Jack the Ripper.

Richard paused dramatically. "And with that signature the legend of Jack the Ripper was born," he said. "But was the letter actually from the Ripper himself? No one really knows. And the topic has been hotly debated for more than a hundred years and will surely be debated for a hundred more without ever reaching a definitive answer. Was the unfortunate truth is that there was no way to know for sure whether the letter was authentic. To make matters worse, it wasn't the only letter the police received purporting to be from the killer. The police were nearly overwhelmed with letters about the crimes, and all of them had to be investigated to determine whether they were real or whether they might provide clues that could lead to the Ripper's capture.

"But no sooner had the police received this first Jack the Ripper letter than the killer struck again, and this time not just one body was found, but *two*. This was the night of the so-called Double Event: September 30th, 1888."

Chapter Thirty-Two
The Double Event

"Sometime around one o'clock in the morning of September 30th, 1888," Richard continued, his tour group listening with rapt attention, "one of the workers from a nearby club turned his horse cart off the street and into a passageway leading to an open area known as Dutfield's Yard. As the man drove through the pitch black passage, something on the ground startled his horse and caused it to pull away in fear. A closer inspection with a lit match revealed the body of a woman whose throat had been cut, and blood was pouring from the wound. The woman was a prostitute named Elizabeth Stride, and that, combined with the fact that her throat had been slashed open, convinced the police that the Ripper had struck again.

"Or had he?" Richard asked, pausing for theatrical effect. "Once the police arrived on the scene and began their investigation, they discovered that, unlike the Ripper's previous victims, Elizabeth Stride's body had not been mutilated. The cuts to her throat were the only wounds she had suffered, and although those hinted at Jack the Ripper being her killer, they wondered why he had stopped there? If it was indeed the work of the Ripper, why had he merely cut her throat and nothing else?

"The answer was obvious. He was disturbed in his work by the man in the horse cart turning into the passage, and so he fled the scene. In fact, because the passageway was the only way in and out of Dutfield's Yard, and blood was still flowing from the body when it was first discovered, it was quite possible that the Ripper himself was lurking nearby in the dark shadows of the passageway as the man driving the horse cart lit a match with shaky hands and crouched over the lifeless body."

"Oh, my god," the girl standing next to me whispered loudly.

"A chilling thought indeed," Richard agreed. "But if that theory is true—if the Ripper was indeed interrupted in his work and was forced to make his escape—then what happened next only serves to confirm that once the Ripper set his mind to killing and mutilation, he would only stop once his thirst for blood was satisfied.

"As I said before, this was the night of what came to be known as the Double Event. Less than an hour later, at 1:45 a.m., the body of a second woman was discovered less than fifteen minutes' walk from the first, lying dead on the ground right here in Mitre Square at the exact spot where all of us are standing now."

Everyone in the group, including me, looked down at the cobblestone pavement underneath our feet.

"Her name was Catherine Eddowes," Richard continued, "another prostitute, and with this victim, the Ripper had time to complete his ghastly work. Her throat was slashed open, and her intestines were strung over her shoulder and arranged around her body. Her left kidney and other organs were removed from her body. Even her face was mutilated, illustrating, I believe, the Ripper's ever-growing lust for blood with each successive murder. It was a terrible scene to witness. And yet, all of this carnage was executed with speed and skill in the matter of just a few minutes.

Everyone in the tour group remained silent, taking it in. "We know that the Ripper worked quickly," Richard said, "because when Police Constable Edward Watkins passed through Mitre Square a quarter of an hour earlier, nothing was amiss, but when he returned less than fifteen minutes later, he discovered Catherine Eddowes's body, and the killer was nowhere to be seen.

"And if this wasn't remarkable enough, the police investigation later revealed that, as usual, no one nearby had seen or heard a thing, including one of Constable Watkins's colleagues who'd passed the entrance to the square just a few minutes before the body was found. At the other end of the square, a night watchman was on duty, himself a former policeman, and he also heard nothing. There was even an off-duty policeman who lived with his family just a few yards away at the opposite corner of the square. None of them saw or heard a thing. The Ripper was not only fast and skilled, but it was almost as if he was a phantom, killing silently before disappearing into the night.

"And that's exactly what he did after killing Catherine Eddowes," Richard said as he prepared to step down from his perch. "He disappeared into the dark streets of the East End. But the police would find one last trace of him before the night was over."

Richard jumped down and gestured for us to follow him to the next stop on the walking tour. We ducked and turned through several narrow streets and came out on a long street with tall modern office buildings lining one side of it and much older three- or four-story houses lining the other. We stopped near some stairs, and everyone gathered around Richard once again.

"Do you see these street signs here?" Richard said, pointing up to the sides of buildings on both sides of the street. "Instead of focusing on the names of the streets, look closely at the signs themselves. Can you see the difference?"

I looked up to see what Richard was talking about. He was right. The signs were quite different. On the side of the street with the modern office buildings, a street sign with a little coat of arms at the left read:

HARROW PLACE E1
City of London

On the opposite side of the street with the older houses, a completely different style of sign read:

COBB STREET E1
London Borough of Tower Hamlets

"As you can see, the design and style of the two signs is quite different," Richard explained. "This is because they are from two different cities. To the west of us, where we've just come from in Mitre Square, is the City of London—a tiny area of land that is sometimes also called the Square Mile. To the east of us, and completely surrounding this tiny Square Mile, is the rest of London—Metropolitan London. The City of London is roughly the area where the Romans had their first settlement in England, and over the ages, it has remained quite separate from the rest of the enormous city that has grown up around it. It is the financial heart of London and perhaps the wealthiest square mile of land anywhere in the world. You can see the difference quite clearly, even here on the street where the eastern side is made up of fancy modern buildings of glass and steel, while the houses on the opposite side of the street are made of brick and are certainly showing their age."

Everyone looked around to see what Richard was talking about. He was absolutely right. In fact, the difference was quite remarkable, and it was one of the first things I had noticed when we'd first arrived there.

"Of course, the City of London was a separate entity even in 1888 when the Ripper was stalking the streets," Richard continued. "Back then, the City of London had its own flag, its own coat of arms, its own Lord Mayor, and most important of all for our purposes, its own police force. To the west and Mitre Square is the City of London with its police force. That is still how it is today. To the east is the rest of London and the Metropolitan Police."

Oh, that is interesting, I thought to myself. Apparently other people thought so too, and they were nodding along with Richard as he spoke.

"You see," Richard said, leaning closer, "until the murder of Catherine Eddowes, the Ripper had been operating entirely on the territory of the Metropolitan Police, including his first victim on the night of the Double Event: Elizabeth Stride. But after being interrupted in Dutfield's Yard, the Ripper then walked east, crossing the invisible boundary between the two cities, and made his second kill of the night on the territory of the City of London. So now, in the dark and early hours of the 30th of September, there was not just one, but *two* separate police forces spreading out through the streets searching for the killer.

"But the Ripper was too clever for them. After his mutilation of Catherine Eddowes, he made his escape, eluding the police of the City of London and once again crossing the invisible line between the cities—perhaps at this very spot. We know he did this, because before he seemed to vanish into thin air, the Ripper left his calling card in a doorway not a hundred yards to the east from where we're now standing.

"Around three o'clock in the morning, a police constable of the Metropolitan Police found a bloodstained piece of cloth in a doorway on Goulston Street. It was a piece of apron that had been cut away from Catherine Eddowes's clothing, perhaps for the killer to use to clean his bloodied hands. What was truly incredible about the find, however, was not the bloody cloth itself, but what was written on the doorway above it. Scrawled in chalk by the killer's own hand were the words 'The Juwes are the men that will not be blamed for nothing.' It was an incredibly cryptic sentence, and to make matters worse, the word Jews was misspelled as j-u-w-e-s, which has led to a century of theories of sinister Masonic connections and the like. But many of the police investigators at the time believed that the killer was merely trying to cast blame away from himself, and because of the predominant hatred of the Jews in London's East End, he was merely trying to cast them in the role of scapegoat.

"Whatever the meaning of the message—if in fact that is what the message said since no less than three different people took note of what it said, each of them recording a slightly different version—the Metropolitan Police Commissioner Sir Charles Warren was soon on the scene and ordered the text to be washed off. For this decision Warren would be roundly criticized for the next hundred years for destroying an important clue, but his concern at the time was that since the city around them was slowly coming to life, and onlookers were starting to gather, he did not want the message to spark a riot against the Jewish residents of the neighborhood. And so the message was washed away.

"With that the Ripper vanished, and the police would never be as close to catching him ever again. With the break of day, the news of the two killings spread like wildfire all across London, and a growing panic among its residents was not far behind. Extra police patrols were added in the East End. Citizen patrols were doubled. Everyone was on the lookout for the killer, and perhaps because of all this, the Ripper went silent. Week after week passed with no new killings, but there were also no new clues as to the Ripper's identity. He was still out there somewhere, and almost six weeks would pass before he emerged from hiding and took the life of his final victim."

Chapter Thirty-Three
Not Exactly What You'd Call A Looker

Richard led us to the final stop on his walking tour through some close and narrow side streets that were already growing dark and gloomy as the sun set behind us. We arrived at a back alley next to a parking garage where Richard finally stopped and waited for all of us to catch up and gather around him before he began to speak.

"Following the night of the Double Event, the streets of the East End were practically deserted," Richard said. "The local residents were understandably frightened and even angry with the police for failing to put a stop to the murders. The police were following up every possible lead in an attempt to catch the killer. They were so desperate that they even resorted to some rather dubious methods of determining the Ripper's identity, including trying to exploit a widely held belief that just before a person died, the final image they had seen would be permanently recorded on the retinas of their eyes. The police in London were so frantic to catch the Ripper that attempts were made to photograph the retinas of the victims to see if the image of their killer had been captured there.

"Of course this entire idea was a fantasy and came to nothing, but on the streets of the East End, the working girls of the area couldn't stay indoors forever—they had no money and nowhere to go to unless they could earn a few pennies to buy themselves a bed for the night. So before long these women soon returned to the world's oldest profession and were back on the streets once again.

"But the Ripper was far too clever to risk making his next kill so openly on the streets of London as he'd done previously. Instead, for his final act of brutal murder, he found a streetwalker who had her own private room where she would take her clients. It was there that the Ripper dispatched his final victim.

"Her name was Mary Kelly, and she was an Irish girl of only twenty five years of age, which made her quite unlike the Ripper's previous victims who'd all been in their late thirties and forties. Mary's body was discovered at number 13 Miller's Court by a man whom the landlord had been sent around to collect the rent. After knocking on Mary's door and receiving no answer, the man peered in through a broken pane of glass in the window and had the shock of his life. Lying on the bed on the opposite side of the room was what can only be described as a mangled and bloody corpse. The list of various mutilations noted by the doctors attending Mary's autopsy are so numerous and repulsive that I will spare you the graphic details and simply say that this time the Ripper had been able to take his time in finishing his savage work, and the result was a body that was hardly recognizable as human."

Richard paused and waited for the effect of his words to sink in.

"In the years to come there were one or two additional murders in the Whitechapel area that some people have argued were also the work of Jack the Ripper," Richard continued. "Some even argue that the Ripper picked up and moved to America where his killing spree continued. But if you asked most of us Ripperologists, we would tell you that these later crimes were almost certainly the work of copycat killers, and that after the killing of Mary Kelly, the Ripper simply vanished, never to be seen or heard from again. But that answer is extremely unsatisfactory to some people, and so the debate goes on even now, more than a century later.

"But who was Jack the Ripper, then?" Richard asked. "I'm sure you're just like me and you're absolutely dying to know—no pun intended! Was it Montague J. Druitt, a mentally unstable schoolmaster who just happened to commit suicide shortly after the last Ripper murder? Was it George Chapman, a Polish Jew who later was sentenced to hanging for poisoning three of his common law wives? Was it Sir William Gull, physician to Queen Victoria and the Ripper suspect that Johnny Depp failed to catch in the movie *From Hell*? Was it the painter Walter Sickert, a suspect recently put forth by the modern crime writer Patricia Cornwell? And the list goes on and on and on."

Richard paused to take a breath before leaning closer to us as if to whisper a secret.

"Do you want to know what I think?" he asked. "I think that if I could build a time machine and go back to the year 1888, I would hide in the shadows of each of the murder sites and finally uncover the true identity of Jack the Ripper. And when the moment of truth finally came and the Ripper was revealed, I would probably look at him and think, *Who the heck is this? I've never even heard of this person before!*"

The whole group laughed, and Richard brought his walking tour to an end., "Thank you so much to everyone for joining me tonight." He nodded and smiled as the group responded with a chorus of replies. "It was my pleasure," he acknowledged. "And for those who are interested in some other tours, please check out my company's website or the pamphlet I've given you. I will be hosting a ghost tour tomorrow evening from the Tower Hill underground station and a Sherlock Holmes tour in the afternoon of the following day. Thank you so much again, and good night."

All of us clapped our hands while Richard took several dramatic bows before jumping down from his perch as the tour group dispersed. A number of people lingered for a while, chatting with him and asking him questions, so I stood off to the side to wait for him to finish.

It suddenly occurred to me that Andrew still hadn't shown up. I'd been so drawn in by Richard's walking tour that at some point I'd stopped looking over my shoulder for both Andrew and Ismay and had just been swept headlong into the world of Jack the Ripper. But now that my head was firmly back in the twenty-first century, I was really worried.

Where the heck is he?!? I asked myself, looking around nervously.

"You're wondering where Andrew is." He said goodbye to the last of the tour group and walked over to where I stood.

I looked up at him and nodded anxiously. "Have you heard from him?"

Richard shook his head. "Not since he texted me and said he'd be late and would catch up with us."

For a few moments, the two of just stood there, silently watching the cars rushing past on the busy street in front of us. Across the street, the clock in the church tower chimed nine thirty.

"You know, if you stand right here where we're standing," Richard mused philosophically, "and you look across the street, right and left, the view you have is almost exactly the same that Jack the Ripper would have had more than a hundred years ago—the church, the buildings, even the Ten Bells pub right over there where the victims of the Ripper once stopped in for a drink. Probably the Ripper himself did too."

I glanced at the corner pub that Richard was pointing at and up the street where a number of prostitutes were busy plying their trade in the gathering dusk.

"Nothing ever changes, does it?" I said, smiling wryly.

Richard laughed. "Not really," he said. "But take a look at that one walking toward us. I wonder how much business *she* gets."

I had to laugh at Richard's cruel joke, but he was right. The prostitute who was lumbering up the street toward us, wobbling drunkenly on her high heels, was not exactly what you'd call a looker (although perhaps something that rhymes with that). In fact, she looked like a man.

My eyes grew wide as I realized the truth of that particular statement. It *was* a man. It was Andrew. And for some reason that I could not possibly fathom, he was dressed as a woman.

Chapter Thirty-Four

You Clever, Clever Man

Richard and I watched, mouths agape and eyes wide as Andrew loped toward us. He was having trouble walking, and who could blame him since he was wearing knee-high leather boots with three-inch heels. Above those he was showing a lot of skin from his bony knees to the hem of his incredibly short skirt. Finishing off his tacky ensemble was a fuzzy faux-fur coat and a blonde wig.

"Andrew! What the bloody hell are you doing, man?!" Richard called out, half laughing as Andrew tottered toward us. "Why in the world are you dressed like a trollop?!"

"We have to get out of here!" Andrew replied, wobbling painfully up the street on his heels. "Ismay's right behind me!"

Richard and I went dead silent and rushed over to meet Andrew.

"What do you mean?" I said uneasily. "Where is he?"

Andrew stopped suddenly in mid-stride and stared right past me, his face turning grim.

"I believe you have something of mine," I heard a thin, cold voice say. I whirled around to find Thomas Ismay standing almost directly behind me, looking gaunt in the harsh light of the street lamps and pointing one bony finger at the painting portfolio that I was still toting around.

"Listen here, my good man," Richard said, stepping chivalrously between Ismay and me. "Why don't you just push off. We have no idea what you're talking about."

"Don't be a fool, *my good man*," Ismay responded mockingly. "These thieves have something that is very valuable to me, and I want it back."

Andrew hobbled up next to me and took up a protective position in front of me and the painting.

"You must be going deaf, old man," Andrew said. "Didn't you hear what my friend here said? We have no idea what you're talking about."

Ismay smiled and shook his head slowly. His smile and self-confidence was unsettling somehow.

"Listen here, my friends," Ismay said, still smiling. "You've had a good run. You almost made off with it. You played a good game. But you also have to know when to admit defeat. So hand over the painting before someone gets hurt."

Richard scoffed. "You can't honestly believe that we're afraid of you," he said.

Ismay laughed a loud and hearty laugh that took all of us by surprise with its ferocity.

"Of course you're not afraid of me!" he cackled maniacally, making me even more uneasy and frightened. "Because you are fools!"

This is creepy, I thought to myself, pulling the portfolio closer to me as if it could protect me somehow. *He's like some comic book villain or something.*

Even Richard and Andrew were taken aback and simply stood there, speechless. Ismay looked past the three of us and nodded almost imperceptibly. I spun my head around and immediately saw a pair of burly thugs standing menacingly on the street corner nearby.

This is completely crazy, I thought. *These guys look like they're ready to break our kneecaps. And for what? A stupid painting?*

But it wasn't just a stupid painting. It was a very important painting that held the clues to a mystery that went back generations. And standing there on that street corner with cars rushing past, it suddenly occurred to me why Ismay had so brazenly refused to let us see the back of it in the first place, not to mention why he was resorting to such desperate measures to get it back. He wanted the treasure for himself.

"Take it!" I said, my face turning red with anger as I laid the portfolio on the ground and kicked it toward Ismay. "Take the stupid thing! We don't even want it!"

Now it was Ismay's turn to be taken aback, and he wasn't the only one. Both Andrew and Richard had also turned to look at me as though I'd gone completely off the deep end.

"Don't you see?" I shouted at them while they recoiled in shock. "He just wants the treasure for himself! He's just a greedy and cowardly old man exactly like his grandfather. If this was the *Titanic*, I'd bet he'd push the three of us straight in the water just to get a seat on the first lifeboat."

It was a cruel thing to say, but I was angry and frightened, and at that moment, I wanted to hurt Ismay as much as I could for making me feel that way. I could see his jaw tighten and his face flush furiously red, but he steadfastly refused to rise to my bait and simply bent down to pick up the portfolio from the pavement.

"That was probably the wisest thing you've done in a long time," Ismay said coldly as he took a couple of steps away from us. "Thanks to this, perhaps when the police arrive they will spare you the indignity of handcuffing you when they shuffle you off to prison."

The police?! I thought, my knees going weak when I heard the faint sound of a police siren somewhere in the distance. *What in the world have I gotten myself mixed up in?*

Ismay heard it too, and grinned a wide, toothy grin. "Here they come," he said ominously. "They might not have caught the Ripper, but they will catch you."

"Hey mate, what's going on over here?" I heard a gruff voice say behind me. I wheeled around quickly to see the two burly men walking toward us, and my heart sank.

"Is this old bloke botherin' you?" the second burly man said to me as he came closer.

What is he talking about? I thought, my head spinning in confusion.

"Oy, granddad, why don't you just bugger off then?" the first burly man said threateningly as he stepped up next to me.

It took me a moment to figure it out, but I quickly realized that they were talking to Ismay. I had assumed that they were a pair of Ismay's goons, but in fact they weren't with him at all; they were simply coming to our rescue. Ismay had been trying to bluff us.

You clever, clever man, I thought with a wicked grin. *Very clever indeed.*

No sooner had I figured that out than a small white delivery van pulled up next to us on the street, and my head was plunged into total confusion once again.

"Oh, my god, I've been looking all over for you, my dear," the girl driving the van said to me as she leaned out the window. "Hop in or we'll be late."

Are you talking to me? I was about to say when I suddenly realized who the driver was. It was Goth Girl, the one who'd made a sketch of me on the subway—a complete stranger who was now coming to my rescue.

"Yes, I'm talking to you, silly," Goth Girl said, gesturing to Richard and Andrew as well. "All three of you jump in or we'll be late."

The three of us looked at each other in stunned disbelief before turning back to Ismay, who was standing there looking even more shocked than we were.

I looked over at Goth Girl and grinned. "Whatever you say, my dear," I replied as I pulled open the back door and vaulted inside. Andrew and Richard were hot on my heels, and within seconds, they were pulling the door closed behind us. Before the door slammed shut, Goth Girl hit the gas and the van squealed off down the street leaving Ismay and the two burly strangers looking after us, scratching their heads in bewilderment.

Chapter Thirty-Five
I Hope Tonight Turns Out Better For Me

"Sorry to startle you like that," Goth Girl called out over her shoulder as she twisted the steering wheel hard to the left and squealed around the next corner. "But I just happened to be driving past, and I recognized you from the train. It looked like you could use a bit of help getting out of there."

There were no seats in the back of the delivery van so the rest of us were forced to hang on for dear life as she made another quick series of turns. Apparently, she worked for some kind of delivery company and was on her way to work when I saw her on the underground earlier that evening.

She made another quick turn and then slowed down a bit as she pulled onto a straight road again. I took the opportunity to pull myself forward so I could kneel down behind the passenger seat and properly introduce myself to the girl who'd just saved us.

"I'm Kitty, by the way," I said, looking at her through the space between the front seats.

"Ellie," Goth Girl replied with a smile, reaching over her shoulder to shake my hand.

"I thought you two knew each other," Andrew said, confused.

Ellie and I looked at each other and laughed. "No, not exactly," I replied. "But let's just say that I'm a big fan of her art."

"You'll have to forgive me for asking," Ellie said, glancing at me in the rear-view mirror with her dark, intense eyes. "But why is your friend dressed up like a prostitute?"

"That's the million-dollar question, isn't it?" Richard observed dryly. "We've been wondering precisely the same thing ourselves."

Andrew blushed a bright shade of red and pulled off his blonde wig. "It's a long story," he said, looking nervously out of the back window of the van. "And maybe the first thing we should worry about is getting away from the police."

"The police?" Ellie asked, looking back at me again.

"The police were coming for us," I said. "Didn't you hear the sirens?"

In the rear-view mirror, I watched her forehead wrinkle into a frown.

"The sirens?" she asked in bewilderment. "That wasn't the police. It was an ambulance. I saw it a few streets back just before I spotted the three of you."

Andrew and I glanced at each other. He slowly shook his head in disbelief. "Incredible," he said. "Ismay must have been trying to bluff us—again!"

I nodded in agreement. It was unbelievable. Ismay sure was a sneaky one.

"You're avoiding the question," Richard said, gesturing to Andrew's trashy clothes.

Andrew blushed again as he struggled to pull off his knee-high leather boots and massage some feeling back into his toes.

"It was the only way I could slip out of the hotel unnoticed," he said. "That's why I was late coming to meet you. When I first left my room, I spotted Ismay staking out the hotel lobby and some suspicious men waiting around the car. I couldn't risk it, so I went back up and called a mate of mine from school to get some kind of disguise for me. He borrowed some clothes from his girlfriend and dropped them by my hotel room."

We all stared at Andrew who was looking quite pathetic as he sat there rubbing his pained feet, and we couldn't help but burst into laughter.

"That's ridiculous!" Richard said. "Not to mention that it didn't even work. The old bloke managed to tail you anyway!"

"Ha ha ha," Andrew said, his voice dripping with sarcasm, but he couldn't suppress a wry smile. "Laugh it up."

"Oh, the irony!" Richard continued, suddenly sitting bolt upright as he had some kind of epiphany.

"Irony?" I asked.

"There are stories that some of the men on the *Titanic* made it into the lifeboats by wearing women's clothing!" Richard explained, slowly bringing his fits of laughter under control. "And the irony of a Murdoch making an escape wearing women's clothing is absolutely delicious!"

"I'm not sure that's irony, actually," Andrew said in a voice so serious that we started laughing all over again.

I glanced up front and saw the narrow slit of Ellie's eyes in the rectangle of the rear-view mirror. That's all I needed to recognize the expression of complete mystification on her face.

"It's a long story," I explained, leaning forward so that I could see her better.

She looked at me with raised eyebrows and a dubious smile as she turned the van onto the ramp of a secured parking garage.

"This is my last delivery of the night," Ellie said as she rolled down the window so that she could talk to the security guard who was making his way over to meet her at the gate. "After that I can drop you off wherever you need to go."

I turned toward the back of the van to see what Andrew and Richard thought.

"What's next, guys?" I asked. "Where do we go from here? Where will we be safe?"

"I think we should stick with Andrew's original plan and go to my place," Richard said. "This old fellow has no idea who I am and won't be able to find us there."

I glanced at Andrew. "Do you think Ismay will still be after us?" I asked. "He has his painting back, after all."

"I have no idea," Andrew said, shrugging his shoulders. "You're probably right. He has no reason to keep coming after us now."

Over on the driver's side of the van the security guard had arrived and was leaning down, hands on his knees, to talk to Ellie.

"I have a delivery for Robson and Associates," Ellie said, taking a thick courier envelope from the passenger seat and handing it out the window.

The security guard pulled out a clipboard and ran his finger down the printouts.

"Your name?" he asked once he found the right entry on the delivery manifest.

"Ellie Stride," she replied. "Commercial Couriers."

The guard nodded and took the envelope. "Thank you," he said. "Have a good night."

"Your name is Ellie Stride?" Richard asked as Ellie rolled up her window and put the van into reverse so that she could back out onto the street again.

Ellie nodded. "Yeah," she replied. "Why?"

"Is Ellie short for anything?" Richard asked, ignoring her question.

"Elizabeth," Ellie said. "Why?"

Richard ignored her question for a second time. "Your name is Elizabeth Stride?!?" he asked, a smile forming at the edges of his mouth.

"Yes," Ellie replied suspiciously, stepping on the brakes so she could turn herself around and look into the back of the van. "Why?!?"

Richard looked at Andrew and me with a big, goofy smile on his face.

"Her name is Elizabeth Stride," he said. "Can you believe it? What are the odds?"

Andrew was looking utterly perplexed, and Ellie glanced over at me to see if I had any idea what Richard was so excited about.

"Can somebody tell me what's going on?" Ellie asked, sounding annoyed and a bit suspicious.

"We don't understand what you're talking about, Richard," I started to say but then it suddenly hit me what Richard was getting at, and I looked at Ellie with a startled expression on my face.

"What?!??" Ellie demanded in exasperation. "What in the world is so amazing about my name? Somebody throw me a bone, here!"

"Jack the Ripper," I said, grinning ear to ear just as Richard already was. Jerking my thumb in his direction, I said, "Richard here is an expert on Jack the Ripper, and Elizabeth Stride was the name of the Ripper's fourth victim."

Richard nodded, his eyes bright and eager, forgetting that not everyone shared his enthusiasm for all things Ripper.

For a moment, Ellie just stared at us blankly.

"Although to be fair, the Ripper's Elizabeth Stride was from Sweden,"

Richard said, "and judging from your accent, I'd say you must be from....?"

"Ireland," Ellie said, finishing Richard's sentence for him as she turned forward and put the van in gear. "And I guess I should probably hope that tonight turns out better for me than it did for my namesake."

Chapter Thirty-Six
Elementary, Is It Not?

I wouldn't have blamed Ellie for kicking the three of us out of her van right then and there, but she seemed to take the whole creepy conversation about her name in stride (no pun intended) and drove us to Richard's flat on Baker Street on the other side of London.

"Why don't you come up and have drink with us?" Richard asked her as we clambered out of the back of the van. "I'll put the kettle on and we'll have a cup of tea."

Ellie looked at me uncertainly. "Please come up," I said. "A cup of tea is the least we can do after you saved our butts tonight."

"We promise not to kill you," Richard said jokingly.

"Richard!" I said, smacking him on the arm and laughing in exasperation. "Stop freaking her out!"

"Okay," Ellie agreed good-naturedly and hopped out of the van. "How can a girl resist having a cup of tea with three complete strangers who might kill her?"

Richard led the way through the bright blue door of an old brick row house and up the stairs to the top floor where he had a small studio apartment. He took our coats and cleared off the sofa, inviting us to make ourselves at home before heading for the kitchen to put on a kettle.

"You live on Baker Street?" Ellie asked, walking over to the front windows and peering down to the street below. "Are you like Sherlock Holmes or something?"

"Not quite," Richard replied, laughing as he took some cups and saucers out of the cupboard. "Sherlock's rooming house was supposedly just up the street at 221b. But I did pick this place based on my interest in the Sherlock Holmes stories."

"So what's your story, then?" Ellie asked, flopping down in the plush chair near the window. "I mean all three of you—what's the deal?"

Andrew went to Richard's bedroom to change into some men's clothes while I sat down on the nearby sofa and gave Ellie the short version of everything that had happened, finishing just as Richard came over to join us with a steaming pot of tea.

"That's quite a story," Ellie said, somehow managing to look impressed and puzzled at the same time. "Stolen paintings, Jack the Ripper, Sherlock Holmes, the *Titanic*—it's got it all. But what are you going to do now that this Ismay fellow has taken his painting back? You still don't know the how to decipher that cryptic writing on the back of it, do you?"

Andrew emerged from the bedroom dressed in a shirt and jeans that he'd borrowed from Richard. He grinned and pulled an iPad out of the oversized purse he'd been carrying as part of his drag ensemble.

"Fortunately, we have a photo of it," he said, flipping through pages until he found one of the pictures I'd taken of the back of the painting. He put the iPad on the coffee table where all of us could see it.

Ellie leaned over to inspect the strange arrangement of symbols and dancing stick figures on the screen.

"So now what?" she asked, looking up at me. "What does all of this mean?"

I shrugged my shoulders, so she looked over at Andrew instead, who simply pointed across at Richard who was calmly sipping his cup of tea.

"I'm hoping Richard will be able to tell us," Andrew said. "Because in addition to being an excellent tour guide, he is also a bit of an amateur cryptographer."

Richard set his teacup down and leaned forward with the rest of us to look at the mysterious symbols on the back of the painting. He examined them for a moment then got up from his chair and walked over to a bookshelf.

"My skills as a tour guide might be more valuable to you than you realize," Richard said as he pulled several books from the shelf. "Those dancing men figures on the bottom are from Sherlock Holmes."

"Sherlock Holmes?!" Andrew and I said simultaneously as we reached down to pull the iPad closer for a better look.

"Absolutely," Richard replied, sitting down on the floor next to the coffee table and placing one of the books he'd chosen on the table in front of him. *The Complete Sherlock Holmes*, I saw on the cover as he opened the book and flipped through the pages until he found what he was looking for.

"Can you figure out what it says?" Andrew asked anxiously.

Richard nodded. "Most certainly," he replied, grabbing a pencil and starting to decode the message behind the mysterious dancing figures.

"Do you have a copy of the original letter?" Richard asked as he continued deciphering the symbols. "The one your family got in the mail in the 1930s?"

Andrew gestured for me to hand Richard the letter from the purse that was lying next to me. I pulled out the *Titanic* postcard and the news clipping and held them in my hands while I waited for Richard to finish.

"These circled characters also seem to have some significance," Richard observed as he continued working through the text one letter at a time.

"Like the Rosetta stone," I said.

Richard looked up at me and smiled. "Precisely," he said. "That's exactly what the back of this painting seems to be—a kind of Rosetta stone."

I blushed and smiled at Richard for a moment before looking away in embarrassment and down at the papers that I was holding in my hands.

"But what exactly are these circled words, then?" Andrew asked. "What do they say if they're so important?"

Richard shrugged. "If the real Rosetta stone is anything to go by, then the two three-letter words are probably the same word," he said. "Maybe all three are the same word, in fact."

"How is that possible?" Andrew asked. "The one on top is much longer than the other two. How can it be the same? And what word would Ismay consider so important?"

As Andrew asked these questions, I stared at the newspaper clipping in my hands.

TITANIC OWNER MAKES GENEROUS DONATION TO BRITISH MERCHANTMEN

London, January 2, 1931

In an effort to express his admiration for the heroic conduct of the officers and men of the British Mercantile Marine in weathering the storm of the Great War, Mr J Bruce Ismay, former managing director of the White Star Line that owned Titanic and survivor of the disaster, has donated £25,000 to the Mercantile Marine Service Association. This munificent gift breaks all previous records for generosity, including those set by Ismay's own late father, Thomas Henry Ismay, founder of the White Star Line, who once made a similar donation of £20,000 more than thirty years ago to the Liverpool Seamen's Pension Fund.

Following the sinking of the Titanic Mr Ismay found himself the target of condemnation for having survived and failing to go down with his own ship. According to his own accounts he was on board the ship only in the capacity of an ordinary passenger and exerted no control or influence over the operation of the vessel itself. Ismay himself maintains that after the ship struck the iceberg he assisted in the loading of lifeboats and when there were no other women or children in sight as the last boat was finished loading he climbed in as it was being lowered away. However, in light of the fact that more than 1500 of his fellow passengers perished in the disaster Mr Ismay was much criticised for his conduct.

The entire affair left Ismay a broken man and after resigning his chairmanship of the White Star Line in 1913 he became a virtual recluse and never again appeared at public functions or discussed the Titanic with anyone. As such he had no statement regarding his generous gift to the British Mercantile Marine but Harold Wilkes, the director of the organisation's Liverpool branch hoped that Mr Ismay's gift will spawn a flood of similar donations to charitable organisations that benefit British seamen and their families.

"This horrific war has devastated our empire," said Mr Wilkes. And has created a crippling drag on the institutions tasked with caring for those in need as well as their innocent widows and children. Our boys went through hell during the course of the war and whether their fate was to crawl resolutely through the Flanders mud or serve courageously upon the high seas, the treasure of our empire can only provide a limited degree of support to them and their families. The responsibility to safeguard their future lies with all citizens whose freedom these brave men defended. We must all do what we can to ensure that these brave men are not left hungry and destitute on the thoroughfares of our great cities. We British have a long history of rising to every challenge with heads held high. Whether slaying the dragons of our mythology or spilling the blood of our youth in defence of freedom, this generosity of spirit is but one of the many virtues that make us British. And as we have just witnessed during the course of this horrendous war, there are those in need, whether within the borders of our own realm or off on some far distant foreign shore, it is our ancient duty to be as unyielding as stone as we stand shoulder to shoulder together against the onslaught like our fathers did before us. We must be ready and willing to sacrifice the many flowers of our generation to nip the plans of evil in the bud and defend our empire. Above all else, we must be British."

DAILY CROSSWORD JANUARY 2ND 1931

FAMED BALLERINA ANNA PAVLOVA FALLS ILL

Famed Russian ballerina Anna Pavlova has fallen ill with pneumonia after catching a chill during a train journey from the French Riviera to The Hague, Netherlands where she is scheduled to perform her legendary Dying Swan. Generally considered to be the greatest dancer of all time, Ms. Pavlova began her amazing career in her native Russia, later to debut on the London stage where audiences were instantly enthralled by her incomparable technique and unequalled grace. Since that time she has given thousands of performances and travelled hundreds of thousands of miles to delight audiences all over the world. Just a few short weeks short of her 50th birthday the celebrated danseuse remains without an equal anywhere in the ballet world. Sources close to the dancer report that she is recuperating in the renowned Hotel Des Indes and hope that she will be back

"Ice," I said, gasping to myself as I suddenly realized what word Bruce Ismay had considered important enough to circle with *cartouches* on his own personal version of the Rosetta stone.

Andrew and Ellie looked at me with bewildered expressions while Richard nodded slowly at me and smiled keenly.

"Exactly, my dear," Richard said, his smile growing wider by the second. "It's elementary, is it not?"

Chapter Thirty-Seven
The Palace On The Boinne

I pushed the newspaper clipping toward Andrew and pointed at the half-finished crossword puzzle that both his family and I had paid so little attention to until that moment.

"Ice," I repeated. "Don't you see? Ismay circled it right here in the original news clipping that he sent to your family. It's like the cartouches used in Eygptian hieroglyphics."

DAILY CROSSWORD JANUARY 2ND 1931

Andrew took the paper, and I watched as his eyes darted across the page until he saw the word ICE that had been circled in pencil under number thirteen down of the puzzle.

"I don't understand," he said slowly. "I mean, I see that it's circled, but what does that mean? And what does that have to do with these dancing stick figures and Sherlock Holmes and all the rest of it?"

I reached over and pointed at the circled sets of symbols on the back of the painting in the photo of it on the iPad. "It means that these two three-letter words are the word ice," I said, looking to Richard for confirmation of my theory.

"Not just the three-letter words," Richard said, nodding in agreement. "But these semaphore characters are enclosed in an Egyptian cartouche at the top, too. Those also mean ice."

Now it was my turn to be confused.

"What do you mean?" I asked. "I tried to decipher that earlier today, and all I got was gibberish."

"Did you use letters or numbers?" Richard asked.

"Pardon me?" I asked.

"In semaphore," Richard repeated. "Did you use letters or numbers?"

"Letters," I replied hesitantly. "But it was meaningless. It said something like Jdaeadieb or some other nonsense."

Richard nodded. "I see where you went wrong," he said as he moved along the floor to get closer to me and pulled the iPad over to show me the line of semaphore text.

"Show me," I replied, sliding down off my chair and sitting next to him on the floor.

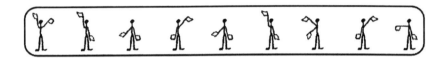

"This first character isn't a J," Richard explained. "It's a signal used to indicate that all the characters that follow are to be interpreted as numbers, not letters. The first ten letters in semaphore code can also be used to represent numbers. A can also be 1, B can also be 2, and so on."

I finally understood what he meant and looked down at the line of little figures of men with flags, seeing them in a completely different light.

"So what does it say?" I asked. "How can a sequence of numbers represent the word ice?"

"That is probably a question better asked of Mr. Murdoch here," Richard said, looking up at Andrew. "The number circled here on the top line is 4—1—5—1—4—9—5—2, which I am willing to bet are the longitude and latitude position of the iceberg that sunk *Titanic*."

We both looked at Andrew expectantly. He shook his head slowly, and seemed to be thinking carefully as he also slid down off the sofa and sat on the floor next to us. Now we were all sitting on the floor, crowded around one end of the coffee table, except for Ellie, who was watching us with curious amusement.

"It's not the position of the iceberg or the *Titanic*," Andrew said. "The reported longitude and latitude of a dense field of ice that lay in *Titanic*'s path was 41.51 North by 49.52 West. The steamship *Baltic* sent Captain Smith a wireless message warning him of it nine hours before *Titanic* struck the iceberg. Captain Smith later gave this warning to Bruce Ismay who carried it around in his pocket for most of the day, showing it off to some of the lady passengers in First Class before giving it back to the captain later in the evening."

"You see?" Richard said, picking up his cup of tea to take a sip. "All three circled words on this painting mean ice."

"Then what about these other two sections of text?" Andrew asked excitedly. "Does that mean you can decode all the rest of it?"

Richard shook his head. "Unfortunately, this big section of squiggles and spirals in the middle is a complete mystery to me," he said. "And it seems as though that is the most important part."

"But you just said that all three circled words mean ice," I protested. "How can you know that if you can't read what this middle section says?"

"Elementary deduction, my dear Watson," Richard replied with a grin. "Since I know what both the top and bottom texts say—and both of them contain a circled word that means ice—it is logical to assume that the circled word in the middle text *also* means ice."

"But what do the bottom lines of text say?" Andrew asked, taking the words right out of my mouth. "You said these dancing stick figures were from Sherlock Holmes, but what does that mean?"

"Etaoin Shrdlu," Richard said cryptically, leaning back with one arm on the seat of the chair behind him as he sipped his tea.

"Who's that?" I asked.

Richard shook his head. "It's not a person," he said. "It's the twelve most common letters in the English alphabet in order of how frequently they are used: E—T—A—O—I—N—S—H—R—D—L—U. And this is precisely how Sherlock Holmes decoded the cipher of these strange dancing stick figures in *The Adventure of the Dancing Men*."

"You're starting to lose me, Richard," Andrew said.

Richard nodded, setting down his teacup before picking up the thick book of Sherlock Holmes stories lying on the table in front of him and opening it to read a section.

> *"As you are aware, E is the most common letter in the English alphabet. And it predominates to so marked an extent that even in a short sentence one would expect to find it most often."*

I was starting to understand where Richard was headed with this and leaned forward to count characters from the last three lines of symbols on the back of Ismay's *Titanic* painting while Andrew peered over my shoulder.

141

"Five," I said after I'd finished counting. "This character here with the man holding the little flag in his left hand occurs five times throughout the whole text, which is more than any of the other letters."

"Eight times, actually," Richard corrected me, pointing to three more instances of similar figures where the man's arms and legs were sticking out at the same angles, but he wasn't holding a flag.

"What do you mean?" I asked. "What about the little flag the man is holding?"

Richard smiled and held up one finger before reading from the Sherlock Holmes book once again.

> *"It is true that in some cases the figure was bearing a flag, and in some cases not. But it was probable from the way in which the flags were distributed that they were used to break the sentence up into words. I accepted this as a hypothesis."*

I looked down at the lines of figures again and saw that Richard was absolutely correct—or rather, Sir Arthur Conan Doyle, the author of the Sherlock Holmes stories was. The men carrying flags were distributed at intervals, which certainly did suggest that their purpose was to separate the text into individual words.

"Okay, so now we know what the symbol for E is," I said. "Now we just have to figure out the rest of Etaoin Shrdlu, right? The letter T is next."

"Unfortunately, it's not that simple," Richard said with a frown and a mischievous twinkle in his eye. He read from the Sherlock Holmes story again.

> *"But now came the real difficulty of the inquiry. The order of the English letters after E is by no means well marked, and any preponderance which may be shown in an average of a*

printed sheet may be reversed in a single short sentence. Speaking roughly, T, A, O, I, N, S, H, R, D, and L are the numerical order in which letters occur; but T, A, O, and I are very nearly abreast of each other, and it would be an endless task to try each combination until a meaning was arrived at."

I wrinkled my forehead and stared down at the lines of text. Sure enough, after the symbol for E, the next most frequently used characters appeared four times each, and there were three of them that did so.

It would be nearly impossible to figure out which one is supposed to be T, I thought in dismay.

I looked over at Richard for help, and Andrew and Ellie did the same.

"So how do we solve it from here?" I asked.

Richard laughed and took another sip of tea. "Because of the small sample of text and the uneven distribution of letters, it would take some kind of advanced computer decryption algorithm to decode a text like this," he said.

"Do you have such a program?" Andrew asked.

"I do," Richard said, nodding with a smug smile on his face, enjoying the suspense.

"Then what are we waiting for?" Andrew asked desperately. "Why don't we plug these symbols in and see what comes out?"

Richard laughed loudly. "We don't have to," he replied. "I told you already that I know what the bottom lines of the text say."

"But how do you know?!?" I asked. "If it can't be solved using the method that you and Sherlock just explained to us, then how can you possibly know?"

"I know..." he said, putting his teacup down and picking up the notebook he'd been scribbling in while decoding the text, "because Sherlock already solved it a hundred years ago."

He held up the notebook so that we could see what he'd figured out.

"The secrets hide in the palace on the Boinne," Richard read with a devious smile, pointing out each word slowly and deliberately.

Chapter Thirty-Eight
The Answer Won't Be That Simple

"Oh, for god's sake, Richard, why didn't you just say that you could read it in the first place," Andrew said in mock exasperation.

"I thought I did," Richard said flatly.

Ellie and I both looked at Andrew and nodded.

"He did say it," we agreed.

"Okay, fine, you win," Andrew said, laughing as he took Richard's notebook from him to examine the decoded text. "But are you sure that's what the message says—the secrets hide in the palace on the Boinne? Didn't you say that the word ice was circled?" Turning to me he said, "Kitty, what did you call it—a cartouche?" I nodded and glanced at Richard as Andrew turned to him and said, "The word ice isn't in there anywhere."

Richard nodded in understanding and leaned forward to point to the original series of dancing figures from the back of the *Titanic* painting.

"You're quite right," Richard said. "The word ice isn't there, but whoever wrote this sentence arranged the words so that the last letter on each line spelled out ice. And that's the three letters they circled as a clue."

Andrew finally understood, and I suddenly had an idea.

"But ice is also circled in the middle section of text," I said. "Can't we use that to somehow figure out what the rest of those squiggles and spirals mean?"

"I thought of the same thing," Richard said, nodding slowly. "And I can try to run it through some different computer programs to see what comes out, but I don't think it will work. Something tells me that the answer won't be as simple as that."

"Why not?" I asked, disappointed.

Richard shrugged. "Just a gut feeling," he replied. "The top and bottom texts—the semaphore and the Sherlock Holmes texts—were encoded from pre-existing and well-known cipher systems. This middle text is something else entirely that I've never seen before. I'd be willing to bet that you're going to have to dig a bit deeper to figure that one out."

Both Andrew and I nodded in reply. Richard was right. Something was telling me the exact same thing—that the answers we'd already found were designed to lead us on to the next, and hopefully final, solution that would lead to the treasure itself. With that in mind, it seemed that we had only one clue to work from—the hidden message behind the figures of the dancing men.

"The secrets hide in the palace on the Boinne," I repeated under my breath, trying to make sense of it.

"What about this place that the bottom text mentions," I asked, looking up at everyone. "The Boinne?

"It's a river in Ireland," Andrew replied. "It's spelled differently here in this text—probably in Gaelic—but I think it means the River Boyne, the site of the famous Battle of the Boyne."

"The Battle of the Boyne?" I asked.

"And so it came to pass on the first of July in the year of our Lord sixteen hundred and ninety," Richard recited melodramatically, doing his best imitation of a patronizing schoolteacher, "that the forces of the Protestant King William the Third of Orange defeated those of the Catholic King James and restored the throne to the victorious King William."

"We learn about it in school," Andrew explained. "It's pretty famous in Britain."

"And what is this Palace on the Boinne?" I asked. "Is it something to do with this battle?"

"Unfortunately, that part I don't know," Andrew replied, shaking his head as he turned to look at Richard.

Richard shrugged his shoulders. "Me neither," he said. "I have no idea what that means."

"It's Newgrange," Ellie said, surprising us by speaking for the first time since she'd sat down. "It means Newgrange."

The three of us stared at her as she sat drinking her tea in the chair by the windows.

"Newgrange?" I asked. "What's Newgrange?"

Ellie leaned forward and put down her cup of tea before speaking. "It's one of the ancient passage tombs on the River Boyne close to where I grew up," she said. "One of the ancient fairy mounds. Brú na Bóinne in Gaelic. It means the Palace of the Boyne."

"Of course!" Richard said, nodding.

"And what are the secrets there?" Andrew asked excitedly, his eyes lighting up in anticipation. "I mean, what secrets is this message referring to?"

Ellie laughed. "There are a lot of secrets there, but not a lot of answers. And I have no idea what secrets this message could possibly be talking about."

"We'll have to go there and find out," Andrew said, his voice serious as he turned toward me. "As soon as we can. Tonight if possible."

"Why as soon as possible?" Richard asked, furrowing his brow. "What's the rush?"

"It's because of Ismay," I replied, nodding in agreement with Andrew. "He has the painting now and before long he'll have figured out everything that we just figured out. And as soon as he does, he'll be on his way to Ireland and the treasure. We have to get there first."

Richard nodded in understanding. "I think leaving tonight is probably out of the question though," he said, looking at his watch. "The last flight of the day would have left hours ago. You could take my car and drive to Wales, but I doubt the ferries from there run twenty-four hours day."

Andrew got to his feet and began to pace the floor, his mind racing.

"What about your plane, Kitty?" he asked.

I shook my head. "It's too dark," I explained. "I couldn't fly until daylight, and by then a commercial jet would be faster anyway."

Andrew nodded and continued pacing.

"Andrew, my good man, what are you so worried about?" Richard asked. "If there's no way *you* can make it tonight, then there's also no way that Ismay can make it, right? You can still beat him there."

Andrew continued nodding furiously. He seemed to agree with what Richard was saying and was about to say something but he was suddenly interrupted by Ellie, who, for some reason, had just burst into tears.

Chapter Thirty-Nine
Is Your Name Really Elizabeth Stride?

In her chair over by the windows Ellie had pulled her knees up and buried her face in her hands, and was sobbing violently. The rest of us looked at each other in confusion for a few seconds before I got to my feet and went over to comfort her.

"I am so sorry, Kitty," Ellie bawled as I put my hand on her shoulder. "And Andrew and Richard too—I am so sorry."

"Sorry for what?" I asked, my voice calm and soothing. "You haven't done anything."

"I have," Ellie said, sobbing even louder now.

"What could you possibly have done?" I asked, wondering whether she was more of a lunatic than we were.

"Ismay!" Ellie cried at the exact same moment that I thought of it myself. "Mr. Ismay is my boss."

On hearing this Andrew's face turned seriously concerned—and angry. He was about to say something, but I held up my palm to stop him and let him know that I could handle it for now.

"Your boss?" I asked, taking my hand from her shoulder.

Ellie nodded. "Yes, my boss," she replied, sniffling loudly as she looked up and met my eyes. "I mean, I go to school and I work for this courier company, but sometimes I do some part-time work for Mr. Ismay as well."

"And?" I asked, my tone cold.

"And today he called me to ask if I could wait outside of your hotel to see if you came out," Ellie said. "And you did, so I followed you."

"On the underground train?" I asked.

"Yes," Ellie nodded.

I shook my head uncertainly. "But you got off the train before I did," I said.

Ellie nodded again. "I know," she said. "You kept looking at me, and I got nervous, so I got off the train and lost myself in the crowd for a few seconds before ducking back on again in the next car."

My mind was spinning, trying to process this information.

"And then what?" I asked, my eyes boring into hers, looking for the truth.

"And then I watched you get off at Tower Hill and wait for Richard's walking tour," Ellie said. "And I followed you as far as Mitre Street, but then my other job called and asked if I could come in and make a few deliveries."

"And where was Ismay throughout all of this?" I asked.

Ellie shook her head. "I don't know," she replied, wiping the tears from her eyes. "Still following Andrew, maybe, I don't know. I didn't even know that Andrew existed at the time."

I thought about this for a second and held up my palm to Andrew again to keep him from jumping in just yet.

"But then you picked us up in your van," I said slowly. "Why?"

"Mr. Ismay told me to," Ellie said, pulling some tissues from her pocket and wiping her nose. "He told me to drive by and pick up the three of you on that corner. He told me to pretend like I was rescuing you or something then to drop you off somewhere and find out where you were going with the painting."

"But we didn't have the painting," I said, determined to keep her story on track.

"I know," Ellie replied. "I saw you kick it over to Mr. Ismay, but I don't think he expected that. I think he was just trying to frighten you into running so he could use me to find out where you were going with it."

I looked over at Andrew in disbelief. Was this Ismay for real? How could anyone be so incredibly manipulative and devious? He was like a cartoon villain.

"And did you tell him?" I asked after I took another moment to collect my thoughts.

"Tell him?" Ellie asked, looking up at me with her dark mascara-stained raccoon eyes.

"Where we were going...?" I prompted. "Here to Richard's place?"

Ellie shook her head. "No," she said, starting to cry all over again. "I didn't tell him. After I met all of you and talked to you... Mr. Ismay told me that you'd stolen his painting and that you three were thieves and... I don't know, once I actually met you it didn't seem like you were that bad after all. You were so nice and funny, and I didn't know any of that. Mr. Ismay told me that you were bad people."

I looked over at Andrew and rolled my eyes. She had a point. We *did* steal the painting. Somehow, I conveniently managed to keep forgetting that rather important little detail.

"You stole his painting?" Richard asked, raising his eyebrows. He had sat calmly drinking his tea until he heard that tidbit, and now his curiosity was piqued.

Andrew nodded and made a guilty face. "We did," he replied. "I mean, *I* did—not Kitty."

"Well done, Andrew," Richard said with a teasing grin. "I wouldn't have thought you had it in you. You're usually so polite and good-mannered."

"I'm guilty too," I admitted, not wanting Andrew to take all the blame. I had, after all, fled with the painting downriver in the middle of a storm.

"Then well done to you as well," Richard said with an admiring nod.

"But what do we do now?" Andrew asked, gesturing over at Ellie who was still scrunched up and sniffling in her chair. "And what about her?"

"It's not her fault," I said, defending Ellie. "She didn't know the whole story, and she was just doing what Ismay told her to."

"But what if Ismay knows we're here?" Andrew asked.

"He doesn't," I replied, looking at Ellie for confirmation. "Right?"

Ellie nodded. "He doesn't," she assured us. "I didn't tell him anything. I haven't spoken to him since before I picked you up off the street."

"And do we just believe her?" Andrew asked incredulously.

"Of course we do!" Richard and I snapped in unison.

"Okay, then, we believe her...." Andrew muttered, looking chastened.

I looked over at Ellie and smiled. When she'd first revealed that she was working for Ismay, I was furious and getting angrier by the second. The only thing that had kept me calm was the need to interrogate her a little bit and get some information so we could assess our situation. But she was right. We *had* stolen Ismay's painting, after all. That *did* make us thieves. But it didn't make us evil, and I believed Ellie when she explained how she realized that and regretted what she'd done. Maybe that meant that I was naïve, but I suppose that's better than being cold hearted and cynical.

Ellie gave me a weak smile in return, and I put my hand on her shoulder again.

"If nothing else, she rescued us from Ismay," I said to Andrew. "That might not have been her intention at the time, and it certainly wasn't part of Ismay's plan, but the end result for us was the same. We got away, and for the moment, we're safe. The only thing we need to do now is figure out how to get to Ireland before Ismay does."

Andrew had calmed down a bit, and now he nodded slowly as he listened to my reasoning.

"Actually, I have one more question for Ellie before I can really trust her one hundred percent again," Richard said.

Ellie looked at Richard for a second then up at me with worry in her eyes. I patted her shoulder and nodded for her to tell him whatever he wanted to know.

"What is it?" Ellie asked, her voice shaky.

"Is your name *really* Elizabeth Stride?" he asked. "Because as a true Ripper fanatic, I would be completely heartbroken if it wasn't."

Chapter Forty
Something Told Me He Wasn't Through With Us

After far too few hours of sleep on Richard's sofa (me) and floor (Andrew), we left him and Ellie behind and headed for Heathrow Airport where we planned to catch the first flight of the day to Dublin.

"Good luck, old boy," Richard said as he saw us off at the front door of his apartment. "I truly hope you will find what you've been searching for all these years."

Andrew smiled a tired smile and gave Richard a rough hug.

"I hope you will find what you're looking for too," Ellie said, looking as though she was on the verge of tears again as she took a few steps toward me to say goodbye. "I am so sorry we had to meet this way. And I am so sorry for everything I did to mess things up."

I grabbed Ellie by the hands and gave her a big smile.

"You didn't know," I reassured her. "You were just doing what your boss asked you to do."

"I know," Ellie replied. "But still...."

I held up my hand and stopped her before she could say anything else.

"No buts," I said. "Everything is going to be fine. I know it. And when Andrew and I are finished in Ireland, we'll come back here to London, and we'll all go for lunch, and we can take one of Richard's walking tours. Okay? A Sherlock Holmes tour maybe?"

Ellie smiled weakly. "Okay," she said, and I pulled her close to give her a hug.

It was hard to say goodbye, and Andrew and I lingered longer than we should have. We would have to hurry to be on time at the airport, so we all hugged Richard and Ellie one last time before rushing down the stairs and out onto the quiet early-morning streets of London.

"Should we be worried that Ismay might be waiting for us out here?" Andrew asked as we walked quickly up the street toward the nearest underground station.

"Because of Ellie, you mean?" I asked.

Andrew nodded. "Do you think she was telling the truth when she said that she hadn't told him where we were?" he asked.

I thought about this for a second then immediately dismissed the possibility.

"Yes, she was telling the truth," I said confidently. "Everything that happened wasn't her fault. Besides, she helped us figure out about

Newgrange and the Palace on the Boyne, remember?"

Andrew seemed to accept this and slowly nodded in agreement. "You're right," he said as we rounded a corner and waited for the pedestrian lights to change so that we could cross a busy street.

"And if not," I said, grinning, "then we've left poor Richard alone with her."

Andrew laughed as the lights finally changed, and we hurried across the street and down into the station to catch the first train.

We spent most of the ride out to Heathrow in silence, surrounded by sleepy morning commuters and tourists heading to catch early flights, the same as we were. Andrew kept looking at his watch nervously, and I wasn't sure why since we had plenty of time. As soon as we stepped off at the airport, however, I understood. Heathrow was enormous and chaotic. It was the busiest airport I'd ever seen, but fortunately, Andrew knew his way around quite well and wasted no time trying to figure things out. He took me by the hand and led the way as we weaved in and out of the crowds, heading for our departure gate with the boarding passes we'd printed at Richard's flat.

"This is a final boarding call for Aer Lingus flight one four nine to Dublin," I heard a slightly robotic woman's voice announce over the sound of the crowds. "All passengers should now proceed to gate sixteen."

"Oh my god, Andrew, are we going to make it?" I asked as we both broke into a run and sprinted the rest of the way through the airport.

"Plenty of time," Andrew replied with a breathless grin as we turned the last corner and finally arrived at the departure gate.

"That was close," the flight attendant said with a smile as we handed her our boarding passes and stepped on board. "We were about to close the doors and head for Ireland without you."

"Thank you for waiting," I said. "We're sorry."

"Don't worry, dear," she replied. "I'm just teasing. You made it just in time."

I followed Andrew halfway down the length of the plane to our seats, and we flopped down just as the crew finally slammed the doors and locked them tight. A few moments later, the plane slowly pushed back from the gate and began the long taxi out to the runway. Through the window, I could see long lines of planes inching along the maze of taxiways, and was again impressed at what a vastly busy and colossal airport Heathrow was. Despite all the potential for chaos and confusion outside, now that we were on the plane, everything was business as usual as we went through all the normal preflight rituals.

The pilot announced that we were third in line for takeoff and should be in the air shortly. Only then did it finally sink in for me that we were really on our way. We'd made it, and there was no turning back now.

"Where do you think Ismay is now?" I asked in a low voice as I leaned over toward Andrew.

"I have no idea," he replied with a shrug of his shoulders. "Maybe he's on this same flight with us?"

"Don't even joke about that!" I said, smacking Andrew on the arm.

Andrew laughed. "I'm sure he's not," he said, grinning, and then his expression turned more serious. "But if he is on this plane, there's nothing we can do about it, I guess."

That thought made my blood turn cold, and I lifted myself up out of my seat to take a quick look around. I couldn't see all the passengers very well, but at least I couldn't see him in any of the rows of seats immediately nearby.

"Well, wherever he is, I hope we never have to see his pale white face again," I muttered as the plane's engines throttled up and we raced down the runway and into the sky.

But even as I said it, I somehow knew that I was hoping in vain. Something told me that Mr. Thomas Ismay wasn't through with us just yet.

Chapter Forty-One
On The Verge Of Uncovering The Secret

The flight didn't take long, and soon Andrew and I were out of the airport and cruising down the freeway in a rental car. It was the same highway we'd driven on a few days earlier when we'd gone to Belfast, but this time instead of continuing all the way north, we took one of the first

exits and headed for the Boyne River valley and the site of the Newgrange monument.

I was surprised at how quickly the world around us changed as soon as we left the freeway. One moment we were speeding along in the midst of a river of modern cars and trucks, the next moment we were bouncing along narrow back roads past farmhouses and ancient rock walls with cows and sheep watching us with curiosity as we drove by. It was like entering a different world or at least a different century.

"It should be up ahead somewhere pretty soon," I said to Andrew as I followed our progress on the GPS on my phone. "Somewhere off to the right."

My navigation was confirmed by a sign that soon came into view, which read:

Brú na Bóinne
NEWGRANGE
300 m

"We're early," Andrew said, pointing to the car's clock as he turned into the parking lot. Ellie had explained to us that the only access to Newgrange was through a visitor's center located on the opposite side of the river from the monument. We'd made such good time from London that we actually arrived before it had even opened for the day. But we didn't have long to wait, so we parked the car and made our way down to the center along a lovely pathway overgrown with plants and trees.

Everything in Ireland is so green, I thought. *It's no wonder they call it the Emerald Isle.*

At the entrance to the center there were a few other people milling around and waiting for the doors to open. One elderly couple gave me a bit of a fright because the man was tall and slim with thin white hair, and for half a second my heart skipped a beat thinking that it was Thomas Ismay.

You have to stop with that, I scolded myself. *Ismay's not some bogeyman constantly waiting to jump out at you from the shadows. He wasn't on the plane, and he's not here now. Just relax and stop freaking yourself out!*

"Oh, my god!" Andrew whispered to me, his body suddenly tensing up. "For a second I thought that was Ismay standing there."

I don't know if it was my nervousness or the excitement of finally discovering what secrets Newgrange would reveal to us, but when Andrew said this, I burst out laughing, and not just one of those ha-ha-and-then-you're-done kinds of laughs. I mean like one of those you-can't-stop-laughing-until-tears-are-running-down-your-face kinds of laughs. I simply couldn't help myself. Even with Andrew looking over at me in horror and the other people staring at me like I was some homicidal maniac, I couldn't stop myself and just continued laughing and cackling until the big wooden door behind me swung open and a short middle-aged lady emerged from the visitor center.

"Watch yourself, dear," she said, smiling brightly as I moved out of the way so that she could swing the door all the way open. "It sounds like you're all having a good time out here this morning."

"Some more than others," Andrew remarked, looking at me like I was crazy.

"Well, come on inside and we'll see if we can give you a bit more fun, then," the lady said, and all of us obediently shuffled along, queuing up to follow her inside to the admissions desk. "The first bus out to Newgrange leaves shortly from a loop road just on the other side of the river. There's no rush yet, but do try to be there a bit early."

Andrew paid admission for the two of us and we decided to head straight out for the bus loop. I was anxious to see what was in store for us. I knew that Newgrange was out there somewhere overlooking the banks of the river beyond the trees, but so far we hadn't seen it.

We went down some stairs and outside again and took a path toward a narrow footbridge across a lovely little river that was winding its way through the beautifully vibrant Irish countryside. As we neared the bridge, the trees opened up and for the first time I saw what we had come there to visit. Through the trees and past some farmhouses I could see an enormous low-lying mound sitting on top of a patch of high ground on the opposite side of the river valley. The mound was wide and flat and covered with green grass so that it looked like a kind of artificial hill, but circling it at its base was a gleaming white retaining wall that made it stand out from everything around it.

"Andrew, look!" I gasped, pointing off toward the monument. "There it is!"

I have to admit that Newgrange was not what I had been expecting, although I have no idea what I had expected to see. I only knew that it was unlike anything I'd ever seen before. We were still quite some distance away from it, but even from there it dominated the surrounding landscape, looking down benevolently across the rolling hills like some mystical ancient guardian.

I couldn't even begin to imagine what mysteries were locked inside that ancient mound and what dramas it had seen unfold during its long history.

The secrets hide in the palace on the Boinne, I remembered, thinking of the cryptic message on the back of the painting. The enormous mound certainly did look like some mythical and magical palace standing there along the banks of the river. It was easy to let my imagination run wild picturing who the inhabitants of that enchanted palace had been.

But as I stood there on the bridge watching the vision of Newgrange floating like a dream on the horizon, I knew at least one thing for certain: somewhere inside that ancient mound was a secret that would lead Andrew and me to the treasure that his family had searched for over so many long years. And now, finally, he and I were on the verge of uncovering that secret.

Chapter Forty-Two

Your Guess Is As Good As Anyone's

A short drive through the back roads and farms brought our small tour group close to the Newgrange monument where we all tumbled out of the bus and met with our guide, Aislinn, who led us up to the very front of the mound itself. As we climbed the hill to the top, I was amazed at the size of the ancient structure spread across my field of vision.

As we approached the front side of the monument, Aislinn gestured for us to join her at a spot just in front of an enormous oval stone set directly in front of an entranceway leading into the interior of the mound. It was part of a circle of huge stones set end-to-end around the entire circumference of the mound, each of them about ten or twelve feet across by four feet high and surely weighing several tons. The entrance stone had a sort of flat front side that was completely covered in a series of intricate carvings—diamond shapes and wavy lines, and most important of all, spirals, particularly a mesmerizing swirling triple spiral that dominated the left half of the great stone.

"Andrew, look," I said, hypnotized by the endlessly spinning patterns. "These carvings look just like the symbols on the back of Ismay's painting."

Andrew nodded enthusiastically as a wide grin stretched across his face. I could almost feel the excitement coming off him in waves, or maybe it was just the cosmic energy of that ancient spot upon which we were standing, but whatever it was, we were both giddy with anticipation.

"Welcome to Newgrange," Aislinn said after we'd all finished gathering around her. "Right now you are standing at the heart of an area that is one of the most important archaeological sites in the world. Stretched out over a few miles along a bend in the River Boyne there are approximately forty separate ceremonial mounds built by the ancient peoples of Ireland. These mounds come in various shapes and sizes ranging from the relatively small, such as the one you see behind you in this farmer's field, to the very large, such as the one standing directly behind me known as Newgrange.

"The mound here at Newgrange is very ancient. Constructed sometime around 3200 BC, it is older than the pyramids of Giza by nearly seven hundred years and older than Stonehenge by almost five hundred years. And when you think about what kinds of technology were available to the people of Ireland at the time, this is a pretty impressive feat of engineering. Particularly since much of the material used to build and decorate Newgrange came from many miles away, probably floated upriver on wooden barges and hauled across land by sheer muscle power.

"And if that wasn't impressive enough, Newgrange is just one of three major ceremonial mounds located here at Brú na Bóinne: The first is Dowth, which is a large mound located to the east of us. The second is Knowth, another large mound located to the west. And the third, of course, is Newgrange itself. The purpose of these mounds is unknown, although they are often referred to as passage tombs. This name may not be quite accurate, however, since very few human remains have ever been found inside of these so-called tombs. Inside Newgrange, for example, the cremated remains of only five or six distinct individuals were found, but those remains are from a much later period than when the mounds were first built.

"So if they weren't tombs, then what exactly *was* their purpose?" Aislinn asked. "Why did these ancient people go to so much trouble to build these structures?"

Aislinn looked at each of us earnestly, her eyes moving from face to face to see if anyone had the answers.

"The simple truth is that no one knows," she said. "Many people pretend to have the answers, but no one really knows. A thousand years after going to the trouble of building Newgrange, it was suddenly and inexplicably abandoned, allowing the earth to slowly grow up over the curbstones and entranceway until it was completely sealed off from the outside world.

"And so Newgrange lingered in limbo for thousands of years, its original purpose long forgotten, but it found new life in myth and folklore. To the locals these mounds were part of the realm of the fairy world, and unless you wanted trouble, you absolutely did not mess with the fairy world. So Newgrange was left untouched for millennia and was only rediscovered again in the late seventeenth century when English farmers moved into this area following the victory of Protestant King William at the Battle of the Boyne.

"In 1699 one of these English farmers decided he needed some building materials and ordered his men to start digging from this large mound of earth on his land. Fortunately for us, the workers starting digging here on the south side of Newgrange and soon discovered the entrance to the interior of the mound that you see behind me. The work was soon stopped, and during the centuries that followed, Newgrange became a bit of a tourist attraction with various visitors leaving reminders of their visit carved into the interior walls as graffiti, mostly during the Victorian era of the late eighteenth century.

"You will see some of this modern graffiti as you move around the site today, but you will also see the artwork that was carved into the stone by Newgrange's original builders. And as you look at all of these various markings that have been carved into the walls and curbstones surrounding Newgrange, I want you to remember to use your imagination and try to come up with your own interpretations and understanding of what they mean."

Aislinn took a step off to the side and gestured at the massive entrance stone and its complex patterns of circles and spirals.

"Just take a look at this curbstone that blocks the entrance here," she said. "These designs were carved on it more than five thousand years ago. What is their purpose? Do they have any meaning, or are they just decoration? These are the questions to which we have no answers, and it's up to each of us to try and find the answers for ourselves."

Wait a minute, I thought, blinking hard in surprise. *Is she saying that no one has any idea what these symbols and patterns mean?*

I looked over at Andrew, and I could see from the troubled wrinkling of his forehead that he was thinking the exact same thing.

"Are there any questions before we go inside?" Aislinn asked.

I had a question.

"Pardon me, did I hear you correctly that you have no idea what all of these patterns and symbols mean?" I asked.

"Yes, that's correct," Aislinn replied. "Because these carvings are so ancient, we've lost any connection to the culture that made them and what their belief systems might have been. For this same reason we also do not know why these enormous mounds were built, other than the fact that they were clearly designed for some kind of ceremonial purpose."

"If you like, I can tell you one of my own personal ideas of what the markings here on the entrance stone might mean," Aislinn suggested.

Everyone in our small tour group nodded eagerly.

"Do you see these wavy lines here at the bottom?" Aislinn said, leaning over and gesturing toward the curbstone. "To me these might represent water—the River Boyne, in fact. And right here, just above the river at the left side is this beautiful distinctive triple spiral pattern. To me these three interlocking spirals represent the three major sites here at Brú na Bóinne: Knowth, Dowth and Newgrange. Each of these ceremonial mounds had its own unique purpose in the belief system of our ancient ancestors, and each of them has its own unique astronomical alignment. Knowth has two tunnels, one east and one west, which appear to be aligned to the spring and autumn equinoxes. Dowth is aligned to the setting sun on the winter solstice. And Newgrange is the most spectacular of all with an incredible alignment to the rising sun on that same day, the winter solstice. I'll explain more about Newgrange's alignment to the rising sun on the solstice once we get inside, but while we're looking at the carvings on the curbstone here, I want to mention just one last thing.

"The winter solstice on December twenty-first is the shortest day of the year. The days leading up to the solstice get progressively shorter and shorter as though the life is being strangled out of the very sky itself, while the days after the solstice grow progressively longer as if the world has been reborn.

"Do you see the spirals on both the left and right sides of this curbstone?" Aislinn asked, pointing down at the great stone. "Those on the left spiral counter-clockwise while those on the right are clockwise."

"Maybe, just maybe these spirals also somehow represent the sun and the days before and after the winter solstice," Aislinn said. "And that's why they spin in one direction on the left and in the opposite direction on the right."

Aislinn paused to let us think this over for a moment.

"But as I said, no one really knows for certain," she said, finishing her explanation. "And your guess is as good as anyone else's."

My mind was racing with different ideas and explanations for these cryptic patterns. It excited me to think of all the nearly endless possibilities that these ancient mystical inscriptions might represent. But I also had to remind myself why Andrew and I were there in the first place. If no one knew what these symbols and patterns actually meant, then how were we ever supposed to decode the messages on the back of Ismay's painting and the *Titanic* postcard that he'd sent to Andrew's family?

"So these squiggles and spirals aren't a language?" I asked. "Like pictographs or some kind of alphabet?"

"Heavens no," Aislinn said, laughing. "The builders of Newgrange might have had fairly sophisticated abilities in engineering and astronomy, but they had not yet developed any kind of written language. These complex drawings might have been used for some form of record keeping or communication, but if there's one thing that these drawings are *not*, it's an alphabet."

160

I looked over at Andrew with a concerned and confused expression on my face. The symbols on the back of the painting and the postcard were almost certainly supposed to be some kind of alphabet. But if the answer to decoding that alphabet wasn't here, then where was it?

Chapter Forty-Three
Deep In The Heart Of Newgrange

Andrew looked as discouraged and disappointed as I felt as Aislinn led our group over the entrance stone and to the opening that leads deep into the interior of the mound. She gave us a few quick pointers on how to best navigate the long, narrow tunnel leading to the inner chamber, and then she unlocked the modern steel gate that blocked the doorway.

"Watch your heads," she said as she led the way inside. "And as you enter, be sure to take note of the rectangular opening that is built above the doorway. This is what we call the light box, and once we're inside, I'll explain its significance."

With that, Aislinn ducked down and through the entrance while the rest of us waited our turn to shuffle single file behind her. Just before I passed through the doorway, I looked up at the light box, which was simply a square-shaped opening between the enormous, flat, slab of stone that formed the roof of the entrance and a smaller piece of carved stone that formed a kind of lintel above it. The front of this smaller stone was decorated with a pattern of X's embossed on it—eight X's in total, all lined up in a horizontal row.

From there I ducked through the doorway and into the tunnel leading deep into the ancient mound.

Aislinn wasn't kidding when she said it was narrow, I thought to myself as I shuffled along, twisting left and right to negotiate my way through the procession of large standing stones that made up the walls of the tunnel. A few seconds later, I reached an extremely narrow section of the passageway and had to contort myself sideways in order to slide through and out into the open chamber beyond.

After the cramped conditions in the tunnel, I was relieved at how open the inner chamber felt when I stepped inside. It was by no means large or spacious, particularly considering that it was rapidly filling with the people from our tour group. But what gave the space a feeling of openness was the twelve-foot ceiling that rose above us, formed by a series of intricately overlapping stones that gradually rose in concentric circles until being capped at the summit by a flat stone.

After gawking around the inner space for a few seconds, I stepped off to one side so that Andrew could squeeze through the last narrow bit of tunnel and come into the chamber behind me.

"Unbelievable," Andrew whispered in awe, taking the words right out of my mouth as he straightened to his full height.

"You are now in the heart of Newgrange," Aislinn said as the last of our tour group stepped into the inner chamber. "As you can see, this chamber is formed in the shape of a cross with three separate recesses surrounding a central open space under this beautiful corbelled roof above our heads, which is still waterproof after five thousand years. Each of these recesses is decorated with various patterns and symbols with carved stone basins where cremated human remains were found when the chamber was discovered in modern times. But as I mentioned when we were outside, DNA testing has shown that these remains came from only a very small number of individuals, and this fact tends to argue against the belief that this place was used as a tomb and instead suggests that its function was more ritualistic or ceremonial.

"Some people believe that Newgrange might have been used in a kind of ceremony of rebirth where the bodies of loved ones would be cremated after they died and brought here to the inner chamber of the mound to be reborn. Once each year the spirits of the dead would ascend into the heavens, and their remains would then be removed and the stone basins washed clean to be used over and over again.

"There is some sense to this idea," Aislinn said. "It would explain why so few individual remains were found inside the chamber despite its having been in use for more than a thousand years. But there is even more compelling support for this idea, which we are about to discover."

With that, Aislinn switched off the electric lights and plunged us into complete and utter darkness.

"Pretty dark, huh?" I heard her disembodied voice ask from somewhere in the darkness. "That's because the tunnel you walked up to get here to the inner chamber was designed to make a series of slight curves to the left and right so that virtually every shred of light from the outside world is blocked. Most of you probably noticed this as you wound your way through the passage. But did anyone notice anything else unusual about the tunnel as you made your way through it?"

I wrinkled my forehead and thought about this for a second. I hadn't noticed anything. I was too busy trying to squeeze my way through to think about anything else.

"No one?" Aislinn asked after a few seconds of silence. "Well, let me tell you then. It's at an angle. The tunnel slopes gradually upward as you make your way through it."

Really?!? I asked myself. I had completely missed that.

"The tunnel actually follows the original slope of the hill upon which Newgrange was built," Aislinn explained. "And right now we're all standing at the summit of that hill under tons of earth and rock, nearly eight feet higher than where we started.

"The angle of the tunnel works to further minimize the amount of outside light that is able to penetrate the inner chamber, but it also has one other very important consequence. It brings the floor of this chamber level with the height of the light box that I mentioned earlier before we came inside. And on five or six mornings each year, from December eighteenth to the twenty-third, a most miraculous thing happens here in the pitch black of where we're now standing."

As Aislinn was speaking, I noticed a bit of light filtering into the blackness surrounding me. At first, I thought that my eyes were fooling me, but after a few seconds of blinking, I realized that I wasn't just seeing things, and a narrow spear of light was slowly coming into focus across the floor of the chamber.

"On the shortest days of the year, the light of the rising sun shoots across the horizon, through the light box, and up through a tiny narrow pathway through the tunnel that we all just climbed up, and straight here into the chamber where we are now standing," Aislinn explained as the light around us grew stronger. "For sixteen or seventeen minutes on those few mornings each year, the light of the sun creeps slowly across the floor and fills this room with an intense and pure golden light. What you're seeing now is just a simulation of this effect using an electric spotlight that we installed at the end of the tunnel. It is just a pale imitation compared to real sunlight, but with our lovely Irish weather it is significantly more reliable, and hopefully gives you some idea of what the real thing would be like."

Aislinn continued to turn the electric beam up to full strength, and as the light grew stronger and stronger, I was absolutely stunned that such an unbelievably beautiful thing as this was even possible. I tried to imagine the ancient people who had possessed such knowledge of the heavens to be able to build this amazing place and create such a breathtaking spectacle of light.

Without thinking, I slid my arm around Andrew's elbow, and for what seemed like an eternity, the two of us simply stood there, speechless as we watched the ancient chamber fill with light all around us.

"This is absolutely unbelievable," I whispered under my breath as I lifted my head to look all around the chamber. In the strange and beautiful light, the mysterious patterns and symbols carved into the rock seemed to take on a surreal glow. As the light grew stronger, I also noticed some of the Victorian-era graffiti that Aislinn had mentioned earlier. Someone named T. B. Naylor had immortalized himself in 1894 by carving his name into the flat stone next to the scratchings of some unknown artist from five thousand years distant.

How could someone desecrate this ancient cathedral of light and rebirth like that? I shook my head in disbelief as I gazed in wonder around the chamber and up toward the ceiling.

And that's when I saw it.

T. B. Naylor wasn't the only person to inscribe his name into these ancient stones. Just above me on the underside of one of the flat stones that made up the chamber's corbelled roof was another example of modern graffiti etched eternally in stone. Above it, there was some other writing from the same author, but it was too small and faint for me to make out from where I was standing.

The name of the graffiti artist, however, was written as clear as day.

Chapter Forty-Four
This Time There Won't Be Any Jet Skis

"Oh my god, Andrew, look," I whispered in Andrew's ear as Aislinn dimmed the lights once again.

"What is it?" Andrew asked, leaning down toward me.

The simulated sunlight was now almost completely gone, and Aislinn had switched on the main lights again.

"Look there," I said, my heart pounding in excitement as I took my hand off his elbow and pointed up at the ceiling. In the brighter glare of the normal lights, part of the text was obscured, but it was still possible to see Ismay's *YAMSI* quite clearly.

"Oh, my god," Andrew said, hardly breathing as he squinted his eyes at the text. "But what does the rest of it say? It's so small. I can't make it out."

"I can't see it either," I replied, shaking my head in frustration. "It looks like some numbers or a date or something."

With the main lights back up Aislinn began to wrap up her tour while Andrew and I stood off to the side and continued to try and read what Ismay had written.

"This place is pretty amazing, don't you think?" Aislinn said. "And if you're interested in seeing the real thing this coming December, please be sure to enter your name in our annual Newgrange Winter Solstice Lottery Draw. Every year some local school children pick fifty names at random, and those lucky winners get a spot for themselves plus a friend on one of the mornings of the winter solstice when the sunrise effect is visible."

Mental note to enter that lottery, I reminded myself as I stood up on my tiptoes, still trying in vain to make out the writing on the roof stone.

Aislinn gestured for everyone to start making their way out, but Andrew and I stayed back while the rest of our tour group slowly shuffled back down the tunnel.

"I can't see it!" I whispered in aggravation. "It's just too small!"

Andrew was a few inches taller than me but he couldn't make it out either. It was clearly going to be impossible without bringing a ladder in there and climbing up to the ceiling.

"Maybe we could take a picture and zoom in on it," Andrew wondered aloud, pulling his cell phone out of his pocket and pointing it toward the ceiling.

"I'm sorry, sir," Aislinn said as she waited for everyone to leave. "No photos inside the chamber, please."

"I'm so sorry," Andrew apologized as he slid his phone back into his pocket. He waited for Aislinn to look away again then glanced over at me and winked. He was too quick for her and got the picture anyway.

Well done, Andrew, I thought, grinning widely as I twisted and squeezed myself back down through the narrow opening and into the passageway beyond.

On the way back out, I noticed that the sloping of the ground under my feet was much more obvious than when I'd gone through the tunnel on the way in. Up ahead a pair of brightly lit rectangles of light marked the exit to the outside world. I was dying to see the photo that Andrew had taken, but I reminded myself to live in the moment, and took a second to run my hand along the smooth stones lining the sides of the passage.

These stones have been standing here since before the dawn of history itself, I thought as I closed my eyes and tried to absorb just a tiny bit of the immense cosmic energy that filled every crevice of that magical place. *Just imagine their hands on these same stones as they carefully lowered them into place.*

"What is it, Kitty?" I heard Andrew's voice behind me.

"Nothing," I replied, and continued down the tunnel to the exit. "Just daydreaming a bit."

"This is the place to do it," Andrew agreed with a laugh as we both stepped back out into the daylight and joined the rest of the group at the front of the entrance stone.

"Thank you very much for your time and attention," Aislinn said as she emerged from the tunnel and locked the gate behind her. "The bus will return you to the visitor's center in a few minutes, but be sure to take a stroll around the back of the mound and see some of the artwork that's carved into some of the other curbstones."

The group gave Aislinn a smattering of applause and slowly broke up to head back toward the bus. I clapped absently as I followed Andrew off to one side where he was already pulling his phone out of his pocket to look at the photo.

"How is it?" I asked, nervous and excited at the same time. "What can you see?!?"

I watched Andrew's eyes as he zoomed in on the photo. His disappointed and frustrated expression as he lifted the screen closer to his face for a better look said it all. The picture was no good. He couldn't see anything.

"It didn't work," he finally said, shaking his head as he handed the phone over to me. "It's too small and faint."

I took the phone and used my fingers to move the image around a little bit, zooming in and out in vain before finally giving up and handing the phone back.

"So what do we do now?" I asked, determined not to lose confidence. "I don't suppose your mother has any connections with the curator of the Newgrange museum, does she?"

Andrew shook his head and stared in the direction of the tunnel entrance with a distant look in his eyes. I could tell that he was already planning our next move and turned to follow his gaze so that I could see what he was looking at. He was looking straight at the steel gate that Aislinn had padlocked tightly shut to keep trespassers out of the interior passage and chamber of Newgrange.

I looked at Andrew and laughed. It wasn't very difficult to guess what he was thinking.

Andrew looked at me in surprise.

"What?" he asked innocently. "Why are you laughing?"

I shrugged my shoulders. "I was just imagining myself making a getaway down the middle of the River Boyne," I replied as I took his arm and walked with him back down to the bus. "Just promise me there won't be any Jet Skis this time."

Chapter Forty-Five

This'll Be A Cakewalk

Andrew and I found a quaint little hotel just up the road from Newgrange that had a couple of rooms available for the night. Neither of us had slept much the night before and we were both exhausted so we checked in and got some lunch before going to our own separate rooms to try to get some sleep. We would have a long night ahead of us so any sleep we could get now would be a blessing but after tossing and turning for a couple of hours, I finally gave up and went to knock on Andrew's door to see if he was awake. When there was no answer, I went to the front desk to ask if anyone had seen him.

"Your friend's not in," the lady at the front desk informed me. "I think he went into town for a little while to get something. He was asking where the nearest hardware shop was."

Hardware shop?!? I thought, and thanked the lady before returning to my room. *What does he need a hardware shop for?*

I flopped onto my bed and stared at the ceiling for a while trying to figure that out until I heard a soft knock on my door.

"Who's there?" I called out as I jumped to my feet.

"It's me, Andrew," I heard a familiar voice say from the hallway.

I opened the door and found Andrew standing there with a brand new black backpack that he'd apparently just bought that afternoon.

"What's all this?" I asked nodding to his backpack.

"Burglary kit," Andrew answered with a grin as he lifted the bag onto a table with a muffled clunk and unzipped the top to show me the contents. "One crowbar, one chisel, one hacksaw, one hammer, one bigger hammer, four flashlights, batteries, a pair of scissors, and an empty Coke can."

"A Coke can?!?" I asked, raising one eyebrow skeptically.

Andrew shrugged. "I saw it on YouTube. But I'm not very confident I can make it work," he said, grabbing the hammer and swinging it menacingly. "Probably better to just do it the old fashioned way."

"And how do we get up to the ceiling to read what it says?" I asked. "Is there a miniature stepladder in that bag somewhere?"

"Ha ha, funny," Andrew replied. "But I figured the easiest thing to do would be to just boost you up on my shoulders. I am sure that will work fine."

"What about security alarms or cameras?" I asked. "Did you notice this morning if there was anything like that around?"

Andrew shook his head. "There wasn't—not that I could see anyway," he said. "I'm sure there isn't. It's not a high-security bank vault after all, just an archaeological site. But to be safe we'll park up the road a ways and go cross-country over one of the farm fields so that we approach it from the back side.

"It sounds like you've thought of everything," I said.

I was impressed. Apparently, Andrew had done his homework.

"So what do we do now?" I asked, glancing at the clock. "It won't be dark for hours yet."

Andrew looked at his watch. "Have you slept at all?" he asked.

"Not at all," I said, shaking my head. "I was too nervous."

Andrew nodded. "We really need to get some rest," he replied. "Why don't we try to sleep, and I'll come wake you up again after midnight, and then we can go."

Sleeping was the last thing on my mind at that particular moment, and I wasn't sure if I could do it, but Andrew was right; we both definitely needed some sleep so that we could be on our toes later that night. We said goodbye and he took his bag of burglary supplies back to his room, and I flopped down on my bed and desperately tried to get some sleep.

One, two, three, four, I counted sheep in my head and did my best to relax for what seemed like hours, but all I could accomplish was to lie there and stare at the ceiling. Thankfully, I finally dozed off at some point, and didn't wake up again until several hours later when another soft knock at the door woke me out of my slumber.

It was Andrew. I opened the door for him, and after taking a few minutes to get ready and get fully awake, I headed down to the car with him.

"Do you know the way?" I asked, rubbing the sleep from my eyes as we pulled out of the hotel parking lot and set out on the dark and narrow back roads.

"Aye," Andrew replied. "I scoped it out earlier today. But it's a long way around to the opposite side of the river, and there are farms all over the place, so we'll have to be careful."

We drove most of the way in silence, bouncing along the claustrophobic roads with trees and tall hedges sealing us in on both sides. I could see what Andrew had meant about the farms. Every few hundred meters or so, we passed a cute little farmhouse. Most of them had no lights on, however, so there wasn't much to worry about. Farmers had to be up early, right? So they all probably had gone to bed hours ago.

"Are you sure you know where you're going?" I said teasingly, trying to lighten the mood a little. We'd been driving for quite some time already, turning left and right and left again through the maze of back roads until I'd lost all sense of direction.

Andrew nodded gravely. "It's not far now," he said simply, and pointed out the window. "That's Dowth just over there."

I turned my head and saw a large mound of earth rising out of the ground on the opposite side of the hedges to my left. It was difficult to make out any details in the dim light, but you could clearly see that it was there—a mass of darkness rising out of the ground, blacker than the sky beyond.

We drove for a few minutes longer and made a few more sharp turns, and then Andrew abruptly switched off the car's headlights before pulling over to the side of the road and parking next to a gate leading into a nearby field.

We sat for a moment in silence before Andrew turned and looked at me straight in the eyes with a deadly serious look.

"Are you sure you want to do this?" he asked. "We might get caught, after all."

I stared right back at him with my best deadly serious look to match his own.

"Who's going to catch us?" I asked. "The cows? Besides, after what I went through in London with that stolen painting, this'll be a cakewalk."

Chapter Forty-Six
What's The Problem With The Gate?

After we got out of the car, we both quietly closed the doors behind us by leaning against them until we heard them click shut. Andrew walked over to my side of the car and handed me one of his flashlights.

"We can't risk using them until we're inside," he whispered, putting a finger to his lips.

His meaning was clear: from this point on, no talking.

I slipped the flashlight into the pocket of my jacket and fell into step behind Andrew as he led the way down a gravel path to a steel gate. I was looking all around, desperately trying to orient myself as my eyes slowly adjusted to the darkness. Andrew had made so many twists and turns on the way there that I honestly had no idea where we were or where Newgrange was relative to us.

I looked up at the sky and quickly found the big dipper and followed it to the North Star. At least now I knew which way was north.

It was a glorious night with only a handful of small clouds chasing each other across the sky. The stars were shining brightly in the heavens above, and a brilliant crescent moon was slowly setting somewhere toward the west.

Through the trees, I caught a glimpse of an enormous low-lying mound looming on the horizon. It was Newgrange just a few hundred meters from us across a wide-open field.

Andrew grabbed the top of the gate and easily vaulted himself over it before turning around to help me scramble over as well. As we headed out across the field, I was amazed at how incredibly quiet the world around us was. Of course, there was the normal nighttime chirping of crickets, and somewhere in the distance, I could hear the occasional screech of a barn owl, but other than that, everything was deathly silent, as though Andrew and I were the only two people left on Earth.

If we were the only two people left on Earth, I thought, *there's no place I'd rather be than right here.*

Somehow, I could sense a kind of ancient cosmic energy surrounding Newgrange, a powerful and elemental energy that seemed to course like a current through the very landscape itself. Maybe it was just my silly imagination running wild, but I really believed this. And I guess the people who had lived on this land five thousand years earlier had felt it too. Why else would they choose to build their sublime temple of light right here at this very spot?

Andrew was continuing across the field just ahead of me, moving fast and making it difficult for me to keep up. I would have to quit my daydreaming and get moving or I'd lose him altogether. But it was tough to stay focused on why we were there, because at that moment, all I wanted to do was climb to the top of the mound at Newgrange and lie back in the grass to watch the stars cycling through the heavens overhead.

Wait up, Andrew! Wait up! I complained silently as Andrew reached the hedgerow running along the side of the field separating us from Newgrange.

What do we do now? I wondered after I finally caught up with him. He was running his fingers through his hair as he examined the thick hedge that stood in our way, trying to figure out how to get to the other side. He pushed aside some of the thick branches and revealed a wire fence on the inside that the hedge had grown up around. With some luck, we could both use it as a ladder and climb over.

Andrew looked at me and clasped his fingers together, indicating that he would give me a boost so that I could jump to the other side. I nodded and stepped up into his hands while I steadied myself with one hand on his shoulder and the other threaded through the branches of the hedge clutching the top of the fence.

Andrew waited a second or two until I was stable then lifted me up and over in one quick, fluid motion. My toes caught on the top of the hedge for an instant, but I landed safely on the ground beyond.

So much for me, I thought. *Now what about Andrew?*

I turned around and watched in stunned silence as he fought and grappled with the hedge and fence, his arms and legs sticking out at awkward angles as he noisily made his way up and over the top and then crashed onto the grass next to me. I struggled to keep from bursting into laughter as he pulled himself to his feet and tried to regain his dignity by brushing the twigs and leaves out of his hair.

So much for being quiet, I thought as Andrew put his finger to his lips again and waved for me to follow him up the ceremonial mound. He was moving more slowly now, walking carefully across the soft grass and staying close to the white quartz wall and enormous curbstones that circled the base of the structure.

As we approached the front entrance of the monument, Andrew slowed down to a dead crawl, cautiously putting one foot in front of the other until we reached the wooden stairs that visitors used to climb over the wall of curbstones to reach the entrance to the tunnel. The stairs looked a bit old and creaky, so Andrew carefully tested his weight on each step as we climbed up and over.

Once we were on the other side, we crouched down behind the entrance stone and breathed a bit easier. Andrew took off his backpack and set it on the ground against the back of the entrance stone so that he could pull out his flashlight. He gave me a grin then gestured for me to follow him as he scrambled over to the entrance alcove where the gate was located.

Staying close behind him, I almost ran into him when he stopped abruptly and suddenly froze in place, his entire body tense and alert.

What is it?!?? My mind screamed as I crawled up beside him. He looked at me with a look of concern and fear.

What?!? What is it?!? What is wrong?!? I pleaded silently with my eyes.

Andrew bit his bottom lip and pointed sharply into the dark shadow of the alcove ahead of him.

I don't understand, I thought with exasperation as I squinted into the darkness. *What's the problem with the gate?!??*

The only thing I could possibly think of was that a much bigger lock was on the gate than the padlock we'd seen Aislinn use earlier in the day. A bigger lock would mean that even with Andrew's clever little burglary kit, we probably wouldn't be able to force it open. But the problem wasn't that the gate was locked too securely. The problem was that the gate wasn't shut at all. It was standing wide open, swinging on its hinges.

Chapter Forty-Seven
A Chilling Thought Indeed

Oh my god, I thought, my blood running cold as I stared at the open gate.

"It's Ismay," Andrew whispered, leaning over and cupping his hand to my ear. "He's been here and gone already."

"How do you know he's gone?" I whispered. "Maybe he's still inside??"

Andrew considered this for a moment, peering up the length of the tunnel and searching for signs of life.

"It's possible," he replied. "But I don't see any lights or anything up through there."

"The tunnel's designed to block light, remember?" I said.

Andrew nodded and thought this over for a few seconds. "I'll have to go check," he said, and he lifted himself up to head for the tunnel to check things out.

Before he could get to his feet, I grabbed his arm and stopped him. I couldn't help it, but then I realized that we had no other option. One of us had to go inside and check or we'd have to abort the whole plan. "Just be careful," I whispered in his ear.

Andrew nodded and held up his palm. "Just wait here," he said and disappeared into the tunnel, instantly swallowed up by the blackness.

With Andrew gone, I was left all alone out there under the stars, nervously waiting for him to return and tell me that everything was all right. Gone were all the silly daydreams of cosmic energy, and with every passing second, my mind nagged at me, telling me that something was wrong.

As I waited, my imagination began to run wild, conjuring up ridiculous scenarios to explain what was going on at the other end of the tunnel and why it was taking so long for Andrew to come back.

Had Andrew stumbled onto Ismay and interrupted him in his work just as he was writing down the secret code? Maybe there was a struggle between the two of them and they were busy throwing each other against the ancient stones as they battled to the death? Perhaps Ismay had pulled out a gun just as Andrew finally overpowered him and wrestled him to the ground. Ismay was defeated and he knew it, so in one final act of desperation, he put his gun to Andrew's chest and pulled the trigger. The chamber exploded in a flash of deadly light, and with a groan, Andrew rolled off him onto the cold stones. As Andrew lay bleeding, Ismay headed back down the tunnel and would soon emerge to finish me off as well.

Don't be ridiculous, I scolded myself. *That isn't what is happening up there. Andrew's just being careful not to make any noise. That's why he's taking so long.*

I knew I was being completely stupid, but my mind wouldn't stop nagging me with all the crazy thoughts that kept materializing in my head.

Suddenly, I heard a faint scraping sound and the scuffle of someone coming down the tunnel directly toward me. My heart jumped into my throat and my body tensed. I prepared myself to make a run for it if I had to when I saw Andrew emerge from the darkness with a big grin on his face.

"It's all clear," he whispered, nodding his head happily in relief.

"Are you sure?" I asked. "Maybe he's hiding in the shadows of one of the alcoves or something!"

"I'm absolutely sure he's not in there," Andrew replied, rolling his eyes and giving me his best give-me-a-break look. "The entire chamber is barely bigger than my bathroom! I am one hundred percent sure that there's no one in there."

Andrew was right. The tunnel and chamber were too small for anyone to be hiding anywhere. Ismay had already been and gone. He'd broken in, got what he came for, and left. And that meant that he was one step ahead of us for the first time since we'd met him in his sitting room in London. We had to get moving if we expected to beat him to the treasure.

Andrew's eyes told me he was thinking the exact same thing, and he waved excitedly for me to follow him up the tunnel. "Let's get this over with quick," he said and disappeared into the darkness. He went up a few yards then switched on his flashlight. The added light made it easy for me to see where I was going as I quickly scrambled up the narrow passage behind him.

But my mind wouldn't stop nagging me.

Something was wrong—very wrong.

But I couldn't possibly think of what it could be as I followed Andrew's light and felt my way with the palms of my hands brushing against the smooth stones that lined the tunnel.

What is it? I thought. *What could possibly be wrong?*

There was something not right, though. I could feel it.

What was it that I'd thought just now as I was waiting at the entrance and thinking crazy thoughts? I thought to myself. *That maybe Andrew had interrupted Ismay as he worked to write down the secret code?*

Something was familiar about that thought—about the idea of interrupting someone in their work.

It took me a second to finally remember. It was something Richard had said the night before on his walking tour. Jack the Ripper's first victim on the night of the Double Event was Elizabeth Stride. She was a prostitute, just as all of his victims were, but unlike the others, her body was not mutilated. In fact, when her body was discovered, blood was still flowing from her only wound—the slash across her throat.

When Jack the Ripper murdered Elizabeth Stride, he was interrupted by the unexpected arrival of the man who would soon be the first to discover the body. Her wound was so fresh, Richard had said, that it was quite possible that the Ripper himself was still lurking nearby in the dark shadows as the man crouched over Elizabeth's lifeless body.

"A chilling thought indeed," Richard had said, and it was.

An equaling chilling thought was that Andrew and I *had* interrupted Ismay in the middle of his work tonight, and that was why the gate was standing wide open.

Andrew was absolutely right when he said that there was no possible way Ismay could have been hiding in the shadows in the inner chamber when Andrew went through the first time. The space was too small, and it took would've taken all of three seconds to swing a flashlight around and see that no one was there. The tunnel was likewise useless as a hiding place for the same reason. It was too small.

The answer was obvious. Ismay could have been hiding out somewhere nearby. There were plenty of dark corners and shadows near the entrance to the tunnel, and there were two wooden staircases for him to hide under as well.

What if we interrupted Ismay just as he was about to close the gate and leave? I asked myself. *What if he ducked into a hiding spot and was lurking just a few feet away from me the whole time Andrew was checking out the tunnel?*

I shivered at the thought of it.

In that case, he was probably just waiting for the two of us to go inside so that he could make his escape, I reasoned. *Why else would he be waiting around out there?*

But there was another reason, and I only realized it when I heard the sound of the steel gate swinging shut behind me.

"Andrew!" I hissed up the tunnel as a wave of panic washed over me.

But it was too late. The next sound I heard was that of a rattling chain and a heavy padlock clicking solidly shut.

Chapter Forty-Eight
I'm Going To Get What We Came For

"ANDREW!" I hissed again, more loudly this time.

"What?" he snapped. "Can you be any louder?!?" Clearly, he was annoyed that I was making so much noise; it wasn't like Andrew to be sarcastic.

"Get back here!" I replied. "Now!"

I heard a loud sigh and the sounds of shuffling and scraping as he came back down the tunnel, the beam of his flashlight jumping and bouncing off the pale stone walls.

"What is it?!?" he said in a loud whisper when he finally reached me.

It's Ismay, I was about to say when we both heard the eerie sound of a familiar voice floating up the tunnel toward us.

"Yoo hoo," the voice called out quietly. "Is there anybody in there?"

I watched the blood drain from Andrew's face. He switched off his flashlight and quickly slipped past me to head down the tunnel to the entrance. I followed right on his heels, neither of us caring how much noise we were making.

Within a few seconds, we reached the opening, and as expected, the steel gate was locked tightly shut, imprisoning us inside the interior passageway. Beyond the gate, bathed in the cold glare of the moon and starlight, was the lanky silhouette of Thomas Ismay standing just outside the entrance.

"What in the world are you two doing in there?" Ismay taunted with a malicious smile on his thin lips. "Did the last tour of the day leave you behind? What a shame."

"Let us out of here," Andrew demanded, his voice low and threatening.

Ismay chuckled and kicked Andrew's backpack full of lock-breaking tools, which was sitting on the ground where he'd left it.

"Too bad all your gear is out here and you're in there," Ismay observed sarcastically. "You do realize that it is a criminal offence to trespass on one of Ireland's cultural monuments, don't you? I'd hate to think what the punishment for that might be."

"I said, let us out of here," Andrew repeated, keeping his voice calm and steady.

Ismay pretended to consider this for a moment then shook his head. "No," he replied. "I don't think that would be a very good idea. It's probably best if I leave the two of you locked up here for the first tour group to discover tomorrow morning. What do you think?"

Andrew stared at Ismay in disbelief, his eyes burning with anger.

"Just forget it, Andrew," I said. "Don't waste your breath talking to him. It's pointless."

Ismay looked over at me contemptuously. "This young lady does have a point," he admitted as he patted his shoulder bag, which appeared to contain some kind of digital SLR camera with a very powerful zoom lens. "But I really must run now. I have what I came for, and I certainly would not want to get caught out here trespassing with the two of you. It would be a shame to put such a damper on my pursuit of the treasure now that I am so close to finally possessing it."

"But why, Mr. Ismay?" Andrew pleaded. "Why? Your grandfather's letter was addressed to *my* family. He obviously wanted us to have it, whatever it is."

"I think it's perfectly clear what the treasure is," Ismay replied. "It's the Rubaiyat! What else could it possibly be? My grandfather must have smuggled it off the ship in her final moments, and it therefore should be mine to do with what I wish."

"If that is indeed what the trasure is, then what use is it to you?" Andrew asked. "With the money your family has, you could buy a hundred Rubaiyats!"

"My family's fortunes are not what they once were," Ismay explained coldly. "Thanks in no small part to the incompetent steering of your great uncle who sent my grandfather's glorious ship to the bottom of the sea and ruined his reputation forever."

I felt Andrew's body tense up in fury. "You know that's not what happened," he said. "You of all people know that better than anyone."

"I know no such thing, my boy," Ismay replied. "All I know is that your great uncle was the officer in command on the bridge of *Titanic* when the iceberg was spotted. And he was the one who gave the commands that sealed her fate. The rest, as they say, is history."

"You take that back!" I hissed nastily.

Ismay glared at me, his cold eyes narrowing to tiny slits.

"You should learn to keep a muzzle on your little girlfriend here," Ismay said. "But her little outburst does remind me that I've foolishly overstayed my welcome here by chatting so long with you. Ta ta for now. Best of luck to you."

With that, Ismay spun on his heels and clambered up the stairs over the curbstones.

"Wait!" Andrew called out in desperation.

Ismay stopped and slowly turned to face us. "By the way," he said. "I wouldn't be surprised if the police were to receive an anonymous tip informing them that the two trespassers they caught up at Newgrange tonight are the same two who were responsible for the theft of a rare painting of the *Titanic*, a valuable family heirloom belonging to Mr. Thomas Ismay of London."

With that final word of warning, Ismay turned and disappeared down the other side of the steps and around the corner. I strained to listen for a few moments after the sound of his footsteps faded, but there was nothing but the incessant buzzing of crickets . Ismay was gone.

Andrew put his hands to his face and slumped against the stone wall, sliding down slowly until he was sitting on the floor. He looked like a broken man who was in need of some motivation. And I knew just the thing.

"What do you think you are doing?" I asked, sounding intentionally confrontational.

Andrew looked up at me in surprise. His expression was so shattered and dejected that I almost slid down right next to him and gave him a hug. But hugs weren't what he needed right now. We didn't have a second to waste sitting around feeling sorry for ourselves.

"What do you mean?" he asked. "What else should I do?"

"I don't know about you," I replied. "But since the police might well be here any minute to arrest us, I am going to head up the tunnel and get what we came here for."

Chapter Forty-Nine
Does Any Of This Look Familiar?

Andrew stared blankly at me for a second until a look of determination slowly crept over his face. "You're right," he said, sliding up the wall again to his feet. "Of course you're right. It would be sheer stupidity and a total waste to just sit around here waiting."

I nodded curtly. *Of course I'm right*, I said to myself while I gave Andrew a conspiratorial smile. Ismay was now one step ahead of us, and we had to be ready to even things up once we got out of there. Trespassing couldn't possibly be a serious enough offence that they'd lock us in jail, so once we paid the fine or whatever we had to do to get ourselves back on the streets, we had to make sure that we knew what the next step was of this seemingly endless scavenger hunt. Besides, if nothing else, it would give us something to do until morning.

Andrew led the way up the tunnel, switching on his flashlights after a few steps so that we could see where we were going. The walk up the passage seemed to take an eternity compared to when we'd climbed it earlier that day. It was as though the tunnel no longer led to the small inner chamber that we'd visited before but instead took us to some deeper, darker hidden place.

At last, we came to the final narrow bit, and I waited for Andrew to squeeze through before I followed right behind him. Stepping into the chamber, I fished my own flashlight out of my pocket, and together we aimed our flashlights toward the ceiling, angling them back and forth like searchlight beams until we found what we were looking for.

By the dimmer light of the flashlights it was easier to see some of the text that had been obscured by the chamber's electric lighting earlier that day. Next to Ismay's name, we could now make out a date.

"The fourth of June, 1930," Andrew said before glancing over at me.

"Apparently Bruce Ismay visited here, long after the *Titanic* disaster."

I nodded and looked up again to see if I could make out the rest of the text that was written above this, but it was no use.

"Can you see what else is written there?" I asked.

Andrew shook his head. "It's too faint," he replied. "But that much we already knew."

He put his flashlight under his armpit and reached into his jacket pocket to pull out his mobile phone. He handed it to me and said, "I'll give you a boost and you take some photos."

"I'm ready," I said. "Let's do this!"

"Just climb up onto my shoulders," he said, kneeling on the ground. I did as he said, and he lifted me high into the air, which brought me much closer to the mysterious and faded writing.

Andrew turned me around until I was facing the text, and while we both shone our flashlights at the ceiling, I craned my neck forward to finally see what Ismay had written there.

"It's some numbers, I think," I said, and I snapped some photos with various zoom settings.

"Did it work?" Andrew asked, looking up at me hopefully.

I flipped through the photos and shook my head. The phone camera just wasn't good enough to get a clear image.

"It's definitely some numbers, but I still can't make them out," I replied, lowering the phone in front of Andrew's face so that he could see for himself.

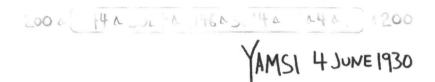

"Dammit," Andrew swore in frustration. "What are we supposed to do now?"

"Too bad we don't have a camera like Ismay's," I said. "But I think I have an idea, although it might be a bit tricky."

"Trickier than this?" Andrew asked, raising his eyebrows doubtfully as he shifted his weight to steady me on his shoulders.

"Move a bit closer to the wall," I said. "And brace yourself by leaning up against it."

Andrew did as I said and then looked up at me with concern.

"You're not going to try and stand on my shoulders, are you?" he asked.

That's exactly what I'm planning to do, I thought as I reached down to put his arms and palms in place to support my body as I pushed myself into a standing position.

"Don't worry," I said. "I can brace myself against you and the wall so that I don't fall."

"But what's your idea?" he asked. "Do you think getting closer with the camera will be good enough?"

"It might," I replied. "But I think my idea will work much better."

"What's your idea, then?" Andrew asked, his voice sounding a bit strained.

"Just a little something I learned in the Florida Keys," I replied as I shakily pushed myself up until I was standing on Andrew's shoulders, leaning against the wall for support and slowly settling into a stable position.

"Are you okay?" Andrew asked, grabbing my calves to support my legs.

"Perfect." I grinned and reached into the pocket of my jacket to pull out my Moleskine notebook and a pencil.

Tearing a blank page from the notebook I carefully lifted it to the ceiling and held it flat against the ceiling stone. With my other hand I took my pencil and rubbed it back and forth across the surface of the paper just like I'd seen Kevin and Kristina Tift do a few months earlier with the silver bars they'd recovered from a sunken Spanish treasure galleon.

"It's working!" I said as I rasped the pencil lead back and forth on the paper. I could see Bruce Ismay's writing materialize before my eyes as if by magic.

Andrew tilted his head back to watch what I was doing. "My god," he breathed. "You're a genius!"

"It's done," I said as I made my last pencil stroke and carefully peeled the paper off the ceiling and tucked it into my jacket so that my hands would be free to climb back down.

"Careful, don't break a leg or something," Andrew warned me as I cautiously lowered myself down again. Once I was low enough, Andrew reached up to grab me under the armpits and slowly eased me to the floor.

Face to face with Andrew and my arms wrapped around his neck, I stretched my toes until my feet were firmly planted on solid ground. He and I were so close that I was sure he could feel my heart pounding triumphantly in my chest, and before I realized what I was doing, I leaned forward and kissed him. At first, I expected him to blush and pull away, but he surprised me by kissing me back, his lips soft and his body warm against mine. It was a magical kiss—so magical that it seemed as if we were in our own private fairy tale. For a few short seconds in that ancient place with the powerful cosmic energy swirling all around us, we shared a kiss like none other I've ever experienced in my life.

"We did it," I said, smiling victoriously.

"You did it," Andrew replied.

I took a step back and reached into my jacket to extract the pencil rubbing. Andrew pointed his flashlight at the paper and moved behind me so that he could look over my shoulder.

"What do you think?" I asked, turning to look up at him. "Does any of this look familiar to you?"

"Familiar? Yes," he said, smiling vaguely as he reached down to hold the paper in his own hands. "But I have absolutely no idea what it means."

Chapter Fifty

Hello? Is There Anybody In There?

Andrew and I climbed back down the tunnel to the entrance to see if we could somehow figure a way out of our unfortunate prison. The pencil rubbing of Bruce Ismay's clue would have to wait until we were safely far away from this place, if that was even possible, of course.

We didn't take any chances with our newfound clue, however, and Andrew took a picture of it with his phone and immediately emailed it to himself, to me, his mother, and even to Richard. That way if we did end up getting arrested, or something bad happened with Ismay, the whole adventure wouldn't have been for nothing. Thanks to modern technology and the very fortunate fact that we were able to get a cell phone signal from inside the gate, Bruce Ismay's generations-old message was easily sent off into cyberspace where it was safe.

"It's no use," Andrew said angrily as he leaned down to examine the chain and padlock securing the steel gate. "Without our tools there's no hope of smashing this lock open."

I sighed heavily. This was not good news since Andrew's makeshift burglary kit was several yards out of reach on the other side of the gate.

"So what do we do now?" I asked.

"I guess we just wait for sunrise..." Andrew said, and after a long pause, he added, "...or for the police to come and collect us."

Andrew slid down and sat on the floor with his back against the wall. He stared despondently through the cold, steel bars of the gate as if he could will it to unlock itself.

I slid down across from him and leaned against the wall. I turned my face to look out toward the stars on the horizon, wishing that we could be like them—a million miles away from here. Actually, just a couple of feet on the other side of the gate would have been enough.

A light breeze was blowing, and the air was refreshing and cool and had a slightly earthy smell to it. I breathed deeply and closed my eyes to think. There had to be a way out of our predicament, after all, and if there was, then I was going to think of it.

"I'm so sorry for getting you into all this," Andrew said, his eyes weary.

I looked at him and smiled. "You didn't get me into anything," I replied. "I wanted this."

Andrew shook his head. "No. You didn't want *this*," he said, gesturing to the locked gate.

"Well, of course not *this*," I replied, laughing. "But it was my decision to come with you on this whole adventure. I wanted to."

"But why?" Andrew asked. "Who knows if we'll ever find the treasure at all. What can you possibly get out of all this?"

I pulled myself over to Andrew's side of the tunnel and slid up next to him.

"Did I ever tell you that I once held a huge uncut emerald in my hand that was probably worth more than half a million dollars?" I asked.

Andrew looked at me. "No," he said, a smile tugging at the corners of his mouth. "You never told me that."

"Actually, I didn't just hold it in my hand," I said, laughing at the memory. "I carried it around in my pocket for a couple of days where it could have accidentally slipped out and been lost."

"Why would you do that?" Andrew asked.

"Because at the time I didn't know that it was an emerald," I replied. "I didn't know that it was worth half a million dollars. All I knew was that it was valuable to me because it was unusual and special."

Andrew just stared at me. "But it was valuable to other people as well," he said.

"But I didn't know that," I continued. "And that's my point. In the past twelve months, I've chased my share of so-called treasures, and I've realized that the real treasures in life are moments like tonight and all the adventures that brought us here. Those are the things that make life unusual and special."

Andrew didn't quite seem convinced. "I suppose not everyone gets to spend the night inside Newgrange," he admitted with a chuckle.

"Exactly," I replied as I reached into my pocket to pull out my iPhone and flip to the photo of the pencil rubbing. "They also don't get to try and solve mysterious and ancient number codes either."

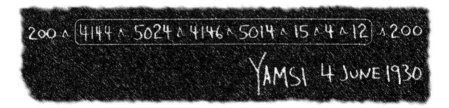

Andrew leaned forward to look at the photo with me. "Another cartouche," he said, referring to the oval box that surrounded the middle series of numbers on the screen. "Just like on the back of Ismay's *Titanic* painting."

"The cartouches from the back of the painting meant ice," I pondered aloud. "You said before that these numbers were familiar. Do they also mean ice?"

Andrew slid closer and leaned over to point to the photo.

"Sort of," he replied. "On the night the *Titanic* sank, she sent out a series of distress calls giving her position to any possible rescue ships that might be nearby. The first two numbers here are *Titanic's* position as reported in the very first distress calls—41.44 North by 50.24 West. After sending that out, the officers on *Titanic* made another more accurate calculation of their position. That's what the second two numbers are; they're the corrected position of *Titanic* that was sent out in all of the later distress calls until she finally sank—41.46 North by 50.14 West.

I nodded. "And the last three numbers are obvious: fifteen, four, and twelve represent the date that *Titanic* hit the iceberg, which was 15 April 1912."

"Exactly," Andrew replied. "And all of that taken together could mean ice, I suppose."

"But what do these other two numbers mean? See the 200 and 200?" I asked. "And what's this little divider symbol between the numbers?"

Andrew shrugged. "I have no idea, but it looks like a pair of legs."

"It's so frustrating," I said. "I thought we were so close, and now it seems like we're stuck again."

I sighed and leaned against the wall again, putting down my phone and sitting quietly with Andrew as we stared out the gate at the sky and stars.

"The sun will come up soon," Andrew observed offhandedly, gesturing to the dim glow of the coming dawn growing at the horizon. "If this was December 21st, the sun would soon be shining through the light box and up through the tunnel to the inner chamber."

My body tensed with exhilaration as I realized the importance of what Andrew had just said. I sat bolt upright and reached over to tug on his jacket and get his attention.

"Andrew! You're a bloody genius!" I said excitedly.

"What'd I do? What is it?" he replied, sitting up straight next to me.

"The light box!" I said, pointing frantically toward the ceiling. "It's right above us."

Finally, he understood. "My god, you're right," he said. "It's not big enough for me to fit through, but I'll bet that you could probably squeeze through!"

The two of us scrambled to our feet and walked a bit farther into the tunnel to examine the wide opening that the ancient builders of Newgrange had installed to let in the rays of the rising December sun.

"Will it support my weight?" I asked, feeling the enormous flat slabs of stone that formed a frame around the opening.

"Of course it will," Andrew replied. "It's been holding up the weight of all this rock and earth for five thousand years. A few extra pounds isn't going to make any difference."

"Give me a boost up!" I replied, more excited than ever. "I'll crawl out and grab the tools then we can break open the lock and get you out of here as well."

Andrew leaned down and cupped his hands together to give me a foothold so that I could climb up into the narrow space that formed the opening of the ancient light box. But before I could step up and crawl through it, I saw a flicker of light out of the corner of my eye.

Andrew saw it too. Up at the front entrance, a light was flashing off the tunnel walls.

"It's the police," he whispered desperately. "Crawl up there quick, and hide. There's no sense in both of us being caught in here. And with any luck they won't even notice you."

I shook my head defiantly. "No way," I whispered. "We're in this together."

"Don't be so stubborn!" Andrew replied and gestured again for me to step into his clasped hands. But it was too late. We could already hear the sound of footsteps on the wooden stairs outside followed seconds later by the beam of a flashlight shooting into the passageway, blinding us with its intense blue-white light.

"Kitty? Andrew?" we heard a female voice call out from the entrance to the tunnel. "Hello? Is there anybody in there?"

Chapter Fifty-One
Let's Hope This Works

Andrew and I looked at each other in complete astonishment, our faces illuminated by the beam of the flashlight shining up at us from the end of the tunnel.

Who is that?!?? Andrew's facial expression said, and I am sure that the expression on my own face was asking the same question.

"Andrew?!? Kitty?!?" we heard the voice call out again.

"What do we do?" Andrew whispered quietly in my ear. "Who *is* that?!?"

I guess we should answer her, I thought, and took a few steps closer to the source of the light.

"Yes?" I called out, keeping my voice low. "It's me, Kitty, and Andrew is here as well."

"Oh, thank god," the voice replied, talking fast and nervous. "When Lizzie told me to come here and help you out, I was so scared, and I told her that I didn't want to come, but she got angry and yelled at me and told me to stop being such a baby and just come over here...."

"Lizzie?" I whispered to Andrew as the voice at the end of the tunnel paused to take a quick breath of air. "Does she mean Ellie?"

Andrew shrugged his shoulders, completely bewildered.

"I was so scared. I didn't know what to do, but Lizzie told me I had to sneak out of the house and take Mom's scooter and walk it up to the end of the lane in front of our house, and when I was far enough away, I could start it and drive over here," the voice continued, off and running full-tilt again. The poor girl was obviously in a panic, and she was making so much noise and waving her flashlight around so much that she was bound to wake up every living person within three miles of Newgrange.

I had to do something, so I pushed past Andrew and rushed down to the end of the tunnel. Standing on the other side of the gate was a frightened-looking teenaged girl several years younger than me with dark black hair and eyes. She looked exactly like a younger and more terrified version of Ellie.

I reached through the bars of the gate and gently put my hands around hers. "It's okay, it's okay, just be calm," I said tenderly, slowly taking the flashlight out of her hands and switching it off. "We have to stay quiet or the whole county will hear us out here."

"I'm sorry... I'm so sorry," she whispered, her bottom lip quivering as she hovered on the verge of tears.

"Don't worry," I replied, my voice calm and soothing. "You did great. You're here, right? And you have no idea how happy we are to see you."

With the flashlight beam finally out of my face, my eyes slowly readjusted to the darkness, and I got a better look at the girl who'd come to save us. With her straight jet-black hair and piercing eyes, it was obvious that she was Ellie's younger sister. The resemblance was quite remarkable. She was wearing a big jacket and Ugg boots, but had obviously just jumped out of bed because she was still wearing a pair of green pajama bottoms with little cows on them.

"You're Ellie's sister, right?" I asked as Andrew walked up behind me to join me at the gate.

The girl nodded rapidly. "Yes," she said. "I forgot that you don't know me. I am so stupid. I'm Karin, Lizzie's sister."

I smiled at her as warmly as I could manage. "You're not stupid," I assured her. "In fact, I think that you just saved Andrew and me from being in a lot of trouble."

Karin looked at me uncertainly. "How?" she asked. "I have no idea what Ellie thinks I'm going to be able to do. That's why I told her I didn't want to come here."

"How did Ellie know we were here?" I asked, trying to keep Karin calm and focused.

"Richard told her," Karin replied. "She said you sent Richard a photo and told him you were trapped up at Newgrange. I have no idea who Richard is, but Ellie called me right away and told me I had to come help you."

"Do you live nearby?" I asked.

Karin nodded. "Just a few miles away down in Donore," she said.

I gave Andrew a look of relief. I couldn't believe it. This was the second time that Ellie had come to our rescue.

"Hi, Karin," Andrew said warmly, reaching through the bars to shake her hand. "I'm Andrew."

"Hi," Karin replied, her voice calmer but still a bit shaky.

"I want you to know how much we appreciate you coming to help us," Andrew continued. "But you also need to get home as soon as possible in case your parents notice that you're gone."

"I hope they don't," Karin said with a nervous laugh.

"Me too," Andrew replied. "So you should head home right away. But there's just one thing we need you to do first. And as soon as you do it, I want you to run back to your scooter and get home as soon as possible."

"Ellie told me to do whatever you needed," Karin replied. "But I don't know what I could possibly do to help. I am so scared."

Andrew smiled at her. "Well, you'll be glad to know that what we need from you is really quite simple," he said, reaching through the bars to point at his backpack, which was still leaning against the backside of entrance stone. "All you need to do is hand me that backpack."

Karin turned and looked down into the dark shadows at the base of the enormous stone. "That's it?" she asked.

"That's it," Andrew replied. "It's stupid, I know. But we need it to break this lock open, and obviously we can't reach it from here."

Karin took a few steps over and grabbed the backpack. She handed it to Andrew who set it carefully down on the ground just outside the gate.

"Are you going to break the lock now?" Karin asked.

Andrew nodded as he kneeled down to unzip the pack and rummage around inside.

"But you need to get going back home, Karin," he said. "Because as soon as I start hammering away on that thing, who knows how much noise that will make, or who might come running."

Karin nodded and took a few steps back, preparing to make a run for it.

"Wait, Karin!" I said, straining to reach through the bars and gently squeeze her hand one last time. "Thank you—really. Thank you for rescuing us."

Karin smiled at last. It was a weak smile, but that was enough for me.

"I didn't really rescue you," she said. "I didn't do anything."

Andrew and I both laughed at this.

"You have no idea how much you helped us," Andrew replied. "Trust me."

Karin turned and was about to go when she looked back at me one last time. "Ellie said that she would come over in a day or two for a visit. Will I be able to see you again when she does?"

I nodded enthusiastically. "Of course," I said. "We'll go get something to eat or just hang out or something. Pizza, maybe?"

"Ellie told me that you have your own plane," Karin said. "And that you're flying around the world."

"I do, and I hope to," I replied, nodding.

"Maybe you can fly me somewhere," Karin suggested. "Just for a look around."

"It would be my pleasure," I said, and Karin smiled again—a real smile this time. And then she turned to go, disappearing over the stairs and out of sight into the darkness.

Andrew and I stood listening, waiting for the sound of her motor scooter driving off before we dared to break open the lock. After a few minutes, we finally heard it, faint and distant as Karin sped off home.

When the sound of the motor had faded into nothing, Andrew pulled out a big hammer and a chisel that he'd bought from the hardware store the previous afternoon. After fixing the chisel into the base of the lock, he raised the hammer and prepared to bust us out of our little prison.

"Unbelievable," he said, shaking his head in disbelief.

"Tell me about it," I replied.

"Well, let's hope this works," Andrew replied, grinning. "Or we'll have to get Ellie to send Karin back again."

And with that he swung the hammer down with all the force he could muster and split the lock straight open with a single clean blow.

Chapter Fifty-Two
I'll Give You A Hint

"Well, that was easier than I thought it would be," Andrew said, looking at me with a surprised expression.

"No kidding," I said. "And quieter too."

Of course, breaking the lock had produced an incredibly loud clank when Andrew had hit it, but it was quick and abrupt and nothing at all like the shuddering and screeching sound of ripping metal that I'd been expecting. If anyone on the nearby farms had heard it, chances are they'd just rolled over and gone back to sleep.

"Come on," Andrew said as he quickly stuffed the tools into the backpack and pushed the gate open. "Let's get out of here."

"Aye, aye, sir," I responded jokingly as I followed him out into the open and up the stairs.

The night air felt absolutely wonderful as Andrew and I sprinted around to the back side of Newgrange. The air was fresh and cold and felt like freedom as we ran across the lawn and over to the hedgerow where we'd first climbed over.

Andrew braced his hands and vaulted me up and over the hedge just like before. He then proceeded to fight his own way over, cursing and spitting leaves out of his mouth as he went.

Finally, he made it over, and the two of us held hands as we dashed across the open field in the direction of our car. I fought the urge to laugh and squeal at the top of my lungs as we went. Faster and faster we ran, as though we were trying to break the surly bounds of Earth and take flight. It was a feeling I knew well from every takeoff and landing I'd ever made, but with the ancient mound of Newgrange looking down on us from behind and the even more ancient stars shining down overhead, I'd never felt so free.

In no time at all, we reached the steel fence near the car and jumped over it easily. Andrew unlocked the doors and we slipped inside, quickly locking ourselves in. We sat breathless and flushed with excitement.

"We did it, Andrew," I said grinning from ear to ear.

Andrew was nodding and smiling deliriously as he looked over at me with his intense green eyes. "We did it," he agreed. "I can hardly believe it, but we did it."

In a rush of adrenaline I reached across and planted a big wet kiss right straight on Andrew's lips. "Now let's get out of here and go figure out what those numbers are supposed to mean," I said with a look of wild excitement.

"Aye, aye, ma'am," Andrew replied and reached for the ignition. He glanced up in the rear-view mirror and stopped short, his smile turning instantly cold as the flash of bright headlights reflected off the mirror and lit up his face.

I turned around to look out the back window. Somewhere on the road behind us, a car was approaching.

"Nothing to worry about, right?" I said. "It's just a car."

Andrew nodded almost imperceptibly and kept an eye on the mirror as the other car drew closer.

"Uh-oh," he said, his face suddenly sagging in distress as his body tensed up.

"What?" I asked. "What's wrong?"

"Police," he said simply as a flicker of blue and red light suddenly filled the car.

Andrew sighed heavily and shook his head dejectedly as the police car pulled off the road just behind us. I watched through the back window as the driver's side door of the car swung open and the dark silhouette of a police officer stepped out.

"Stay cool," I said calmly. "We're not doing anything wrong here."

Andrew looked over at me as though I'd lost my mind.

"What do you mean?" he asked. "What possible explanation do we have for being parked out here in the middle of nowhere?"

I rolled my eyes and gave Andrew a mischievous grin.

"What do people *usually* do when they're parked out in the middle of nowhere?" I asked teasingly as I reached over to mess up Andrew's hair a little bit. "And I'll give you a hint—breaking into ancient archeological mounds isn't it."

Andrew gave a snort of laughter, and smiled but he was tense as the police officer walked up to his side of the car and gestured for him to roll down his window.

"Good evening, officer," I said, leaning forward and putting my hand on Andrew's shoulder. His name badge flashed in the light of his car's headlamps for a second, and I was able to read his name: Seamus MacNamara.

"Good evening, folks," Officer MacNamara said. "Can I please see some identification?"

Andrew reached for his wallet and dug out his ID card while I reached into the inside pocket of my windbreaker, pulled out my passport, and handed it over.

"It's a bit late," Officer MacNamara said as he flashed his light on our IDs and pulled a pen from his breast pocket to take down our details. "What are you two doing out this way so late at night?"

"Just... ummmm," Andrew said, flushing bright red in embarrassment. "Just watching the stars."

"The stars, eh?" Officer MacNamara replied with a chuckle. "Fair enough. Say no more."

"We were actually about to head home," I said. "Just as you were pulling up."

Officer MacNamara leaned over and looked in through the car window, his intelligent eyes scanning the interior carefully. "That might be a good idea, I think," he finally said. "Where's home for the two of ye?"

"The Newgrange Lodge," Andrew replied.

"Fair enough, that's not far," Officer MacNamara said as he handed our IDs through the open window.

"Not far at all," Andrew agreed.

"Listen here, we had a report of some funny business up at the Newgrange Monument tonight," Officer MacNamara said, leaning down to look us both straight in the eyes. "Daniel O'Shea up at Newgrange Farm reported seeing a skinny old fella with white hair jumping the fence a half hour ago. If you ask me it was the drink talking—he sounded like he'd had a few too many—but I don't suppose the two of ye saw anything unusual while you were sitting out here, did you?"

Andrew and I looked at each other in surprise.

"Actually, we did," Andrew said. "We saw a thin old man with white hair drive past here not too long ago. He slowed down to take the corner here, and I got a pretty good look at him."

"Is that a fact?" Officer MacNamara asked, taking note of this in his notebook. "And did you see where he went from there?"

Andrew shook his head. "Sorry, no," he said. "He just drove past, and that was it. I didn't see where he went after that."

Officer MacNamara nodded and snapped his notebook shut. "Well, it's probably nothing, but I'll have to head up and have a look around all the same," he said, leaning down to give us a wink. "Thanks for your help, and make sure you drive straight home, won't you? No more stops at the side of the road."

"Absolutely," Andrew agreed with a smile. "Straight home."

"Brilliant, drive safe," Officer MacNamara said and headed back to his car as Andrew rolled up his window.

"Oh, my god, Andrew!" I whispered as soon as the window was all the way up. "That was so close!"

Andrew sighed in relief. "Tell me about it!" he whispered. "I thought our goose was cooked for sure there."

"Well you heard what the good man told us," I said as I patted Andrew on the shoulder. "Straight home so we can finally make some sense of these bloody numbers."

Andrew nodded and reached for the ignition again, but stopped short for a second time when he glanced in the rear-view mirror.

"Oh no, what now?" he said as I turned to look out the back window. Officer MacNamara was coming back around again on Andrew's side of the car.

"I think you might have been right," I whispered. "Our goose might be cooked after all."

Andrew rolled down the window again and put on a smile as he turned to face Officer MacNamara.

"I'm terribly sorry, folks," Officer MacNamara said. "I'm afraid I can't let you head home quite yet."

My heart fell into my stomach.

"What is it, officer?" Andrew asked innocently. "Is something wrong?"

"I just got a radio call that one of the night patrols up in Slane picked up a white-haired old man driving like a bat out of hell through the middle of town," Officer MacNamara said. "I'm about to go pick up Daniel O'Shea from his farm and bring him over there to see if it's the same man he saw jump the fence up at Newgrange. I know it's not convenient, but I'll need you to follow me there to identify the man and see if he's the same fellow you saw earlier."

Andrew slid his eyes over at me with a look of utter disbelief on his face.

"Whatever you need, officer," he said. "We're at your disposal. Just lead the way."

Chapter Fifty-Three
Maybe There Is No Treasure

"I guess figuring out those numbers will have to wait a bit," Andrew mumbled as he pulled out and followed Officer MacNamara's car down the dark, narrow country lanes.

"I guess so," I replied hesitantly as I watched Andrew's eyes focused on the road ahead. "But what's our plan here, Andrew? I mean, what if it *is* Ismay that they've caught over there in Slane?"

"What if?" Andrew asked, glancing over at me.

"What are you planning to do if it *is*?" I asked. "Are you going to lie and say that it was him that you saw?"

Andrew shrugged. "I think Mr. Ismay deserves a little bit of payback for locking us up tonight," he said. "Besides, it's not much of a lie to try and convince the police that Ismay is the guy that farmer saw jumping the fence at Newgrange tonight. He *is* that guy. Ismay *did* break into Newgrange."

Andrew had a point—a good point, actually. I just wasn't comfortable with it somehow.

"It's not like he'd end up going to prison," I said, thinking aloud. "At worst he'll just have to pay a fine or something."

"Exactly," Andrew said. "And while he's busy sorting all that out, it buys us a bit of time to finally figure out this last clue and get to the treasure."

I nodded. "We'd better start figuring it out right now, then," I said, pulling my phone and the pencil rubbing out of my pocket.

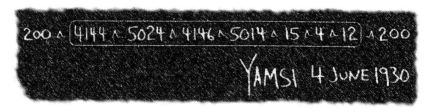

As Andrew drove, I stared blankly at the enigmatic sequence of numbers and symbols, desperately hoping for some kind of epiphany or inspiration that would help me solve it.

"Okay, so there's 4144, 5024, 4146, 5014...." I read aloud as I wrinkled my forehead in concentration. "And then there's that date—15, 4, 12. April 15th, 1912. And then we have 200 and 200. What on earth is all of this supposed to mean?"

"Maybe they're hieroglyphics?" Andrew suggested. "The middle numbers have a cartouche around them. Didn't you and Richard say that these oval cartouche things are from Egyptian hieroglyphics?"

"They are," I agreed, nodding. "But as far as I know, the Egyptians didn't use the same symbols for numbers that we do. Egyptian numbers would probably be the same as their other hieroglyphic symbols—little pictures of trees or birds or whatever."

I grabbed my phone and Googled the words Egyptian Numbers just to be sure I was right. I clicked on the link for Egyptian Numerals on Wikipedia and skimmed the article.

"See?" I said, holding the phone up and scrolling through it so that Andrew could see. "The number one is a stick, one thousand is a flower, one hundred thousand is a bird or a frog, a million is some dude with his hands in the air, and so on."

"And what about the legs?" Andrew asked.

"The legs?" I replied.

"That little symbol between the numbers in Ismay's Newgrange clue," Andrew said. "The one that looks like a pair of legs out for a walk."

Now I knew what he meant, and I picked up the pencil rubbing to stare at it some more.

"I don't know," I said. "I have no idea what that is supposed to mean."

"What are you talking about?" Andrew asked, confused. "It was on the Wikipedia page you just showed me."

"It was?!?" I snatched up my phone again to scroll quickly through the page from top to bottom. "I didn't see that!"

"Right there," Andrew said, reaching over to point out the tiny image of a pair of legs on the screen.

"Andrew, again you're a bloody genius!" I cried. "Look at what it says!"

Addition and Subtraction

For plus and minus signs, the following hieroglyphs were used:

and

If the feet pointed in the direction of writing, it signified addition, otherwise it signified subtraction.

"So what does that mean?" Andrew asked. "Are we supposed to add the numbers together?"

"I bet that's exactly what it means!" I replied in growing excitement as I flipped to the calculator app on my phone and began punching in the numbers. "Let's do the math and see what we get: 4144 plus 5024 plus 4146 plus 5014 plus 15 plus 4 plus 12 equals 18,359."

"What about the 200's?" Andrew asked.

I shook my head uncertainly. "I'm not sure about those," I replied. "See the one on the left? The little legs next to it are walking to the right as if to signify addition. But the legs next to the 200 on the right are pointed in the opposite direction, signifying subtraction. The two hundreds cancel each other out: 18,359 plus 200 minus 200 is still 18,359."

"So what are they there for, then?" Andrew asked, even more confused.

"I don't know," I replied.

"And what is significant about 18,359?" he asked.

"I don't know," I repeated. "I have absolutely no idea."

"Stumped again," Andrew said, and he laughed cynically. "Maybe there *is* no treasure. Maybe it's all just an endless string of increasingly cryptic and confusing clues."

I stared at the numbers and shook my head in frustration.

"I don't understand this," I said. "Why is this so difficult? Didn't Bruce Ismay actually *want* you to figure this out? Is this some kind of revenge on your family or something?"

"Of course he *wanted* us to figure it out," Andrew said calmly. "And the news clipping and *Titanic* postcard and the painting and these numbers here—all of it is somehow part of the solution. We just have to figure out how they all fit together."

"And how on earth do we do that?" I asked as we reached the outskirts of a tiny village nestled along the banks of the river.

"I have no idea," Andrew said as he made a turn and followed Officer MacNamara's car down a long hill then across a bridge into the center of town.

A few more turns through some deserted side streets brought us to the local police station—the Garda as they were called in Gaelic—where we pulled up past a blue lamppost with the Garda shield emblazoned on it, and from there we turned into a small parking lot. Officer MacNamara and a stout middle-aged man who I assumed was Daniel O'Shea got out of his car.

"There ye go," he said as Andrew pulled up next to him and switched off the ignition. "Welcome to Slane. Now if you'll all just follow me inside, we'll get this over with nice and neat and quick for ye."

Chapter Fifty-Four
If You Don't Believe Me, Just Try It For Yourself

Officer MacNamara led us through a set of brightly painted blue doors and inside the tiny police station.

"How are ye, Patrick?" he called out to another policeman who was manning a radio set at a sort of reception desk near the entrance.

"None too bad," Officer Patrick replied cheerfully. "I suppose you're here to see the old fellow."

"That we are," Officer MacNamara replied as he led us through a cluster of desks to a sort of lunchroom near the back of the building.

"I'll call Conor and have him bring the old fellow up to room one," Patrick called after us as he picked up a phone and dialed a couple of numbers.

Officer MacNamara gestured for Andrew and me to take a seat at one of the tables in the lunchroom. "Now, if the two of yous can just wait here for a wee minute, I'll take Mr. O'Shea in first to see our suspect," he said. "Is that all right with ye?"

"That's fine," Andrew replied for the both of us.

"There's coffee there on the counter and some water if you prefer. Just help yourself," Officer MacNamara said as he and Mr. O'Shea headed out the door, and before we knew it Andrew and I were alone again.

"Do you want some coffee?" Andrew asked as he took a few steps over to the small kitchen in the corner of the room.

I shook my head. "No thanks," I replied. "Just some water maybe."

Andrew poured himself a cup of coffee, sniffing it dubiously as he added some cream and sugar, then he filled a glass with water from the tap.

He walked back over and joined me at the table. "If we're going to figure this out," he said quietly, "I think we need to start at the beginning and see if there's anything we're missing."

I nodded in agreement, and using my fingers, I counted off the various clues we'd found. "First there was the envelope that your family got in the mail in the 1937," I said. "Inside that envelope was a newspaper article with a kind of riddle that hinted at a treasure."

"The storm that breaks after the flood," Andrew recited from memory. "Drag the innocent through the mud. The treasure lies not with dragon's blood but where ancient stone like flowers bud."

"The place where 'ancient stone like flowers bud' must refer to

Newgrange," I said. "A place where once a year the life-giving light of the sun pierces deep into the mound and gives light to the ancient stones of the inner chamber."

"Makes sense," Andrew agreed.

"Which brings us to the second thing that was inside that envelope," I said. "A postcard of the *Titanic* with an indecipherable message on the back of it written in a strange, squiggly writing. And on the front was a hidden clue written in Morse code using what looked like portholes lining the side of the ship."

"Turn Yamsi's Tragedy Around," Andrew said, still listening and following my train of thought. "That clue led us to Ismay's painting— Yamsi's *Tragedy*."

"And on the back of that painting was three different kinds of cipher writing," I continued. "Two of those ciphers were relatively well known and easy to figure out, but the third cipher was completely different. It was the same kind of strange squiggly writing that was used on the back of the postcard."

"And that writing," Andrew said, picking up where I left off, "bears a striking resemblance to the symbols and carvings that are etched into the stones at Newgrange. And although those ancient carvings might possibly be a primitive attempt at a kind of writing, we also know that they are most definitely not an alphabet."

"Bruce Ismay must have seen those carvings while he was living in Ireland," I reasoned, my excitement growing. "He must have been some kind of amateur cryptographer—as a hobby or something. And then one day he visits Newgrange and is so inspired by the ancient designs there that he uses them as the basis for his own secret alphabet."

Andrew nodded hesitantly. "That sounds about right," he said cautiously. "When I was a child, I also tried to invent my own secret alphabet so I could pass secret messages back and forth with my mates. But our secret alphabets always had a key so that all of us could decode it."

"But that's exactly what the back of Ismay's painting is," I said. "Like Richard said when we were back at his flat in London, the painting seems to be a kind of Rosetta stone that holds the key to unlocking the entire mystery."

"Except that the clues on the back of the painting led us further," Andrew said. "To Newgrange where we found this strange sequence of numbers that adds up to 18,359."

"But what in the world does the number 18,359 have to do with the *Titanic*?" I wondered aloud.

"Or with ice," Andrew reminded me. "Don't forget that the numbers were circled with a cartouche, the same as we'd previously seen around the word ice."

"It's obvious what ice has to do with *Titanic*," I said, chuckling. "But what either of those has to do with the number 18,359 is completely beyond me."

Andrew sighed heavily and leaned back in his chair. "Maybe we're simply not *supposed* to be able to solve it," he said. "Maybe it's all just a trick."

I shook my head. "I don't think so," I said. "Bruce Ismay clearly meant for your family to solve this. But with every successive clue becoming more and more difficult to crack, it seems that he certainly didn't want it to be easy for you. Maybe it was meant to be a secret that took years to solve."

"Maybe the people in 1937 had all the time in the world to solve this," Andrew laughed. "But we certainly don't. In a couple more hours, at most, Thomas Ismay will be back on the streets again."

"The people in 1937 might have had all the time in the world to figure this out," I said, "but we have something they didn't."

"What's that?" Andrew asked.

"The Internet," I said, reaching for my iPhone to open one of the web browser apps. "Every clue thus far has led us somewhere. Maybe if we're lucky, I can figure out where we're supposed to go next."

"Maybe this last clue isn't supposed to lead us anywhere else at all," Andrew said. "I mean, isn't Newgrange the place 'where ancient stone like flowers bud'? Doesn't that bring us back to the riddle where all of this started in the first place?"

I considered this for a second as I waited for Google to open. "If that is true, then what is the 'storm that breaks after the flood'?" I asked. "And how does it 'drag the innocent through the mud'?"

"I always assumed that it referred to the public outcry that occurred after the sinking of *Titanic*," he said. "Bruce Ismay was vilified by the press and the general public for climbing into a lifeboat and surviving the disaster."

"Okay, let's find out what the words Titanic and ice and the number 18359 have in common," I said, typing the three search terms into Google as I spoke.

"Maybe 'the storm that breaks after the flood' means something more specific," Andrew said distantly, staring at the ceiling, lost in thought.

I hit Search on the iPhone screen and waited for the search results to come up. It took a few seconds, but when they finally appeared, I had one of the biggest shocks of my entire life.

"Maybe it refers to the *Titanic* inquiries," Andrew and I said at exactly the same time.

Andrew sat bolt upright and looked over at me with a look of surprise.

"What did you say?" we asked each other simultaneously, then burst into laughter.

"You go first," I said, giggling.

"What I said was that maybe 'the storm that breaks after the flood' refers to the *Titanic* inquiries," Andrew explained. "Both the Americans and British held commissions of inquiry after the disaster to figure out what happened. And during those Bruce Ismay's reputation was certainly 'dragged through the mud.' "

I nodded excitedly. "I think you may be right," I said, my heart pounding in excitement. "Because what do you think Titanic and ice and 18359 all have in common?"

"I have absolutely no idea," Andrew replied with a look of utter confusion.

"This," I said triumphantly, turning my iPhone around to show him the list of Google search results. It took him a few seconds to see what I had seen, but then he understood. Right at the top of the list, one in particular had jumped right out at us.

<u>Testimony of Joseph B. Ismay, cont.</u> - **Titanic** <u>Inquiry Project</u>
www.**titanic**inquiry.org/BOTInq/BOTInq16Ismay02.php ▾

18359. Did you understand from that telegram that the ice which was reported was in your track? - I did not.

It was so absolutely unbelievable that I could hardly trust my eyes. Maybe you can't believe it either? But just try Googling it for yourself and you'll see what I mean.

Chapter Fifty-Five
Please Tell Me It's Seventy-Nine

"My god," Andrew gasped, his jaw dropping in astonishment as he reached for my phone to get a better look. "Is it true? Is this even possible?"

I let Andrew take the phone then just sat there watching him as I grinned from ear to ear.

Andrew clicked on the link to take him to the website of the *Titanic Inquiry Project* website then navigated around for a while, reading aloud as he went.

"In the wake of the sinking of the R.M.S. Titanic on 15-16 April 1912, both the United States Senate and the British Board of Trade held inquiries into the causes of the disaster," Andrew read. "The British hearings, following a standard legal practise of the time, numbered each question and answer sequentially throughout the entire proceedings. The testimony of witness Joseph Bruce Ismay, Managing Director of the White Star Line and International Mercantile Marine, on inquiry days 16 and 17, dated 4 to 5 June 1912, can be found in questions 18224 to 19073."

"Question number 18359," Andrew continued. "Right in the middle of a discussion about the ice warning from the *S.S. Baltic* that Captain Smith had given to Ismay earlier on the day of the disaster."

Andrew read aloud again. "Question to Ismay: 'Did you understand from that telegram that the ice which was reported was in your track?' Answer: 'I did not'."

Andrew looked up at me, smiling broadly.

"Ice!" he said, his voice filled with excitement.

"Ice?" I asked, confused. "What do you mean?"

"Ice!" he said again and turned the phone so that I could see it.

18359. Did you understand from that telegram that the ice which was reported was in your track?
- I did not.

I still didn't understand what he was talking about, but as I stared at the question and answer on the screen, it slowly dawned on me.

"Ice!" I said, almost leaping out of my chair. "Where is the picture of the back of the painting? Do you have it?"

Andrew nodded like an excited little kid on a sugar rush as he reached for his own phone and flipped through to the photo I'd taken of the back of the painting. Pulling his chair next to mine, we placed the two phones on the table side-by-side and compared the two images.

"You count the letters from the question and answer, and I'll do the same for the cipher message," Andrew said, leaning forward, eager to start counting. "If the word ice appears at the same point in both texts, then...."

Andrew was so excited that he couldn't even finish his sentence.

"Then we've found the solution," I said, wide-eyed with excitement.

We must have been quite a sight, the two of us sitting there, crouched over the tiny screens of our phones, carefully counting under our breath. I finished mine and sat up straight to wait for Andrew.

"What'd you get?" he asked after he finished counting, his voice full of anticipation.

"Forty," I replied. "The word ice starts at the fortieth letter."

"Yes!!!" Andrew exclaimed in pure elation. "Same for mine!"

"We should count how many letters there are for each," I suggested, "just to be absolutely sure."

"Good idea," Andrew agreed, nodding happily as he bent over to start counting again.

I was so excited that I was finding it difficult to count and had to start over again several times before I finally was able to finish. By the time I did, Andrew was already waiting and looking at me anxiously.

"How many?" he asked nervously. "Please tell me it's seventy-nine."

I grinned and nodded ecstatically. Excluding spaces and punctuation, that was the exact number of letters, which meant that the two texts were the same—the question and answer from the *Titanic* inquiry was the same as the cryptic message in squiggly characters on the back of Ismay's painting.

Andrew heaved a huge sigh of relief and ran his hands through his hair.

"You did it!" he said, looking over at me with awe. "You solved it!"

"Me?!?" I replied, my voice going up an octave. "You're the one who solved it! I was just fooling around on the Internet and got lucky."

Andrew smiled and shook his head. "We *both* solved it, let's just leave it at that," he said. "But do you know what this means?"

I nodded solemnly. I knew exactly what it meant. It meant that we would be able to finally read the message on the back of the *Titanic* postcard. For the first time since Bruce Ismay himself had written the message in 1937, a member of the Murdoch family would finally know what he'd been trying to tell them. The secret that would lead us to the treasure would be revealed at last.

It wasn't going to be easy, of course, especially not when Andrew and I were sitting in the lunchroom of a tiny police station in Ireland. I would have preferred to print out some of the photos and scribbled detailed notes all over them, but I was too excited to wait for even one more second.

"Okay, you write down the letters as I figure them out," I said, sliding my notebook and a pencil across to Andrew. I lined up everything I needed on the table in front of me. First the original *Titanic* postcard at the far left, followed by Andrew's phone with the picture of the back of the painting, and finally my own phone with the text from the transcript of Ismay's testimony before the British *Titanic* Inquiry.

I took a deep breath then got to work. The first character from the postcard was a circle with a kind of upside-down horseshoe inside.

Searching through the symbols in the photo of the back of the painting, I quickly found the same character eight letters in from the beginning. Turning to question and answer number 18359 from Ismay's testimony, I quickly counted eight letters in.

"M," I said. "The first letter is M."

Andrew nodded and scribbled that down on the piece of paper he'd torn from my notebook.

Turning back to the postcard again I moved on to the second character, which looked like a sideways number 8.

That one was easy. There were two of those right next to the symbol I'd just looked at on the picture of the back of the painting.

"U," I said, and Andrew quickly wrote that letter down as well.

This isn't so bad, I thought as I settled into a nice steady rhythm of decoding the message one letter at a time.

"R... D... O... C... H," I continued before looking up at Andrew to give him a grin. "Murdoch, it says!"

Andrew nodded and smiled a goofy punch-drunk happy smile that made me want to just wrap my arms around him and give him a big hug. But there was no time to lose with such silly flights of fancy. We had a message to decode and a treasure to find.

Working my way through the rest of the characters much more quickly, I lost track of the words and letters in my head, and by the time I finished, I had no idea what I'd just spelled out.

I looked up at Andrew expecting to see that same happy goofy smile on his face that had been there before, but to my surprise, his face was heavy with emotion, and his eyes were swollen with tears.

"Andrew—what is it?" I asked with concern. "What does the message say?!?"

Andrew stared vacantly at the paper in his hands and looked up at me with a confused and flustered expression. He opened his mouth to say something, but at that very moment, the door opened and Officer MacNamara stuck his head in the room.

Chapter Fifty-Six

Right Here, Right Now, Tonight

"We're ready for you folks now," Officer MacNamara said, leaning into the lunchroom and waving for us to follow behind him. "You can just come with me."

Are you kidding me?! I screamed to myself. *Why now?!?? Couldn't you have waited for two more minutes?!?*

Andrew quickly composed himself, wiping the tears from his eyes with his sleeve, tucking the message in his jacket as he reached for his phone.

"No worries," Andrew said, and he gave me a solemn look as we stood up and walked to the door.

"Sorry to keep you waiting so long there," Officer MacNamara said as we followed him down a dimly lit hallway that ran along the windows at the back of the building. "I'm afraid that Mr. O'Shea wasn't exactly what you would call a reliable witness."

"What do you mean?" Andrew asked, acting more calm and collected than I would have thought possible under the circumstances.

"Oh, I don't know," Officer MacNamara said. "First of all, he's a lot drunker than we thought he was. In fact, he's downstairs right now sleeping it off in one of the holding cells. But of course he was so far gone that he couldn't remember what the old fellow he saw earlier tonight looked like. So we still don't know whether we've got the right man or not. And as if that weren't bad enough, O'Shea and our suspect got into a bit of a shouting match, and we had to break it up and separate them."

"A shouting match?" I asked, confused. "Were they able to see each other and talk to each other?"

Officer MacNamara laughed heartily. "Of course they were, darlin'," he said. "We were all standing in the same room together. Were you expecting some Hollywood interrogation room with one-way mirrors and the like?"

"Actually, yes," I replied, suddenly very nervous about coming face-to-face with Thomas Ismay.

Officer MacNamara laughed again. "That kind of fancy thing is for the folks in Dublin, maybe," he said as he opened the door at the end of the hall and led us through. "But don't worry. Just ignore him if he talks to you, and we'll get in and out of there as quick as a wink."

I glanced over at Andrew to see what he thought of all this. He looked as cool as ever and put his arm around my shoulder.

"Don't worry," he said with a nod and a perfect smile. "Everything's going to be fine."

I hardly knew how that was possible, but Andrew's strength and warmth made me feel safe and protected as Officer MacNamara led us down to a locked door at the end of the next hallway. Through the windows, I could see the first rays of the sun filling the sky in the east, bringing life to a brand new day, and I knew that Andrew was right. Everything was going to be fine.

"Step inside folks," Officer MacNamara said, knocking lightly on the door before twisting the handle and ushering us inside.

We stepped into a small, bare room with bright fluorescent lights and pale yellow walls in need of a fresh coat of paint. The only furniture was a single table in the middle of the room with a few chairs pulled up to it on each side. Seated at the table in front of another police officer was the unmistakable figure of Thomas Ismay, looking meaner and angrier than ever. He was clearly extremely unhappy about being locked up in that tiny, barren room.

"Oh, for the love of god," Ismay said, smiling a thin, cruel smile as he saw us enter the room. "Where on earth did you find these two?"

"Quiet down, you," the officer standing behind Ismay said, tapping the table threateningly with his nightstick. "Don't go making any trouble like you did with the last one."

Ismay threw his hands up in frustration and leaned back in his chair without another word. He sat there fuming and angry, staring at us defiantly, daring us to challenge him. Andrew stepped up close beside me and threaded his warm fingers through mine, giving me another boost of much-needed reassurance.

"Well, what do you say?" Officer MacNamara asked, looking expectantly at Andrew and me. "Is this the fellow you saw out by Newgrange earlier tonight?"

I nodded and opened my mouth to say yes when I suddenly felt Andrew squeeze my hand tightly. I turned to look at him with a quick glance of uncertainty, as he simply looked down at me and smiled before looking at Officer MacNamara and shaking his head no.

"It's not him," Andrew said, much to my shock and surprise. "It's not the same man."

Officer MacNamara nodded. "Are you absolutely sure?" he asked. "I mean, do you think you got a good enough look at the fellow earlier tonight to be sure you'd recognize him again if you saw him?"

"Absolutely," Andrew replied, nodding confidently. "I remember his face perfectly, and I am absolutely sure that this isn't him."

Officer MacNamara nodded again and thought this through for a second before turning to face Ismay. "Well, Mr. Ismay, I'm terribly sorry to have inconvenienced you like this, but like I told you before, we had reports of a man fitting your description sneaking around one of our treasured cultural monuments tonight, and we had to be sure it wasn't you."

Ismay narrowed his eyes and looked suspiciously at Andrew before answering. "I do understand, officer," he said, finally. "And I certainly do hope that no damage was done up there at...?"

"Newgrange," Officer MacNamara said. "And no harm done. One of our men was just up there to take a look around. He found one of the gates standing wide open with the lock busted all to hell, but no other signs of vandalism or the like."

"I'm glad to hear it," Ismay said, shaking his head disapprovingly. "Imagine what kind of miscreants would do such a thing."

"I couldn't agree more," Officer MacNamara said. He gave a curt nod to the other officer and said, "Mr Quinn here will take you down to collect your valuables and then escort you to your car."

"Thank you," Ismay said, sliding back his chair and getting to his feet, still looking suspiciously at Andrew and me.

"And no more speeding around like the devil on wheels," Officer MacNamara scolded. "Keep it under the speed limit."

Ismay smiled thinly and put his hand over his heart. "I wouldn't dare think of it," he replied. "I've learned my lesson."

Officer MacNamara gave Ismay one last look before turning to Andrew and me and gesturing for us to follow him from the room.

"Thank you for your time this morning," he said with a tired smile as he led us through to the front of the station and back out to the parking lot. "I really do appreciate your cooperation and patience."

"Not a problem, officer," Andrew said. "We're always glad to help however we can."

"Good night to ye and thank you again," Officer MacNamara said, giving us one final nod before disappearing into the police station and leaving us standing alone on the empty parking lot with the village slowly coming to life around us.

Andrew smiled at me and took me by the hand, leading me back to where our car was waiting. I was bursting with curiosity and wanted to just shake him and ask what the heck had just happened back there, but somehow I was able to hold my tongue until we were in the privacy of the car.

"What was *that* all about?!??" I asked as soon as the car doors were safely closed behind us. "Why did you let Ismay off the hook like that?!? How do you know he hasn't already figured out the code and is halfway to the treasure by now?!?"

Andrew looked at me with a warm and beautiful smile. "Do you remember that story you told me a couple of hours ago about the emerald?" he asked. "When we were still locked inside Newgrange?"

I was taken aback for a second.

"Of course I do," I replied hesitantly.

"You said that at the time you didn't know that it was an emerald," Andrew continued, still smiling that same overwhelmingly beautiful smile. "All you knew was that it was unusual and special, and that's what made it valuable to you."

"Yes," I said, unsure of where he was going with this. "I remember that."

"You also said that it made you realize that the real treasures in life are things like everything that happened to us tonight," Andrew said. "And everything that led us here to this very moment, right here, right now, tonight."

I nodded solemnly. "Exactly." I agreed.

Andrew kept smiling and reached into his jacket to pull out the torn-out page from my notebook with the decoded text from Bruce Ismay's 1937 *Titanic* postcard scribbled on it.

"This is the real treasure," he said, his eyes welling up again with tears as he handed the page over to me.

I looked at Andrew uncertainly as I slowly took hold of the paper and held it close, feeling Andrew's warmth as it lingered on the corners of the page.

"I don't understand...." I began to say but Andrew gently put his index finger to my lips and stopped me in mid-sentence.

"You will," he said, nodding down at the paper that I was clutching in my hands.

With one last deep look into Andrew's intense green eyes, I slowly turned the page over and finally read what the message said, becoming the second person in more than eighty years to read what Bruce Ismay wanted the Murdoch family to know.

MURDOCH IS INNOCENT
AND DIED A GENTLEMAN

"Murdoch is innocent and died a gentleman," it read.

E.P.I.L.O.G.U.E. One

The Real Treasures In Life

One week later, I found myself on the western edge of Ireland at the summit of the sheer cliffs that stand sentinel over the North Atlantic. The cold wind swept viciously off the ocean, howling mournfully like some disembodied spirit.

Seven days had passed since Andrew and I had finally reached the end of his family's long search for treasure and truth, not one of them ever realizing that the two were, in fact, the same thing.

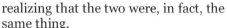

In the end there had been no treasure, at least not the kind that buys expensive flashy things whose value is measured in mere dollars and cents. The gift they got instead, as Andrew had said, was the *real* treasure. After more than a hundred years of uncertainty, doubt, and hurtful slander, the Murdoch family had finally learned from the pen of Mr. J. Bruce Ismay himself, the managing director of the White Star Line, that Andrew's revered great uncle William Murdoch was not to blame for the tragedy. He had died with honor as the mortally wounded *Titanic* slipped out from under him and into the deep, dark sea.

On hearing the news from Andrew, his mother had immediately flown to Dublin to meet us, clinging and hugging me as though we'd known each other for years although we were actually just meeting for the very first time.

"If only your father was still with us," Andrew's mother cried hysterically as she wrapped her arms around the two of us at Dublin Airport. "Bless his soul—how he would have loved to have lived to see this day."

As the news spread, the Murdoch clan converged on Ireland from all over England, Scotland, and beyond. Andrew's mother somehow arranged with some real estate friends of hers for all of us to spend a week at Bruce Ismay's former country estate on the Connemara coast. The home was an absolute palace with endless rooms and sprawling grounds, and even with the seemingly constant influx of Murdochs coming and going throughout the week, the house never seemed to run out of space.

Professor Flynn also came to stay for a few days, driving out from Belfast with a car full of books about *Titanic* and spending endless hours with the various members of the Murdoch family telling stories and bringing the legend of the great lost liner to life through his words and his enthusiasm for the subject.

Richard came as well, flying in from London to spend a few days exploring the countryside and taking immeasurable delight in frightening everyone sleepless with terrible ghost stories told around the dim light of a crackling fire late at night.

Also flying in from London was Ellie, who picked up her sister Karin along the way and brought her to spend some time with all of us. Andrew and I were so thankful to Karin for having come to rescue us at Newgrange that we lavished attention on her the entire week. And of course, as promised, I took her up in my trusty De Havilland Beaver for an unforgettable flight across the jagged cliffs and pounding surf of Ireland's dramatic coastlines.

On our last night together, we all came together, family and friends alike, for one final raucous meal around an enormous rectangular table in the estate's grandiose dining room. For hours, we all laughed and joked together, telling stories and making toasts as we gorged ourselves on deliciously robust and hearty homemade Irish delicacies.

As the talk continued late into the night, Andrew and I were forced, for the umpteenth time, to tell the story of how we had made what the Murdoch family had begun to call "the Discovery."

"There's just one thing you've left out," Professor Flynn said as we finished our story.

"And what would that be, you rascal Flynn? I already mentioned how important your help was to us, didn't I?" Andrew replied, making everyone laugh.

Professor Flynn slowly shook his head. "Not that, my good boy," he replied. "Although if you could make me sound a bit more handsome in future tellings, I'd be much obliged."

"Then what is it?" I asked, trying to think of what part of the long and complex story we'd left out.

"This!" Professor Flynn said, holding up the pencil rubbing that Andrew and I had made in the cavernous chamber at Newgrange. "You've forgotten to explain the meaning of these strange 200's at either end of your cartouche here in the middle."

I looked across the table and nodded slowly in realization. Professor Flynn was right. In all the excitement of making "the Discovery," and in the hustle and bustle of the last week, Andrew and I had forgotten all about those.

"I don't know whether they actually *do* mean anything," Andrew replied with a shrug. "Like we already explained, feet pointing to the right means addition, and feet pointing to the left means subtraction. 18,359 plus 200 minus 200 is still 18,359, right?"

Everyone around the table nodded in agreement and turned to see what Professor Flynn had to say about that.

"But did it ever occur to you to check the transcripts of the British *Titanic* Inquiry for the question and answer to number one eight *FIVE* five nine?" he asked. "The one that is two hundred questions after the one that helped you crack the entire mystery?"

Andrew looked over at me and shook his head. "Actually, to be honest," he said, "it never occurred to us."

"Well it occurred to me," Professor Flynn said with a grin. "And you'll be surprised to learn what it is."

Andrew raised his hands and kowtowed jokingly toward the professor. "Please tell us, oh wise one, what the plus 200 question and answer say," he intoned in mock worship that made everyone laugh all over again.

"I most certainly will, you insolent whippersnapper," Professor Flynn said, grinning. "But first a wee lecture about *Titanic*."

Everyone around the table groaned, having learned firsthand that week that although Professor Flynn's stories were always informative and entertaining, they were also frequently longer than one might otherwise be happy with (to put it as nicely as possible, of course).

"Oh, you ingrates," Professor Flynn replied. "It won't take but a minute."

"Please go ahead, Professor," I said, smiling. "I, for one, would be glad to hear whatever you have to say."

"Thank you, my dear," Professor Flynn said with a gracious smile.

"Just keep it short," I quipped and set off another round of laughter.

Professor Flynn took all of this in stride, of course, and laughed along with us. We were all family there, somehow—the big extended family that I'd never had in my normal life.

"Well, the story—a short one—that I want to tell is about a book called *Futility*," Professor Flynn said. "It was published in 1898, fourteen years before the sinking of the *Titanic* and long before that ship was even conceived of by Bruce Ismay and the directors of Belfast's Harland and Wolff shipyards. The book featured a fictitious ship called the *Titan*, a brand new ship that was the marvel of her day, the largest thing ever to be set afloat. On her maiden voyage, the *Titan* struck an iceberg one cold April night on the North Atlantic. That collision doomed the ship because despite being considered 'practically unsinkable,' the *Titan* was about to sink after all, and without enough lifeboats to save everyone on board, more than half of her passengers and crew would soon find themselves sent to a watery grave."

"You're making this up," I gasped in disbelief.

Professor Flynn shook his head. "I'm afraid not, my dear," he said. "But it is a shocking premonition of what actually occurred fourteen years later, isn't it?"

"And then what happened?" Andrew asked. "In the book, I mean."

"Oh, well, from there the book gets quite ridiculous," Professor Flynn said with a chuckle. There are Eskimos and polar bear fights and people living on icebergs. But the reason I mention it is because there is a message there, coming to us from across the years, about the arrogance of man and his belief that his machines can withstand the forces of nature. But there is also a lesson about humility, and as we sit here tonight eating dinner in this lovely dining room where J. Bruce Ismay himself once ate, I can't help but think of him and his own journey from arrogant pride to humility."

Everyone around the table nodded silently.

"And for J. Bruce Ismay, that journey began with a split-second snap decision on a cold morning in April 1912 when he stepped into one of the last lifeboats to leave *Titanic* and chose to save his own life." Professor Flynn said, pausing to take a sip of his drink before continuing. "As we all know, Ismay was later crucified by the press and by the public for this decision. But as we gather here tonight celebrating the restoration of the Murdoch family's honor, I thought we might also take a moment to remember the man who made it all possible, and who himself had one last thing to say to us about the restoration of his own honor."

Professor Flynn cleared his throat and put on his glasses as he prepared to read from a scrap of paper on the table in front of him.

"Question and answer number 18,559 from Mr. J. Bruce Ismay's testimony before the British *Titanic* Inquiry," he began. "Question: 'Would you tell us what happened after you got the women and children in?' Answer: 'After all the women and children were in and after all the people that were on deck had got in, I got into the boat as she was being lowered away'."

Professor Flynn removed his reading glasses and looked solemnly around the table at each of us.

"Now, at the risk of ruining a good party," he said quietly, "perhaps we could have a moment of silence for all the victims of the *Titanic*. Not only for those who died that cold April night, including, of course, the great and honorable William Murdoch, but also for those who survived the disaster and carried the weight of that terrible tragedy with them for the rest of their days."

"Amen to that," Andrew's mother said, her voice barely louder than a whisper as she reached out to grab hold of the hands of those who were sitting on either side of her. The rest of us followed suit, joining hands and bowing our heads as we sat there for a long, silent moment and simply remembered.

Hours later, deep in the dark early hours of the next morning after everyone else was fast asleep, I stood along the cliffs overlooking the sea and took another moment to remember the victims. As I stared out across the sea I imagined *Titanic* steaming away from Ireland toward the west and the setting sun on her cruel collision course with fate. The next day all of us would leave this place and go back to our respective homes and fates, including me. It was time to bid farewell to my new family and friends and continue on my journey around the world. As I headed east, endlessly chasing the rising sun and that elusive place where every new day is born, I would also be on a collision course with my own fate. I had no idea what that fate might be. No one ever does. But if I'd learned one thing from my adventures in Ireland and at Newgrange, it was this: as the light of the rising sun breaks across the horizon, it has the potential to pierce deep and to bring light into all the dark and hidden places inside each one of us. Every new day brings new life and possibilities. As I turned my back to the cliffs and the sea and faced the coming dawn, I could hardly wait to see what this brand new day would bring.

Epilogue Two
Some Interesting News

From: Charlie Lewis <chlewis@alaska.net>
To: Kitty Hawk <kittyhawk@kittyhawkworld.com>

Subject: Some interesting news

Hey Kitty!

I was so glad to see your name in my inbox last night and hear all about the amazing experiences you've had in London and Ireland. Adventure definitely seems to follow you wherever you go.

I also have some great news and a little bit of an adventure of my own to tell you about. Some people from the UN World Food Program have contacted me and a few of the other fisherman back here in Alaska and they've asked us to come to Rome in a few weeks for a conference on fishing and food security in third world countries. Can you believe it? I'll be going to Rome!

We have to meet up. I'd really love to see you. I'll take you out for some great Italian food and you can tell me all about your adventures in person. What do you think?

Thinking of you always,
Charlie

Some Further Reading (if you're interested)

Why is it called the "R.M.S." Titanic?: You often see the *Titanic* referred to as the *S.S. Titanic* (as in "Steam Ship") but more properly she was designated as the *R.M.S. Titanic*, which stands for "Royal Mail Ship". Ships with this designation were those that were under contract to carry mail for the British Royal Mail service and were seen as being particularly reliable. As a ship with the R.M.S. designation the *Titanic* was naturally carrying thousands of pieces of mail onboard when she sank. In fact, during the early moments following the collision the postal clerks down in the lower parts of the ship worked furiously to move the mail to higher decks in an effort to save it from the rising seawater. In modern times this tradition is carried on by British Airways and you sometimes see the crest of the Royal Mail on the fuselages of some overseas flights.

Tales of Premonition: The various stories of premonitions of disaster as told to Kitty by Andrew at the beginning of this book are all true and based on allegedly real accounts of survivors of the disaster. Likewise the various details regarding the sinking of *Titanic* are also based on real events and accounts. Most people will have seen the *Titanic* film and the computer-generated graphic sequence showing the ship's collision with the iceberg and subsequent sinking, however in 2012 National Geographic and James Cameron produced an up-to-date CGI sequence that is quite excellent and is worth taking a look at. In this sequence you can even see the various lifeboats being put off the ship, which is quite fascinating. Try searching "Titanic CGI 2012" on YouTube.

Newspaper Articles and Crossword Puzzles: The scrap of newspaper that plays such an important role in this book is obviously made up, but the incident described of J. Bruce Ismay donating money to the British Merchantman association is based on a real occurrence that took place just after the First World War. At that point in time, however, the crossword puzzle had yet to be invented so the newspaper article in our story is dated a little more than a decade later. It was interesting for me to learn during the writing of this book that newspaper crossword puzzles were more-or-less invented by Adrian Bell, the father of BBC Journalist Martin Bell. From 1930 to 1978 Mr Bell created more than five thousand such puzzles for the London Times.

Dragon's Blood: The reference to Dragon's Blood in this book is a strange one but among the many items of cargo on board the *Titanic* there was indeed a shipment of this bright red powdered resin.

The Rubaiyat of Omar Khayyam: Another famous item of cargo on board the *Titanic* was the so-called Rubaiyat of Omar Khayyam. Anyone who's read about the *Titanic* has probably heard of this fabled and bejeweled book of poems. Due to its exotic and seemingly valuable nature, added to the fact that it was lost when the *Titanic* sank, the book is an irresistible element to writers of fictionalised *Titanic* books. In truth, it was not all that valuable, perhaps worth tens of thousands of dollars, but since it was the closest thing to a real treasure lost on *Titanic* it tends to pop up quite frequently (including in this book, of course).

SOS versus CQD: It is true that the *Titanic* was one of the first ships to ever use SOS as a distress call. However, as noted in this book, she was hardly the absolute first ship to have done so. That distinction apparently belongs to the

Cunard liner *Slavonia* which ran aground off the Azores in June of 1909 and sent the first SOS call. Prior to the adoption of SOS as the standard global distress call the Marconi wireless company used the call CQD. Both of these sets of letters are often believed to be acronyms: "Save Our Souls" or "Come Quickly Distress". The truth, however, is that neither of them actually stand for anything in that sense. "CQ" was the Marconi company's standard call for all stations and adding "D" to the end of it signalled that the message to follow was urgent. As detailed in this book, SOS was chosen because the combination of the three letters in Morse Code (dot-dot-dot-dash-dash-dash-dot-dot-dot) was simple enough for even amateur wireless operators to recognise. On the night *Titanic* sank she transmitted her distress calls using both of these standard calls.

The Titanic Quarter in Belfast: If you ever have a chance to visit Belfast I can highly recommend checking out the so-called Titanic Quarter. In addition to the excellent Titanic Belfast museum where you can learn about *Titanic* and see the outlines of their hulls on what remains of the original slipways, you can also check out (just like Kitty Hawk did) the drydock where *Titanic* was fitted out in preparation for her ill-fated maiden voyage.

The *Californian*: As described in this book the actions (or inactions) of the nearby ship *Californian* and its Captain Lord remain a controversial topic to this very day. There are many theories and arguments about what actually happened and what the officers of *Californian* saw or didn't see on that fateful night, but to my mind all of that discussion is largely academic in nature. It is an indisputable fact that the officers on the bridge of *Californian* (by their own admission) saw rockets being fired by some unknown ship on the horizon, a clear indication of a ship in distress, and yet they took no action. The subsequent destruction and apparent falsification of their ship logs to place themselves further away from the disaster than they actually were also did not help their efforts to maintain innocence in the storm that followed. However, as also detailed in this book, even if they had taken swift and immediate action this would likely have not have resulted in saving everyone on board the *Titanic* either. They were close, but not *that* close, after all. But this fact does not excuse them from having taken no action whatsoever and I think that history has rightfully condemned them. I also find it interesting to note that the famed *Titanic* historian Walter Lord (no relation to *Californian's* Captain Lord) has said that if he could use a time-machine to travel back in time to 1912 that he would not place himself on the decks of *Titanic* herself to see how history actually unfolded. Instead, he would put himself on board of the *Californian* so he could see with his own eyes what exactly was going on over there on that infamous ship as the *Titanic* foundered nearby. To him, a man whose life was greatly devoted to the history of the *Titanic* disaster, I think that this wish is immensely telling. If you're interested in reading more about this particular contentious issue I can highly recommend the book "The Other Side Of Night" by Daniel Allen Butler.

YAMSI versus ISMAY: As described in this book, the pseudonym "Yamsi" was one that was actually used by J. Bruce Ismay in wireless communications from aboard the *Carpathia* following the disaster as they steamed for New York City. If you're interested in seeing some of these actual messages or any of the *Titanic*-related wireless messages (including distress calls) then I suggest you check out the following excellent website which has them all collected together:

http://markpadfield.com/marconicalling/museum/html/events/events-i=51-s=0.html

<u>J. Bruce Ismay</u>: The painting that haunts Bruce Ismay in this book, the *Tragedy*, is not a real painting but virtually all the other details of his life are. From his homes in London and Ireland, his activities after the disaster, even his habit of collecting newspaper articles, are all based on real accounts by those who knew him. In my opinion he is somewhat of a tragic figure. There was no reason why he should have been expected to go down with the ship, after all. But with so many women and children still on board when he slipped away on one of the last lifeboats it does raise the question of his character to have done such a thing. In maintaining his innocence on this score Ismay consistently explained that at the time his lifeboat was put off the ship there were simply no women or children around so he simply saw his chance and took it. This has always puzzled me. How could it possibly be that on a sinking ship, even one as large as *Titanic*, with more than one thousand souls still on board that there was no one around? And yet, this is precisely the situation as described by several witnesses to the disaster. Can it be that as the ship plunged lower and lower in the water that most people, many unable to navigate the maze of passages leading to the boat deck, simply headed for high ground at the back of the ship? It seems to me that *if* this were the case then Ismay may not be quite the despicable character that he is often portrayed as in films and books.

<u>Shakespeare's Globe Theatre</u>: In this book I have tried to convey a sense of some of my favourite things about the city of London. One of those things is Shakespeare's Globe Theatre, an authentically reconstructed Elizabethan age theatre on the banks of the Thames not far from where the original Globe theatre once stood. Tours of the theatre are available all day and the plays of Shakespeare and others are frequently performed there. Check out www.shakespearesglobe.com for details.

<u>The Abbey Road Crosswalk</u>: Abbey Road Studios is one of my favourite recording studios in the world and in addition to having recorded there several times I also make a point of visiting the crosswalk there from time to time when I am in London. Perhaps it's a bit silly, but there's something very magical about the place to me and you can generally amuse yourself quite well watching tourists take an endless variety of crosswalk photos throughout the course of the entire day. If you're interested in some of the music that I have recorded there (including an unplugged live performance) please check out my music website for free downloads at www.secretworldonline.com.

<u>The British Museum and the Rosetta Stone</u>: Another favourite haunt of mine in London is the British Museum. Not just because it's free, of course (most museums in London are), but because it is a wonderful place to spend a couple of hours, poking around in previously undiscovered corners, and getting in touch with the foundations of what we call civilisation. As described in this book, one of the real rock stars (pun intended) of the museum is the Rosetta Stone. This simple block of stone was the key to unlocking the secrets of one of the most fascinating civilisations in our world.

<u>Egyptian Hieroglyphics</u>: This sacred system of ancient Egyptian writing is a hundred times more interesting than I have been able to describe in this book. The depth and layered complexity of this writing system is endlessly fascinating to me, despite the fact that I am only the most basic of mere amateurs when it

comes to understanding it. There are hundreds of books on the subject, of course, but check out the following website which has some good information and delves into such concepts as the phonetic, logogram and determinative nature of hieroglyphs as well as a kind of hieroglyphic dictionary: ancientegyptonline.co.uk.

Cleopatra's Needle: The spot along the banks of the River Thames where Kitty finds herself confronted with sphinxes and hieroglyphs in the middle of the night is a real place that is commonly referred to as "Cleopatra's Needle". The obelisk there is a real Egyptian obelisk, but actually has nothing to do with Cleopatra at all. The name is simply a misnomer since the obelisk actually dates from 1450 BC which is more than a thousand years before she was born. This obelisk and another just like it which now stands in New York City's Central Park once stood in the ancient Egyptian city of Heliopolis and were recovered from the ruins of that city in the 19th century and given away as gifts by the ruling powers of Egypt at the time.

The River Thames: As described in this book the River Thames is a tidal river, which means that it experiences two high and two low tide cycles per day. It is easy to forget this as you walk the streets of busy London in modern times but the actual location of the city itself is very much based on this fact. When the Romans built their first settlements in what is now London they located them based on the extent of the tidal reach upriver. For thousands of years to follow ships of many empires rode the tidal currents up and down the river from London to the sea. Ships still do, in fact. A rather odd modern side-effect of the tidal nature of the Thames is the British pastime of "mudlarking". Take a look down along the banks of the Thames if you're ever in London at low tide. If you see some people in rubber boots down there, picking their way through the disgusting mud with latex gloves on their hands, you will probably wonder what in the world they are doing. What they are doing is beachcombing the Thames and looking for artefacts (ancient or not so ancient) that have been washed free by the tides. On any given day a mudlarker can find remnants of clay pipes, pottery, Delft blue tiles, old-fashioned glass bottles, and so on. If you're interested in learning more about mudlarking or even trying it for yourself, please be aware that there are very strict rules about what you can and cannot do as a private unlicensed mudlarker (the most important of which is that you cannot dig *down*, but must only retrieve things you find at the surface). I can also suggest taking a Thames Beachcombing walking tour with a professional archeologist to help you decipher the provenance of what you find. Check out www.walks.com.

Jack The Ripper: And while we're on the topic of London walking tours (www.walks.com) I should also suggest one of my favourite walking tours to take while in London - the Jack the Ripper Walk. There are a lot of such walking tours available from different guides and companies but for as long as I've been visiting London the most popular one has always seemed to be the one led by Donald Rumblelow from the London Walks company. On this tour you will be able to get plenty of information about The Ripper as well as purchase and autographed copy of Mr Rumblelow's excellent book.

Sherlock Holmes and The Adventure of the Dancing Men: The system of basic cryptography from one of Sir Arthur Conan Doyle's Sherlock Holmes stories is exactly as described in this book. Try Googling this story to read a copy of it for free online. Plus, if you've never read Sherlock Holmes before I can also highly suggest that as well. The short nature of most of the stories make for perfect reading as you lie in bed trying to fall asleep.

Newgrange, Knowth and Dowth: As described in this book these ancient mound tombs in Ireland are older than Stonehenge and the great Pyramids of Giza. If you are ever in Dublin please take the time to visit these ancient structures. You won't regret it, I promise. In addition to the main mound at Newgrange that I have described extensively in this book there are also two other major mounds located at this particular bend in the Boyne river. Just up the road from Newgrange are the smaller mounds of Knowth and Dowth. Of these, Knowth is by far the most impressive with an incredible assortment of megalithic artwork decorating the site. Both Knowth and Newgrange are accessible only via the nearby visitor's centre and there are several tours throughout the day. Dowth is accessible privately, although there isn't much to see there. While you're there be sure to do as Kitty Hawk herself did and enter the annual lottery for a spot inside the tomb at Newgrange during the sunrise mornings of the winter solstice. But even if you aren't one of the lucky ones, the demonstration of the experience using electric lights that each visitor on the tours gets is an experience that you will never forget.

The Newgrange Cipher: The substitution cipher used by J. Bruce Ismay in this book is, of course, purely invented. However, the individual characters used in the cipher are absolutely real and are found at the various ancient carvings on the walls and kerbstones of Newgrange, Knowth and Dowth.

The Titanic Inquiries: Following the loss of *Titanic* both the United States Senate and the British Board of Trade held extensive inquiries into the disaster. The transcripts and various other information relating to these two fascinating inquiries can be found at the following excellent website: www.titanicinquiry.org

William McMaster Murdoch: For as long as I have been interested in *Titanic* I have always found the ship's first officer Murdoch to be one of the most interesting characters in the tragedy. I suppose that's why I centred almost an entire book around him. The family members in this book are of course entirely fictional, but the controversy surrounding the man himself is not. His hometown of Dalbeattie, Scotland is fiercely proud of their native son and even took offence at his portrayal in the James Cameron film about *Titanic*. You can read more about that particular episode in the history of *Titanic* and Dalbeattie on the town's website: www.dalbeattie.com/titanic/apol.htm. For more information about Murdoch himself there is an exceptionally good website with more information that you could ever want: www.williammurdoch.net.

Just in case you enjoyed this book, please allow me to try and entice you into reading another one by providing a sample of a new book series that I am working on and have already finished the first book of:

The Guild of the Wizards of Waterfire

Prologue

The guilds had existed for two and a half thousand years, and it certainly wasn't the first time that tragedy had struck and claimed the life of an Elemental before their time. It had happened before, and it was sure to happen again, but for Virginia Soul, it was the first time that tragedy had struck so close to home in her own small world.

Since ancient times, the lighthouses had been the secret symbol of the elusive Guilds of the Waterfire Wizards. Standing strong as beacons of safety and stability where water meets fire, each one held the destructive power of the other at bay.

In the beginning, the lighthouses themselves had served the wizards as secret meeting places; each guild had constructed its own place of gathering and refuge. But as the guilds spread throughout the world and into places far from the sea, the image became more symbolic. The iconic form of the lighthouse began to appear everywhere—on walls and signs, over doorways, or cleverly hidden in corporate logos—just look around and you'll see what I'm talking about. But for those in the know, each lighthouse marks the location of a guild's secret meeting place.

Virginia's guild was no exception. Every Thursday at seven o'clock, she would ride out to the Shurgard Mini Storage building close to her home, type the access code into the keypad next to the entrance door, and climb the stairs to the secret room under the building's pretend lighthouse that the uninitiated simply dismissed as one of the company's marketing gimmicks.

But on this particular Thursday, Virginia wasn't there. She was somewhere else instead—the last place in the world that she wanted to be at that particular moment. She was standing in the rain in a cemetery wishing that she and the other mourners were in their secret room, safe and warm as they watched the rain streak down the windows outside. They would drink some hot tea and talk and laugh while playing games—Catan or Monopoly, maybe, or perhaps even the ancient guild game of Pharos.

Every guild must consist of five members, or the guild must disband.

That was the rule, and it had been the rule since long before Virginia was ever born. It was a rule that stretched back as far as the very existence of the guilds themselves, for two and a half thousand years.

Earth, air, fire, water, and ether.

Love and strife.

Everything had to exist in balance.

But at the moment, the only thing Virginia could feel was strife plunging its painful needles of memory deep into her broken heart. She looked across at Memphis Grey, her best friend, standing next to her at the side of the grave. Memphis was a mess, alternately wiping tears and raindrops from her face as she stared down at the lonely casket being lowered slowly into the ground. Strands of her intense blonde hair fell over her shoulders from underneath the fabric of the black hoodie that was pulled up to cover her face. She didn't want the others to see her cry. Virginia didn't care about that and just let the tears flow like rivers of sorrow. She cried just like the dark clouds that were hanging overhead.

Flickers of lightning licked at the corners of the sky, splitting the air and bathing the mourners in a stark, harsh light for an instant before another wave of thunder rumbled through the ground and sky.

Virginia leaned forward and looked past Memphis to the smaller figure at her side with tousled brown hair hanging wetly down into his eyes. Ithaca was Memphis's little brother, and seeing the two of them standing there in tears made Virginia's heart rip in two all over again. Ithaca was only two years younger than Memphis, and he was old enough to understand what death was, but just like the rest of them, it was the first time that something so tragic had struck so close and taken someone they loved so dearly out of their lives forever.

Virginia turned away from the sight of them and buried her face in her hands, sobbing loudly and coming close to completely losing it. Her eyes darted around the cemetery in a panic, looking for a way to escape. If only she could just push her way through the crowd of black-dressed mourners and make for the cover of the nearby trees. Then she could be alone with her thoughts and just sit and listen to the sound of the rain, and remember.

As she grew anxious and was about to bolt, a warm hand patted her gently on the shoulder, instantly calming her and helping her to get her breathing under control. Virginia looked up to see Memphis and Ithaca's great-uncle, Winston. Winston Eric Waters was her mentor, and the leader of their guild. With droplets of waters dripping from his gray, speckled goatee, he smiled down at her, his brown eyes full of kindness but just as flecked with pain as hers were. He patted her on the shoulder again then left his hand there, its warmth and weight solid and reassuring against the rest of the world that seemed to be descending into chaos around them.

All of them were there—Virginia, Memphis, Ithaca, and Winston, and below them in the coffin that was now slowly settling into the muddy earth lay the lifeless body of the fifth member of their guild—Christian.

Christian had been a big brother to the three youngest members and a kind of adopted son to Winston. The five of them had been as close as family—closer even, growing up together and learning from each other's mistakes as they trained and explored the world around them and the fabric of the universe that held it all together. They'd laughed and fought and cried with each other, and together they had somehow shouldered the great responsibilities that came with being an Elemental.

But now, all that was finished. Three nights ago, on a dark, tree-lined street, Christian's life was snuffed out in a flash of tires and screeching metal. He was dead, and for nothing more than a stupid car accident, the kind of tragedy that strikes friends and families a hundred times a day all across the world. Christian was dead, and if losing their friend wasn't traumatic enough, the very existence of their guild was in jeopardy. Everything they'd worked so hard to accomplish was in question.

Virginia had absolutely no idea what they were going to do.

She reached into her pocket and squeezed the petra stone that she always carried with her; she could feel its power, and took comfort in it as she closed her eyes to block out the tears and falling rain.

What are we going to do? Virginia asked herself.

Christian would have to be replaced; otherwise, their guild would fall. But how could anyone ever replace him? They could never love anyone the way they had loved him.

When the priest finished the ceremony, the mourners began to shuffle slowly back to their waiting cars. Some of them stopped by with words of wisdom and comfort for the four of them—how sorry they were, how time heals all wounds, and how no one can know the sometimes terrible cost that all of us have to pay for being human. But none of the mourners had any idea what the five of them had been through together, or how Christian's death threatened to unravel all of their lives.

Virginia's father leaned down to whisper in her ear. He and her mother would wait in the car, and she should take all the time she needed to say good-bye. He smiled at her—a weak and helpless smile full of love and caring—before Virginia's mother gave her a hug, and the two of them walked off, melting into the crowd of other black clothes and umbrellas making their way through the forest of gray headstones.

"I know it seems impossible," Winston said after everyone else was out of earshot, and just the four of them were left standing by the grave that was cut like a scar into the side of the hill. "But we'll find another to take his place. The guild will live on, and so will Christian's spirit."

The three of them looked up at Winston as he gazed off distantly toward the horizon. A slash of lightning cut through the sky in the east followed by a peal of thunder that washed over the landscape like a thunderous, breaking wave.

Winston was right. There was no other choice, and they all knew it, but that didn't make the lacerating pain of loss any easier to bear.

Every guild must consist of five members, or the guild must disband.

They all knew the rules. They'd been living by them all of their lives.

A MESSAGE FROM THE AUTHOR

First off, thank you so very much for buying this book and reading it. You have absolutely no idea how much that means to me. And maybe reading this book has piqued your interest in learning a bit more about what you now know is one of my favourite topics - *Titanic*.

There are literally hundreds of books about the *Titanic* and the various events surrounding the disaster but if you were to ask me to cut through the crap and just recommend a few of these, these would be my top picks.

"A Night To Remember" by Walter Lord: This is the book that got me (and thousands of others) first hooked on *Titanic*. First published in the 1950s it remains the benchmark against which all other *Titanic* books are measured.

"The Night Lives On" by Walter Lord: As the godfather of all *Titanic* buffs, Walter Lord revisited the subject in the 1980s with this excellent additional book on the subject.

"Shadow Of The Titanic" by Andrew Wilson: While the two books above deal with the story of the *Titanic* herself and the events surrounding her sinking, this book focuses instead on the stories of the survivors of the disaster and the life and death that awaited them back on dry land.

Finally, a book I already recommend before in the Further Reading section: "The Other Side Of Night" by Daniel Allen Butler. This book focuses on the events surrounding the mysterious ship on the horizon that failed to come to *Titanic*'s aid on that fateful night - the *S.S. Californian*.

And with that yet another Kitty Hawk book comes to an end. And good timing too, since just last night I typed the final words on what will be my next book (as soon as it's back from editting) - The Guild Of The Wizards Of Waterfire. I am pretty excited (and simultaneously nervous) about this new series of books and it was interesting to take a bit of a sidetrack from the Kitty Hawk universe and write about something more fantastical instead. More than likely, however, the next book I will write will bring me right back into Kitty's world and continue with her adventures flying around the world. What will be next for her, you ask? I have a few ideas up my sleeve. Some of them might even be *good* ideas.

Talk to you again soon... in the next adventure.